THE
SUNFORGE

Also by
Sascha Stronach

The Dawnhounds

THE
SUNFORGE

THE ENDSONG
- BOOK TWO -

SASCHA
STRONACH

SAGA PRESS

LONDON SYDNEY **NEW YORK** TORONTO NEW DELHI

AN IMPRINT OF SIMON & SCHUSTER, LLC

1230 AVENUE OF THE AMERICAS, NEW YORK, NEW YORK 10020

First Saga Press trade paperback edition August 2024

SAGA PRESS and colophon are trademarks
of Simon & Schuster, LLC

Simon & Schuster: Celebrating 100 Years of Publishing in 2024

For information about special discounts for bulk purchases, please contact Simon & Schuster Special Sales at 1-866-506-1949 or business@simonandschuster.com.

The Simon & Schuster Speakers Bureau can bring authors to your live event. For more information or to book an event, contact the Simon & Schuster Speakers Bureau at 1-866-248-3049 or visit our website at www.simonspeakers.com.

Interior design by Yvonne Taylor

Manufactured in the United States of America

1   3   5   7   9   10   8   6   4   2

Library of Congress Cataloging-in-Publication Data
has been applied for.

ISBN 978-1-9821-8707-1
ISBN 978-1-9821-8708-8 (ebook)

For Don,
catch you down the line

My daughter is a demon who lives in the forest. Her muscles are lean; her claws are long; her teeth are a broken mass of pulp and enamel. Her fur is a testament written in scars, a dark scrawl in the incomprehensible calligraphy of violence. When she comes for your children, she eats only their softest parts; she tears the tenderness from them as it was torn from her; she takes their stomachs and lungs; she leaves their muscle and bone to fester on the forest floor. My daughter is a poem written in blood. My daughter is a reckoning. My daughter burns like the sun and you will never catch her.

Some distant beast screams, harsh and mechanical, and in the fractured seconds after Kiada jerks out of her nightmare, she finds herself tangled in her lover's arms, a gentle cage that moments ago felt like iron shackles. The nightmare lingers: the air is heavy and dark, the ship's timbers on the roof above her have split open in an awful mock grin with layered rings of teeth like a hagfish, and her throat prickles. It should've been the first clue, but in the half-light, for a half moment only, she is still partly asleep and the sheets feel like chainweight, the burlap of prison-robes, the long quiet coming back to claim a fugitive. She shouts, but her throat chokes it back down, muscles constricting, keeping her safe from herself. She knows, with the certainty of a dreamer, that she is dead and her body hasn't caught up yet. The mouth in the ceiling is still there, split open and suppurating, slick with a clear pus-like sap, and as she stares, it begins distending downward in a grotesque riot of muscle and tooth, and that's how she knows none of it is real. She coughs through the haze filling the room; it hurts, and she has never hurt in a dream

before. A bead of salivary pus forms and drops down onto her shoulder, and it feels very much like the first raindrop of a storm. The cat has gotten into the cabin somehow, and it is yowling, pressed against the wall with back arched and eyes wide.

Kiada is many things, but she is not slow. She is on her feet before her mind can fully process the danger, dragging Yat with her through the smoke, snatching up the cat under one arm, barreling out into the hallway, some part of her knowing that Yat should be awake by now but pushing the thought down. There is no awful mouth in the hallway, but there is plenty of smoke, mingling with roiling steam that seems to be coming from everywhere at once. The smoke is flowing downward from the deck, seeping through the boards. There is no greater danger to a sailing ship than fire; everything is flammable, and there is no escape but the deep. Even a bioship like the *Kopek*, a chimera of cellulose and flesh, is susceptible; wood is wood, even if it no longer has roots. The ship reeks of burning flesh, and she cannot tell whether it's from the timbers or the crew. A sailor pushes past her, carrying salves and bandages. Another is tapping the ship's stoma system, shouting that it's not working; her chin and neck are coated in blood, her skin is red and peeling, and her shouts turn into shrieks of *It's not working, it's not working.* Kiada drops the cat and grabs the woman with her free hand and tries to speak to get her to calm down, but her throat is so dry from smoke that only a wheeze comes out.

Yat lifts her head for only a moment, inspects the woman, and says in an awful cracked voice that is not her own, "Microwave damage?" then seems to look shocked with herself and says in a voice that Kiada actually recognizes, "What's happening?" And then her eyes flutter and close, and she goes totally limp.

"What? What is she talking ab—"

It's a problem for another moment.

"Fire?" says Kiada. The woman stops and nods once. In the dim light belowdecks, the blood makes her look almost like she is a feasting predator, but her eyes are wild and fearful.

"You," says Kiada, aware of how much each word costs her as it tears up through her scorched throat. "Sick bay. Now."

The woman darts away, and Kiada lays Yat down against the wall and begins to work the stoma system. It is part of the new ship refitting, interconnected musculature accessible by a system of holes in the ship's walls. Access to any part of the ship from any other part of the ship. In theory, at least. Kiada reaches into the hole and lets the muscle close around her forearm. There is something wrong with the flow of magic throughout the ship, something feverish, and she navigates through it, tearing open knots of magic, shoving the dancing liquid-gold currents into places where they're needed. The ship is in terrible pain, the fire spreading down from the mycelia holding the sails in place and out across the deck. Its source is unclear, but the ship is not engaged by an enemy, as far as she can tell; there is no life off-ship for a hundred miles, not even seabirds. Even the deep ocean is never quite so empty.

The stoma tightens with such speed and violence that Kiada's arm breaks and she screams. She tries to pull away, but her arm is stuck fast as the ship closes around it, grinding bone against bone. She grits her teeth and tries to keep her arm steady as her magic reweaves the bone (nothing worse than healing wrong and needing to break it again later), and she rips a guttering stream of magic from the stoma. Its muscles go slack, and she withdraws her arm. There are deep gashes along her forearm that look like tooth marks, and the entire thing is slick with pus.

5

She puts her palms flat against the wall and works the old-fashioned way. It is rough, less direct access than the stoma, like calling to somebody through deep water, but she soothes the beast just long enough to locate the ship's fire suppression system and slam as much magic into it as she can. The stoma in the ceiling open up and lymph rains down, viscous and heavy with pus, coating everything, reeking of stale beer. It's hard to perceive much of what's happening above deck, even with the sight of magic, but something changes, and Kiada allows herself to slump down against the wall beside Yat. The air scrubbers have come back online, pulling the smoke into their mucus membranes, engineered chloroplasts feasting on carbon and ejecting the rest outside, but it still surrounds them and stains their nightclothes black. Kiada is suddenly exhausted, the adrenaline falling away. The cat nuzzles against her. Out of the corner of her eye, she swears she can see a silhouette watching her, an absence shaped like a woman, a living ache, and she does not understand. As the ship weeps its bitter, heavy tears down onto her, she falls into a sleep as deep as death.

In dreams, my daughter drifts down through the night. There is a single hole in the center of her skull where the nail went in, an impact point that the cosmos screams through, a dent in heaven itself. The way the light roils through her, the way it warps the darkness around it, she is like and totally unlike a star, like a new sun blooming in the monstrous bottomless sky. She opens her eyes and she drifts down headfirst and she sees a tree, its bark the deep red of old bad blood, its gnarled trunk so broad that she can barely see the shadows as it begins to curve away on the horizon. It is covered in ridges and trenches, scars as valleys, cancerous keloid growths like the spines of distant mountains. She is screaming, but there is no air; there has never been air. As the abyss calls out to her, she tries to reach out, and the scars on the tree's trunk split open to reveal a thousand eyes, all watching with a hunter's intent.

I need to warn her, but I cannot speak while I am stalking. It is a rule. Each syllable is a snapping branch, a second's reprieve from

my gaze. I could break my rule, but a clever hunter does not need to. Instead, I reach out and take words from the air, falling loose from another's mouth, and I reach out to my dear, dear daughter and ask one thing:

Can you keep a secret?

TWO YEARS AGO

F ucking Vuruhi," said Nyree. She scraped up the last bit of cold cream from the sides of the jar, applied it to a tissue, and started to carve peach lines into the flat white pan of her stage makeup; her night makeup sat arranged carefully off to one side, ready to go on the instant she had her real face back. One of the lightbulbs alongside her mirror guttered for a few seconds, casting long shadows across her face.

The Bokoura Theater had been a grand old girl, once upon a time. Finest in Radovan, finest in the damned Empire. They still kept the facade tidy, but the dressing rooms were all peeling gold paint, all fingers of lichen creeping up the windows, no visible mold but the sense of it behind every faded painting. No matinees, nothing during the week: shows on Rāfray and Rāfraksdag evenings only. *Mārū and the Firebird* was a good show—a classic, never failed to

have the audience laughing at the funny bits and weepy at the rest. Never failed to fill seats, until recently. Same crowd every night now: Vuruhi lads, spread out across the empty rows, leering, razor-clean scalps and nice tan shirts from that tailor over in Irapuki who had the big wolf's head up on the wall, who refused to work for women, little black-and-gold wolf's-head patches on their shoulders, which made her think less of soldiers than boys playing dress-up. If there were any Vuruhi inside, there'd be more outside, lurking around the doors and in the street, quietly threatening to make a scene.

The Vuruhi never broke the law—they just existed in a space where they were visibly willing to break the law, and they'd never be charged for it unless they were really obvious. They knew it, and they knew everybody else knew it, and so they hung around the theaters and the bars and anywhere else they thought they might find a degenerate to harass—to kill only if they had an excuse, but they were so very good at finding excuses. The Bokoura had already fallen on hard times before they showed up, of course; everybody had fallen on hard times.

Nyree had been a child when Hainak broke off from the Empire, but old enough to be paying attention. She remembered the shrieking headlines, the thudding of boots in the square, the young men defacing the statues of brotherhood and unity. Hainak left first, then the Garden Cities, then the Oxhead, until Radovan the Lion stood alone. You couldn't have an empire of one city, but they held on to the name anyway, as though one day they might actually push down from the Syalong Cherta, retake the Garden Cities, push on Hainak itself; they spoke as though Radovan were an empire going through a rough patch, not a corpse that lacked the dignity to stop kicking. In the twilight hour, the wolves had arrived to circle the

carcass—the Vuruhi were a symptom, but they desperately wanted to be a cause.

Boots in the hallway, stepping soft. Nyree froze, the tissue and a wad of cold cream halfway to her cheek. She wasn't ready to become another missing person. She looked around her desk for a weapon; she could probably give somebody a right jab in the eye with a spoolie brush, but it seemed like a long shot. Around the room, around the room. Desk drawer? On rails, wouldn't come out. Chair? An antique, the intendant would have her head. Her eyes settled on a vase of flowers from some anonymous admirer. Magenta lilacs, perfectly tasteless, but in a conveniently solid vessel. She darted over and snatched it up, ready to strike, ready to kick and claw and bite and—

"Fucking—" said the voice. "Fucking shit, hold on."

She recognized it and lowered the vase a little.

"Ari?" said Nyree.

"Yes, miss," he said. "Gotcher stuff. Just gimme a minute."

She let out her breath and felt her head spin, just a little. She laid the vase down on the end table with the bad leg, where it wobbled accusatorily up at her.

The door swung open to reveal Aritama Kolamona, smuggler and self-professed cad extraordinaire—or at least to reveal his arms and legs: the rest of him was behind a tottering stack of cardboard boxes. She knew once he put them down, she'd see a Faiadino kid with olive skin, thick brown hair, and ritual scarification that marked him as one of the wasteland nomads, though she'd never known him to live anywhere but Radovan. He could've been thirty, but he could've equally been a weathered nineteen, and she had money on the latter. Depending on who you asked, he was either the best or worst crook in the Empire. She'd known him long enough to realize it was a little

bit of both: he had a sharp mind and a big heart, and he was too poor to afford either of them.

Each box had APPLES: FOR EXPORT and a big red stamp with RA-DOVAN PORT AUTHORITY printed on it. They did not contain apples, and they did not come from Radovan. She helped him take the boxes over to her desk, removing them from the stack one by one until his flat cap poked out, then his angular face, and finally the filthy piece of wool and cheap dye that he referred to as his Nice Vest. He'd sewn dozens of extra pockets into it, each one in a totally different fabric. She was removing the last box when he cleared his throat.

"Got some bad news, miss: price has gone up. Need a silver per unit now. Blockade's getting tighter. I know a crew who can run it, but they don't come cheap."

Of course he'd waited for her to unload before telling her. There was a note of apology in his voice, but a note of something else, too: a little hunger. He was going to ask for something else, and she wasn't eager to find out what. She hustled him into the room, closed the door behind him, then spun around in full diva mode: a juggernaut of offended propriety and altogether too many ruffles.

"Do you know what happens if my people can't get their medicine, Ari? They die. Their voices change or they get a little shadow on their cheeks and some fucking Vuruhi notices, and they end up with their throat cut. You're not selling hats here, Ari; those vials save lives. We had a deal."

She'd backed him into a corner. She wasn't particularly tall, but neither was he. He was a rough lad, but she knew he had no interest in hitting a lady. He glared back at her, then his face settled.

"You're one of them," he said, "you know. Whatsits." He spun his hand vaguely in the air.

"Spit it out," she said with a frown. She got chasers hanging around the theater from time to time, had to give more than one of them a ringing slap to get them to back off. Ari hadn't seemed like the type, but nobody ever *seemed* like the type until suddenly they were.

His brow furrowed, then he shook his head.

"No, miss, not like that. Thought you knew me better than that. I mean you're one of them, you know, like, if I say, 'C-sharp,' you know which one that is and you can sing it. Like that."

"Pitch-perfect?" she said. She slumped a little and gave him a smile, and even she couldn't tell whether it was real or forced: she hadn't had reason to smile in a long time, and it felt unfamiliar and uncomfortable. He studied her with wide, anxious eyes, then bristled, as though shaking off goose bumps.

"Yep!" he said. He gave a slight nod, apparently to himself, then he reached into his pocket and pulled out a piece of yellowing paper. "C-sharp," he said, peering at it over his cracked spectacles. "D one octave above the treble clef, F-sharp one below."

He didn't need the spectacles, but he'd told her they made him look refined; she thought they very much made him look like a boy wearing his father's spectacles. "Can you sing that?" he said.

She had a good range. Was famous for it, really. It would still be a stretch. But that was it: no price raise, just a free show at some little cousin's Mazana or something. The Nightingale of Radovan, one night only in an uptown union hall. Might get a ribbing if any other performers found out, but worth the price. A silver a unit was almost double what it had been last time. She knew the war was getting ugly again, but she'd have to start selling things that mattered if she wanted to afford the medicine from Hainak, and she didn't have a lot left that mattered.

"Give me the sheet music and a week or so," she said, "and I can sort it out."

She didn't need a week for the music, but she might need a week for her heart to stop slamming itself against her ribs. He handed her the slip of paper. It had three notes written on it, not even on a stave. "I need the whole thing," she said.

"That is the whole thing, miss."

She'd heard some of the backstage lads talking about it one time, in bits and pieces. Something about stealing radio waves with music. It sounded like magic, or nonsense, or both. Nonsense for kids, grifters, and the unfashionably rich; the sort of nonsense that wasn't against the law only because the law hadn't caught up to it yet. "Ari," she said, "are we doing something illegal?"

He became a wellspring of No Comment; the sudden stoniness of his face would've impressed the statues in Nahairei Park. She changed tack.

"Is anybody going to get hurt, Ari?"

He perked up at that. "No, miss, not one soul. Promise. But we need to do it tonight."

She sighed, then settled back down at the mirror and wiped off the rest of her stage makeup. It took several minutes, and she did not look at Ari. In the mirror she could see him dutifully putting the boxes away in her hidden stash in the closet. She applied as little makeup as she thought she could get away with—civic camouflage, a certain sort of vulnerable girl's best friend—then stood up and shouldered her bag. As she stepped out into the hallway, she saw a leaflet on the floor, a pregnant blond woman holding a baby while standing in a field of golden wheat. She had no shoes on. WOMEN OF RADOVAN, it thundered, WHERE IS THE WORLD YOU DESERVE? JOIN

THE VURUHI PEOPLE'S MOVEMENT. She rolled her eyes. *Good luck with that one, lads,* she thought, and tried not to dwell on how it had gotten there in the first place. She put her elbow around Ari's and pulled him a little closer. His figure wasn't exactly large, but it made her feel a little safer. A little.

"Show me to the mischief," she said. Maybe her night wasn't going to be so bad after all.

NOW

Kiada does not wake in the sick bay, and that's the first sign some-thing is off. Her muscles ache and burn, and her first attempt to stand puts her straight back on her ass. Yat is not next to her any-more, so she tries to stand for a second time, works through the pain, and hobbles down the smoke-stained hallway toward the galley. She can hear voices ahead, that sort of flat post-panic burbling you get from some folks after they've been at the fringes of a fight, empty words just tumbling out to fill the space. She approaches them, pushes open the door, starts to admonish the sailors standing there, and then registers their injuries. Extensive burns, barely treated and still weeping. Rikaza and Ken Set-Xor, both old hands, both excep-tionally hard people to shake. The burns are worst on Xor's palms—Kiada glimpses bone and cannot bring herself to look any harder.

"Captain where?" she says. She cannot find a way to soften the words, which erupt from her like bullets.

"I don't know, ma'am," says Riz. "She hasn't been seen since the attack started. Ajat is acting cap, and she's topside."

Kiada points down the hallway. "Yat's missing," she says. "Find her."

Riz nods, all business. Xor tucks her palms into her armpits and mutters something that Kiada does not care to hear. Her nerves are frayed, and finding out will just piss her off, so she does her best not to find out and heads up the stairs onto the deck. As she emerges into the open air, the reek hits her. She thought it was bad belowdecks, but topside it is so much worse. Burning doesn't have one smell; it has a thousand. It is not just the *Kopek* on fire, it is the entire horizon, the familiar Radovan skyline rendered hazy and incomprehensible in smoke, a curtain of it that seems to drink in the city, to pull its houses and towers upward and spread them across the sky in a great dark cloud of greasy ash. When a city burns, it burns in so many ways that they run together and overwhelm the senses. Kiada cannot tear herself away from it, but she must. On the deck, sailors cluster around the railings, pulling up buckets of water to treat their burns. The mainmast is missing entirely, only a jagged crown of bone shard piercing up through the deck where it once stood. The burn patterns are all wrong: there is evidence of fire, but a lot of the burns seem to have erupted from *inside* the ship, boiled up, and burst outward. Steam burns, like she sometimes saw on the factory floor when the rusted pre-war infrastructure broke back in a life she does not care to remember. Nobody gave a shit about the factory blanks; many of them lived with horrific injuries, and so long as the injury didn't interfere with the work, it went untreated. The uneasy memory makes the scene before her even

harder to handle, but she has a job to do—she'd be a terrible bosun if she didn't attend to the crew in front of her before the dead men in her head. She still feels half trapped in a dream, weightless, but she sets to work directing repairs. Somebody needs to be strong, and it's always her. It's apparent even at a glance that the ship is going nowhere. They have enough mycelia in the hold to fix the shrouds and sails, but the mainmast is done for: even if they could pull it up out of the water and reattach the severed muscle and bone, there wouldn't be enough steroids in the whole of even Hainak Port to get it functional again, much less here in Radovan where everything is steel. Thankfully, the foremast is still mostly intact—a couple of days and the crew could get it working again, and then maybe they could limp to safer waters. Five sailors are trying to drag the ruined topgallant of the mainmast back out of the water. She orders them to the foredeck. One starts at her command, and she realizes she is shouting and cannot stop herself from doing so over the roaring of her own blood in her ears.

The crew drops the mainmast into the water and hustles over to the foredeck. Up on the forecastle, Ajat is pacing. She glares down at the sudden flurry of footsteps, and Kiada glares back and stomps over, doing her best to weave through the wounded crew and up the stairs to the foredeck. Her heartbeat has slowed somewhat, though as she approaches the front of the ship, she sees the ruined city in full and recognizes some of the buildings amid the smoke—the opera house, the marble facade of the old imperial palace, houses on houses on houses, the mile-high tangled steel pinnacle of the doppler control array looming over it all. She needs to return to the crew, but she has a single question that needs answering, and as she approaches Ajat, it bursts out of her.

"What the *fuck* just happened?"

TWO YEARS AGO

They went through Nahairei Park, where the ivy-covered statues of Empire glared down at Nyree: Queen Niwa the Uniter in her flower crown and gorgeously carved robes; Vuru the Wolf in furs, his hunter's axe notched from another skull; Irgmatei II the Lion, proffering a generous hand down to some nameless and shirtless Hainak native with shark teeth around his neck; even a surprisingly well-maintained statue of Wihiki the Blacksmith; plus kings and queens and second cousins to the seneschal and anybody else who could afford the services of a mason and enough ground to put a statue on. The park was maddening: built across a dozen levels, connected with ladders and stairs that seemed to go nowhere. Some rich settler had purchased the whole thing for the city in perpetuity, only to for it be sold by the inch for the installation of Cultural Artifacts and Sundry Beautiful Places. When Nyree was younger, it had been

the park of a thousand nooks and good places to kiss. Now it was filled with shadows. Vuru stared down at her with sightless marble eyes, and Nyree did her best to stare back.

The statue was new and clearly well kept; anybody tagging it might find themselves getting a nighttime visit from the lads with shaved heads. She wished they'd taken the subway, but Ari had been insistent that they couldn't be seen.

Ari smoked a cheap cigarette, of which he seemed to always have an endless supply. He led her down a winding wooden staircase and up to a wire fence. She could see the bulk of a rusted radio tower tottering drunkenly over the nearby cliffside. This was definitely the place. Ari was tugging at the fence, muttering to himself, until he found a piece of it that came away, and he pulled until the hole was wide enough to admit her.

"After you, ma'am," he said with a cocky half smile. A ferro-cat was lurking around the fence line, licking at some exposed wiring on one of its paws.

Her dress caught on the wire, and she had to stop to untangle it. The cat's features shifted and clicked together in something that felt a little too close to mocking. She worried Ari would be watching, but she turned and saw him staring at the staircase, suddenly alert and very quiet. She followed his gaze and saw nothing. She tugged at a ruffle, heard the fabric tear, swore as quietly as she could, and stepped through the fence. Ari followed her without a sound and closed up the hole in the gate—the cuts to the wires were perfect, and it was as though they'd never been there at all.

The ground around the tower was muddy, and she hiked up her dress as she stepped across it. Her shoes were ruined, but she could always steal another pair from the wardrobe department—the Bokoura

had long since started accounting for petty theft as part of its expenses. For a moment, she saw a constellation out of the corner of her eye, and she turned to face it and gasped. It was the city: Radovan the Lion, laid out beneath her, so beautiful and peaceful that it hurt. A reflection of the night sky, a thousand little stars laid on the fabric of the night. The moment passed: Ari tugged at her elbow, and she followed him over to the dark brick building at the base of the tower.

He knocked twice on the door, staccato, and the same strange knock replied. The rust-red door swung open, and they stepped inside. The building seemed taller than was possible from the outside: multiple levels of gangplanks and scaffolds going up three stories. At least half of the tower was indoors, and at the top level, there was a girl.

She was filthy and wore heavy, dark woolen clothes. She had bags under her eyes. She'd almost certainly cut her own hair, so short that she'd probably stabbed herself with scissors at least once. She was smoking a cigarette identical to Ari's, which—considering he rolled his own—meant it had almost certainly come from him. She couldn't be more than fifteen. She stared out a grimy window, looking back into the park.

She said something in Faiadino without looking away from the window. She didn't shout, but her husky, oddly reedy voice carried throughout the structure, echoed off the cramped walls. She sounded annoyed.

Ari nodded and gave her a thumbs-up. He leaned in and whispered into Nyree's ear, "Don't mind Mārek. She's only like that on the outside, and maybe the inside just a little bit."

The whisper carried throughout the entire structure. Mārek gave him a look that could strip paint, then pointed at a box attached to a

nearby wall. "Make the fuckin' noise, Nightingale," she said. "Target inbound with doppler, thirty seconds."

A doppler? She thought they were stealing audio recordings, maybe listening in on some rich man's phone line to see if they could dig up dirt, but they wanted the whole karetaozi, the actual machine. What did they need a blasted humanoid robot for?

Ari opened the box and took out a telephone. He held it up to Nyree and nodded expectantly. She shrugged, then took the phone and sang the three notes into it. She had barely finished and heard a quiet click on the other end when Ari snatched the phone out of her hand. In an instant, his whole posture changed: shoulders back, head forward, more lines in his face somehow—that tightness that comes from vinegar and old worry. Nyree spent her days around actors, and she'd never seen anybody get in character so quickly. Ari was a natural.

"This is Nikoze, trunk six," he said, his voice deeper, more authoritative, a sort of tired lilt to it: a bored engineer just trying to finish his shift. "Got a doppler in Nahairei just walking in circles babbling about nothing. Looks like it probably got too many orders at once and got stuck in a loop; you know what the mk2s are like. Give our tower repair permissions, and I can have it fixed in no time."

He paused, and Nyree strained to hear the tinny response on the other end. She couldn't make out words, only short confused barks.

"No, trunk six. Nine is scrap metal, you know that." A pause. Ari sighed and pinched the bridge of his nose. "I dunno about your diagnostics, I just know what I'm seeing. You've got my token, just zero on that—look, no look, some toff is about to call the main trunk shouting that his doppler is broken, and then we'll be hearing about it for weeks; that new manager they've got at HQ doesn't know shit about

shit, but he wants us to smell of roses. I'm here on-site, I can have it fixed before the toff's butler can find a phone booth and save us both a week's paperwork."

Another pause, then Ari grinned. "Yep," he said, "yep, mum's the word. I'll erase the logs on this end, you get it on your end. Look, I know a guy at a distillery, and I'll send you through a little thank-you; if a gas can shows up at your door, it's not gas: it's the good stuff. Single malt."

He waited for a response, then tilted back his whole head and let out a deep belly laugh that lasted several seconds. It was a voice deeper than his frame, but he lived entirely inside it. "No problem at all," he said. "Stay safe out there."

He hung up, and suddenly Mārek was a frenzy of activity, moving from box to box, dancing across high catwalks, hitting switches and reorganizing plugs. In another life, she'd have made a wonderful ballerina. She finished at the mains box, bounced up and down a little, clearly counting under her breath, then shut down all the mains at once, and instantly fired them back up. She stood for a moment, totally still, and Nyree realized it was the first time since they'd met that Mārek wasn't swinging her leg or tapping her foot or making curls of her ragged hair; she was as serene as an angel on a church roof.

"Why'd you go horizontal?" shouted Ari. He'd slumped back into his usual self: low shoulders, but clever and jittery eyes dancing from thing to thing.

Mārek came out of her reverie and scowled at him.

"I'm just saying," he pushed on like a dinghy plowing into a hurricane, "you escalate vertically, and we could take the whole network. Open a back door, come back whenever we like."

It didn't make sense to Nyree, but she caught enough on the tail

end to feel a chill run down her back. Take the whole network—surely not? There were thousands of dopplers in Radovan, in every noble household, in every government ministry, in the palace itself.

"Yōhua," said Mārek, "let every linesman in a thousand miles know we're here. Why not break down the director's door with a sledgehammer while we're at it? We minimize our exposure—no unnecessary attack surface. We leave a tunnel, not a door." Her voice went up in pitch, nasal and mocking. "Leave it open," she said, "so we can come back whenever we like."

She returned to pacing, moving across the haphazard planks like they were the flagstones in Unity Square. They watched her for a while, until she noticed them watching. She peeked out at them from under the brim of her cap and glowered. She was very good at glowering, which is to glaring as mulled wine is to grape juice; there were prima donnas with thirty years of leading roles behind them who couldn't muster even a posset's worth of the same dull crimson malice.

"Sent it to Auntie's place," she growled down. Her words echoed down the tower, unexpectedly loud.

Ari grinned, then turned to Nyree. "Auntie is gonna love you," he said. "Latest shipment of that special medicine is on me. You keep your friends safe, yeah? And if you ever need a discount in future, well—"

She knew Ari couldn't be rich, and the shipments usually cost her almost every cent she had—if his cut of tonight covered it and then some, it was worth more money than she could've possibly guessed—certainly more than she'd ever made for three notes. Ari gestured around the room, up at Mārek and the jungle of loose wiring above them.

"—you know who to ask."

26

G'day 妹妹. *Sorry I'm late; it's been a rough forever.*[1] *Had to drive through the whole* ~~my daughter is a demon who lives in the forest,~~[3] *almost missed the turnoff. I know what you're thinking: So it starts here, right? And yeah nah, I mean, sort of.*

It starts with a girl fleeing hounds through an olive grove. It starts in a café by the sea. It starts on a sick man's ship, sinking down into dark water. It starts in a place where the oceans are red and the bone

---

1. Understatement of the fuckin' year/epoch/fucklot[2] right there.

2. I cannot believe you people still don't have a word for this unit of time, like just because you think it doesn't matter to you personally, it's not worth conceptualizing. And like, you're the ones in it. I'm not even chrono-locked anymore, marching onward as the weight of history bears down from behind. I quit that gig ages ago. All irony, since now there are teeth entering my eye. Whatever, I'm just gonna call it a "fucklot," okay?

3. Mate, you sound like a sack of bees fucking a dial-up modem, what even is your deal?

27

spires whistle with wingbeats. It starts with silence. It starts with two brothers on a gibbet. It starts with the biggest drill in the known universe. It starts with a dying city. It starts with a broken vial. It starts with a secret. It starts with a crane; it starts with a girl; it starts with a weeping tree. It starts with a kiss, or a shipwreck, or maybe a lost girl on a wide dark lake.

Which is to say, like, y'know, nothing starts anywhere, because everything starts everywhere; there is a music to that endless cascade of history; everything happens because something else happened; anything could happen, because something happened.

So, meimei, to your question: Is this where it starts?[4]

Yeah nah, of course not.

But it'll have to do.

---

4. Well, fuck me for trying to start with the action, I guess. All right, have at it.

ONE YEAR AGO

Ari's place was nice, though it wasn't *really* Ari's place. He'd told Kiada the widow who'd lived there had died and her children would be bickering over the property for thirty years and none of them had the key anyway. She suspected he was lying—there were signs that he wasn't the only one inhabiting the place—but he was a charming liar, and she didn't think it was worth pushing. She'd met Mārek once and kept an eye out on subsequent visits, but the girl was clearly not a conversationalist and tended to stay out of sight. Good kid; Kiada saw herself in her.

The teacups were Hainak porcelain, with living patterns writhing beneath the surface, activated by the heat of the tea. They probably cost more than either of them earned in a year. He offered her milk, but she hadn't seen a fridge, and the place had no power anyway.

Scented candles provided most of the light. The place smelled like somebody's old kōma who'd been doused in machine oil.

It looked like the widow had been a hoarder, and Ari had been only too happy to carry on the tradition. Knickknacks lined every spare surface. Kiada idly played with a toy armored car, rolling it back and forth with a single finger. She liked the little rattle of its wheels, though she'd never say it out loud—if she showed enthusiasm for anything, Ari would never let her hear the end of it. She'd be finding toy cars in every shipment from here until Worldsend.

The house had the same sort of cozy Ari-ness that pulled people into his orbit. It was cluttered but well lit. Ari was shamelessly in love with every little damned thing, the sort of sentimentalism that didn't work out at sea. She was unaccustomed to it, but she couldn't bring herself to hate it.

"More ships in the harbor," he said, "with those new grub-cannons. Wild. I heard they can eat through steel. Which is, y'know—the old ones couldn't do that, but science marches on, and it's worrying to be in the crosshairs, though it's still fascinating. What do they eat when they're dormant? A metabolism like that, it's gotta be something, but I haven't seen any additional feeder pods on the ships, so I guess they've figured out some new high-density protein mix or, like, you know—uh, oh, more tea?"

She hadn't even clinked her empty glass down on the saucer, but he knew somehow. She handed it back to him.

"Thank you," she said. She tried not to smile, but he made it hard. What a wonderfully expressive little man. While he was filling the glass, she reached into her pack and pulled out the latest samples, then put them on the table. They'd already dispensed with the usual trade. Three crates sat in the corner of the room.

"New stuff from Hainak," she said. "Experimental. Higher potency, injectable. Easier to slip under the wire in any useful quantity. Still not well-tested, but nobody's grown anything they shouldn't've."

"Ajat using it?" he said.

She tried not to let her surprise show. She didn't even know they'd met, but of course they had. Ari knew everybody.

"Would that change anything?" she said.

"I trust you," said Ari, "and so, I trust your friends. If they're using it, I trust it."

For a moment, she was ready to lie. They badly needed the sale. The endocrinologist who'd hawked it to them had promised it was custom-built for the blockade, easier to smuggle. Might finally mean some damned overhead, instead of constantly running the red and stealing to fill in the gaps. She sighed.

"I don't know what she's using," she said. "I can ask, but right now, I can't promise it's this."

"Was that candor, Miss Kiada?" he said. "Does that make us friends?" He was grinning. She pursed her lips and forced down a groan.

"Got no friends," she said. She tried to sound serious, but it was hard to come off as surly with a porcelain saucer in her hand.

"Oh, yes, hrmm," said Ari, "of course, none at all. There is not one person on that boat you're friends with, not even Ajat or Iacci or Rikaza or Sibbi, no friends at all, like a lone wolf who smokes broody cigarettes in the rain—you're a cigarette wolf, Miss Kiada, a nicotine saddo, who does *not*, under any circumstances, absolutely love the opera. I have never seen you cry during an aria, not once, and definitely not at least four times including during the third act of *The Violets of Spring* when the lovers Oroiji and Wāhima reunite after

31

being torn apart by hardship, and *definitely* not when Donq the Oaf sings that he lives in a world of iron and dreams of a world of gold."

"Ari," she said, "I am ready to commit violence on you."

He was about to say something clever when somebody rapped on the door. It wasn't a knock, nothing so polite; it was a closed fist, quick and intense, the sort usually followed by a boot. There was a stained glass saint above the doorway. The top of a shaved head brushed against the saint's feet. Not the owners, then. She clasped her hands together and felt her threads spread out into the room, felt the threads of the man on the other side of the door (angry but triumphant, a dangerous, plodding sort of anger), felt Ari's panic and did her best to soothe it, to push into his head a *Calm down, follow my lead*.

Ari took a step toward the door, and—from outside—a heavy shoulder hit it with a bone-rattling bang. Ari's anxiety spiked, and Kiada had to push harder to keep him calm. Tiger Weaving was powerful, but it wouldn't work if he didn't act natural. The shoulder rammed the door again, and the frame splintered. She could sense the man on the other side, and there was no rage there, just the satisfaction of a full mousetrap. She searched and found names, faces, a precise time, date, and location. The door creaked open, and the Vuruhi stepped inside.

He was broad as a brick shithouse and had to stoop to get under the lintel, but his face was strangely round and boyish, with a half-grown patch of blond peach fuzz around the edges. As he stepped inside, his satisfaction evaporated, and Kiada couldn't help but let a little smile play out across her lips. *Gotcha.*

He stepped right past Ari and over to the kitchen table, picked up the samples, and turned them over in his hands. She could feel his

curiosity spiking, feel that predator's instinct at spotting prey, and she caught the threads, forced them back down, smoothed them out, turned the foreground into the background. He seemed to freeze, then he put the samples back down where he'd found them, almost carefully.

"Wrong house," he muttered. He turned to Ari, and the surge of fear almost knocked Kiada over. Her power over the man wobbled, and she could feel a twinge of something in him, a *wait, what*–ness, and she pushed it down, let Tiger's gift roll through him, let him see everything and nothing at all.

He pulled out a paper banknote and handed it to Ari. "Sorry to bother you, sir," he said. "That's for the door."

He stepped out as quickly as he'd come in, then Kiada let him and Ari go. Ari turned to her. *What the fuck*, he mouthed. She shrugged. Ari had seen too much just now, but she had a trick for that, too. She reached inside him, found the thoughts percolating in his head, caught them and flattened them out until they took on the same gray as the wallpaper. His face slackened, just a little, then he turned his head and nodded to himself.

"We got lucky," he said.

"Yeah," she said, "really lucky."

"What did he think the samples were?"

She shrugged. "Something else," she said.

"Something else?"

Catch the thread, push it away.

It's nothing. It doesn't matter.

It hurt to do to a friend, but it was an ugly world made for ugly people. It was her world, a world of the dead, a world of iron, a world without toy cars or scented candles. He was nodding to himself,

stitching together his own story. She couldn't hide what was there, but she could change how important it was, and she let the thoughts of wild luck sprout and grow and kept the others quiet. It was not an evil. It was a kindness.

"We got lucky," he said again. They sounded less like words than a mantra, like a magic spell he could use to still his beating heart. He seemed to perk up, then he reached into his pocket and pulled out a ticket.

"Speaking of lucky, got myself a ticket to see the Nightingale sing tonight, but Auntie's making me work. It's for *Mārū and the Firebird*, a real tearjerker. You're stuck here until morning, so you might as well. You can still make it if you take the subway. That new Hineinui Tepe Station is just around the corner."

She didn't ask how he knew her schedule. She could've plucked the thought from his head, but she'd done enough of that for today. She felt dirty. He waggled the ticket in front of her face. "Mhm," he said, "back row, so nobody can see you weeping like a big sad nicotine puppy dog."

"Fuck off, Ari," she said. He smiled at her, and she smiled back. She took the ticket, slid a brown paper envelope across the table, then packed the samples back into her bag. She tried to leave without saying anything else, but Ari stepped in her way and pushed something into her hand. It was the toy armored car. She gave him a look that could wilt a cactus, and he drew his thumb and forefinger across his lips, a traditional Radovan street salutation that meant many things, but most broadly meant *I'm no snitch*. She nodded at him, just once, then put the car into her pocket and stepped outside. The crisp Radovan evening greeted her: streetcars and electric lights. She looked down at the ticket, then set out into the city.

Lwakes up somewhere in the belly of an animal, and for a moment, he does not understand, but then he sees that it is a ship grown wildly, cancerously—something wrong with its thyroid injectors, perhaps?—and he looks down at his body and sees that it does not belong to him, that it is *other* in a way that settles into him like a splinter. The other sailors in the sick bay are covered in the same microwave burns he saw earlier, in the instant he'd awoken from his long sleep and not understood. He understands now. He takes the body, dresses it in clothes he has only ever interacted with secondhand, then goes to the mirror and sees the reflection. He does not consider himself a man of great passions, but the face stirs something in him, a revulsion. It is a demon he barely recognizes. His lip curls ever so slightly. He takes the body out of the room and stumbles as the floor moves beneath his feet. He hasn't needed sea legs in a very long time.

He arrives in the mess hall, a scene of panic, crewmen suffering from burns and abrasions. Sailors scratching at themselves, rubbing their wrists and forearms and not knowing why. Some sort of

weapon, perhaps? Not a terribly effective one. And then it occurs to him that he has not seen a microwave emitter in decades, that there's only one woman in the universe who knows how to build something like that, and he feels twin pangs of pain and longing, and knows that he must find her, that he needs Vic. Things have gotten out of control; it's what she would call "project creep" in that wry way she had that always made him feel a little off-balance, like she knew the words were ridiculous but enjoyed using them just to watch him squirm. How he missed it.

The sailors cluster around a table, and two women—one whom he'd awoken beside earlier, both with the look of officers about them—are arguing over a map. They fall silent as L enters, and the redhead stomps over to him, embraces him roughly. He returns the hug as politely as he can. The deception is necessary, but the embrace is uncomfortable. The woman pushes her face up to his and stares deep into his eyes.

"You okay?" she says.

He nods. "Quite fine."

Partner, then. Pressure point. Would've been good to know the first time. L knows there will not be a third opportunity. His reconstruction was slow and painful. On a nearby bench, two sailors are performing wound care. The woman is muttering, "It's not that bad, it's not that bad," and the crew seem to take reassurance from it, which is dangerous. He's seen residents make that mistake in the OR, though he's proud to say he's never seen it twice. He owes these people nothing, though, least of all his experience, and helping would be dangerous. There is no statute of limitations on a Hippocratic oath, but he nonetheless feels it is long expired, gone to dust with a world that is no longer even memory.

The redhead has stepped back. She is looking at him, studying him, and though he finds little intelligence in her eyes, he does see a subtle cunning that worries him deeply. She is a rough woman, clearly. A soldier, perhaps, lean and muscular, some sort of postwar steroid recipient, with none of the chemical scarring he's come to expect but plenty of other scars. He takes a gamble: he leans in and kisses the woman on the cheek, slipping his arm to intertwine with hers. She blushes and hisses *Not now* at him, and he knows all he needs to distract her. He will not escalate it, of course: that would be distasteful. He simply understands that she is baffled by affection, mollified, easily manipulated. She is strong and white, and those things have done her well enough that she hasn't needed to develop anything else. The red hair is a rare mutation, and he admires it for a moment, wonders how it even got into this gene pool. But, ah, of course, to say Fergus had gotten around back then would be an understatement. None of the other crew are watching them, and he unhooks his elbow and smiles as demurely as he can.

"I'll go and get some clean bandages," he chirps, and then the world tilts as he falls forward. The redhead catches him, and people are shouting, and . . .

L is standing ankle-deep in dark water while the night stretches out in all directions. A solitary monolith emerges from it: a dentist's chair, four improvised ligatures for the victim's wrists and ankles. He knows the bindings came later, but memory is a strange beast: the chair is not real anymore. Somewhere in the distance he can hear hoofbeats, and he suppresses a scream. He tries to run and the water rises up and coalesces into a wall, into a window looking out over the street where he died the very first time. He pounds on the glass and screams and screams but he cannot break it. It is tacky and

membranous, and the real window was not. It comes away on his fists in clumps, but there is always more, and he does not remember when he started screaming but he cannot stop, knows he cannot break the window because he did not break the window, knows he cannot leave this place, and in the street below he sees a pale man on horseback, a man with a dreadfully dull name whose crisp indigo-blue uniform is entirely free of dust, sees the man pulling behind him a machine of steel and teeth so broad and heavy it will cover continents and render them gristle and myth, and L knows that in an hour the entire operatory will reek of blood so badly that it penetrates even his stupor of pain, that he will relive this day again as he has a thousand times before and if he wants to get away, all he needs to do is break the window (the stairs are not an option, there is a man on the stairs already, the one who caught him, the one who rode ahead of the rest and had already dismounted by the time L even noticed hoofbeats), though he has never succeeded in breaking it, not one in a thousand times, and so he throws himself against it even as its residue begins to soak through his clothes. He strikes it again and again, screams, grabs for a chair that materializes beneath his hand as he reaches out, hurls it and watches it melt back into dark water, and at last he falls to his knees, too empty to do much else but weep. He rolls over, puts his back to the wall—he will look the milk-white devil in the eye this time, even if it takes everything from him—and sees a woman staring at him with tears in her eyes and he says, *That's not right, you weren't here*, and then . . .

Yat is in Kiada's arms, and her throat hurts like she has been crying. Something clings to her, the residue of a dream, and she curls her fingers protectively into her palm and does not know why. She tries to remember, but it is like pushing a splinter deeper, and she cries

out. Everybody is staring at her, people are rushing over, somebody is lifting her clothes, checking her body for wounds, and despite the fact that she cannot stop the juddering hot-cold tremors, this is one indignity too far, and she pushes away, holds up her hands.

"I'm fine," she says, and she can hear the lie, hear how raw her voice is, and she knows everybody else can hear it, too. They back up anyway, and there is nobody touching her but everybody is still staring.

"Check her eyes," says Ajat. There is a twinge of fear in her voice. A look goes between her and Kiada, and then Kiada shakes her head.

"She's just shaken up," she says, "we all are."

"No," says Ajat, "not now, of all fucking times. Not—"

She looks around, sees the crew staring at her, then takes Kiada by the elbow and drags her into the galley and slams the heavy door. When they emerge, Kiada is pale. She walks up to Yat, takes her gently by the hand (she is rarely so gentle, even when she is trying to be, it is as though the whole world is made of glass and she is trying desperately not to break it), and says in tones as flat as tombstones, "Kahurangi mai, I need to look at your eyes."

Yat straightens her back, lifts her chin. She does not know what is happening, but she'll face it with dignity nonetheless. Kiada approaches, lifts the left eyelid and peers in, lifts the right, then mutters that Vic's in town, and Yat feels something inside her surge up involuntarily, phantom fingers pushing up from her guts into her throat, and she does her best not to let it show, but she sees Kiada's pupils widen, just a little, and she knows she's done for. They are touching, closer even than they do at night, and a single thread runs between them, one thought crisp and clear: *You know I love you, right?* She still can't say the words aloud, but it's as close as she's come.

Kiada turns and says, "She's clear."

"All right," says Ajat, "but she sleeps in the brig anyway, just to be safe."

Kiada moves as she does when she's about to strike; there's an argument about to burst from her. "Not happening," she says. "She's been weaving for, what, six months? She's a talented beginner, but you're all acting like she's a nuclear bomb. What exactly do you think she's going to *do*? Tell me."

Yat does not comment that Kiada's "tell me" sounds half-sincere, like she's scared, lost, and trying not to show it, and the fear makes her feel sick. She hates feeling dangerous, like she's both the powder keg and match.

"*Aue*, the audacity," says Ajat. "Auntie grows white girls in a lab and sends you all to test me."

Yat puts a hand on Kiada's shoulder. "It's fine," she says. "I've slept in cells before."

She knows something is wrong with her. She doesn't know what, but over the years she's cultivated the ability to sleep almost anywhere. She knows what's about to happen, and she doesn't want to let somebody else do it for her, so she puts her free hand against the wall of the ship and drains herself into it, empties herself of magic almost entirely. She does it so quickly nobody has any time to react, then raises both hands.

"We good?" she says. Ajat nods and carries on.

"Nobody except Weavers are allowed in the brig while she's down there," she says. "I can cut off the ship's weave around her cell, but if the bosun's wrong and one of you goes down there at the wrong time, then you're a walking battery just waiting to get drained. Only Weavers down there, and they need to stay on their fucking toes. Riz,

you escort her down. If shit changes, you don't go in with fists, you go for the drain, got it? Kill, don't injure. It's a risk I'm asking you to take on."

"Yes, Captain," says Riz. "C'mon, greenhorn, let's get you downstairs."

They're frowning, and their wounds (wounds? Where had she seen wounds?) seem healed. Rumor has it Riz had once punched a train clean off the tracks, and Ajat's choice has clear implications: not somebody cruel or hateful, but somebody who would absolutely put her through a wall if she acted out. They don't talk as they make their way down through the bowels of the ship. Only when Yat is in the cell and the lock has sealed itself does Riz actually look her in the eye.

"I like you, kid," they say, "but if Ajat says you're dangerous, then you're dangerous. Her judgment has saved my life more than once, and I'm trying to stay calm here, but I am not feeling it, not in my heart, not in my head, not in my godsdamn eyelashes. Just don't give me a reason, okay?"

Yat undertook the same routine herself more than once in her days as a cop. *We're friends, right? But we're not friends at all, not when I've got the keys and all the weapons. It just hurts less to pretend we're friends.* She nods, and Riz leaves.

Only when the brig door has slammed shut and the retreating footsteps are gone entirely does Yat turn to the other figure in the cell. He is half-cloaked in shadow, but she'd know his silhouette anywhere. She sees it in her nightmares sometimes, pushing the barrel of a gun right between her eyes. He seems to shimmer and glide, as though he is made entirely of dark water. He emerges from the pitch-black. She expected sharklike teeth and a crisp dark police uniform.

Instead, she sees pinched cheeks, a high collar, a bowler hat, round wire glasses, a deep gray frock coat, and matching slacks. She's seen clothes like that a thousand times in temples all over Hainak, in her father's greenhouse looking over the planters. Traditional alchemist's clothing, as worn by every depiction of Luz, Son of Crane: Luz of medicine, livestock, the harvest. Luz, in whose name every alchemist utters praise. Luz, brother of Hekat the Hunter. As he steps toward her, the shadows peel off the walls and move with him, and she feels them cold and slick, wrapping around her ankles. She tries to cry out for Riz, but no sound comes out.

"Constable," says the god Luz, "I think it is time we got better acquainted."

ONE YEAR AGO

The seat was awful, but that didn't matter. With a few false starts and little bit of finesse, Kiada's particular gift got her backstage. The crew moved around her without acknowledging her, never quite managing to see her anywhere but out of the corners of their eyes. She made her way into the wings. Performers moved back and forth around her, never questioning her presence.

It was a strangely intimate thing to watch a show from the wings. She could see the mechanisms and wires, the quick costume changes, all the artifice, and love the thing anyway. It was honest, as much as theater could be. One or two performers seemed to notice her as they passed, something inside them registering the break in routine, the unfamiliar face, but she caught the golden threads of magic moving between neurotransmitters and pushed them away before they had time to grow. It started to tire her somewhere toward the end of the

first act, so during intermission she clambered up onto the catwalk, handled the lighting technician's curiosity, then settled in beside him with crossed legs and watched the second act play out.

She didn't speak the dialect of High Radovangi it was performed in, but she'd heard the story before, long ago: it was about a young man, Mārū, who found a strange egg in the woods and took it home to his village, hoping to sell it. It hatched, and the firebird's emergence burned the town down, and the townsfolk hunted Mārū and the bird out into the forest. Mārū sought to protect the firebird, whom he felt he had wronged, but he failed, and the townsfolk butchered them both. The bird sprang back to life (marvelous pyrotechnics, like nothing she'd ever seen before, shooting so high they warmed her feet), but she could not raise Mārū from the dead. Her tears fell on him, filled with magical promise . . . and did not raise him. The bird wrote a beautiful song to call his spirit, and that did not raise him. She cried out to the gods themselves for intervention, but that did not raise him.

Part of the show—woven in seamlessly—was the crew panicking, wandering onto the set, trying to move Mārū's actor, who did a wonderful job at playing dead. As the firebird failed to raise Mārū for the third time, the director came onstage and told the audience they needed a minute to speak with the authorities, then sent the audience off into the final intermission chattering among themselves about how much of it was real.

When the curtains closed, Mārū's actor sat up. A makeup artist came out and did some work that was hard to discern from above. She worked quickly, and by the time the sounds of audience chatter began to fill the theater again, she was gone. A crew member checked something beneath Mārū's shirt, nodded in satisfaction, and placed something in his hand, which the actor closed a fist around. Mārū lay back down.

After a few moments, the lights dimmed and the curtains parted. Mārū lay still. Did he squeeze the object in his hand? It was hard to say, even from her special little viewing spot. The firebird announced that while the audience had been away, she'd found a secret song that would help them raise Mārū, but she needed the audience to stand and sing along. It was "Hunter, Hunter," an old folk song they'd all learned as children, about the city's founding. It wouldn't have worked with a high-street crowd, but the Bokoura was a bit rowdier and more accommodating, and the audience stood and began to sing along.

Between the lights, the band, the firebird onstage encouraging them to new heights, it was a belter. They stamped their feet, waved their hands, whooped and cheered. They stayed standing when the song finished, and the firebird went to Mārū and lifted his head. Kiada couldn't see his face, but she could see the audience, hear the gasp run through them. The actor quietly dropped the string that had been in his hand, and Kiada realized what it was: a great big squib taped to his chest somewhere, filled with something that looked very much like old dark blood. There had been a good few minutes since he'd popped it, and it'd had time to soak, so when the firebird lifted him, the puddle congealing beneath his chest spilled out and over the boards.

Somebody stormed out, raving angrily. The room was otherwise deadly silent, and she could hear his every word: *That's not how the story goes, that's not how things work!* The rest of the audience sat and did not speak. Somebody was crying near the back in small, hitching sobs. They'd come to the theater to be moved, and they had been moved, and they hated it. But of course, there was still the rest of the third act to go, and where to go from here? It was a classic opera,

everybody knew where it ended: Mārū was meant to come back from the dead, to discover he was secretly a prince, to go and reclaim his kingdom from his wicked and ugly uncle. Would he be a good king? It didn't matter after the curtain fell; if he'd been a good man, for all it mattered he was a good king. Instead, the firebird quietly buried his body (a clever trick with a trapdoor) and sang a long lament for him, then set about returning to the town and finishing the job. With the town burned, she sang of triumph, of work yet to do, then took off on hidden wires that rattled beside Kiada's head, and disappeared behind the proscenium and out of sight. The orchestra fell silent, and the curtain just fell. Kiada barely had time to register what was happening when the show's star actress landed on the catwalk, saw Kiada, and screwed up her face.

"You're the new girl?" she whispered.

Kiada nodded. She'd been seen, too late to work her magic now. Best say as little as possible, play the part. Even without her gift, she'd always had a talent for going unseen. The trick was to look like you belonged, to smile and nod and know where the exit was just in case things went wrong.

"Well," said the firebird, turning around and showing Kiada her back, "help me out of this. It's too damned tight, I swear I can barely sing in it. I keep telling Sogi that women's sizes are different, and he tells me he has a wife and he'd know if women's sizes were different, and it's not worth having that argument. Anyway, zip, please."

Kiada helped with the zip, blushed a little at seeing the woman's brassiere, got mad at herself for blushing, pulled the zipper down a little too hard, and got it jammed on one of the teeth. She tried to unhook it, which only made it worse. The firebird was letting out little notes of annoyance that were getting less subtle with every passing

second. She was a striking woman, tall and fine-boned, pale as porcelain, with a beautiful sharpness to her. Her wig was flame-red, but up here, up close, a little blond hair poked out from beneath the false hairline.

"I, uh . . . It's—" Kiada tried to let the zipper up, but it was firmly stuck around the teeth. "It's broken, miss," she said. "Ma'am. Your . . . firebird?"

It was quite a thing to see the woman round upon her. Kiada could handle herself in a fight. She'd once punched every single one of a man's teeth out. It hadn't been a plan or anything, but she'd hit him in just the wrong way that every single one of his remaining rotten teeth ended up in his throat or on the floor. She was, nonetheless, totally unequipped to deal with a prima donna in full flounce. The woman put a single finger beneath Kiada's chin and pushed it upward so they were face-to-face. She was very tall. Her eyes were a deep blue, flecked with little dark imperfections like tea stains or little drops of blood. She pursed her lips and leaned in close, then stepped back and released Kiada from her strange spell.

"You're not the new girl," she said. "Who are you?"

Kiada was a lot of things. A good sailor, a better brawler, inexplicably tongue-tied. What she *wasn't* was a snitch. "Broke in," she said. "Through the back door."

The firebird sighed. "Tell Auntie she doesn't need to spy on me, she can always just ask," she said. "I'm an open book. There's no man in Radovan who doesn't know my dirty secrets, haven't you heard?"

"Auntie?" said Kiada.

"Oh, come on, dear," said the firebird. "You're filthy, you're covered in scars, and you managed to get yourself onto the catwalk without the crew noticing. I know one of Auntie's spiders when I see

one. You're prettier than the last one she sent, for what it's worth. Not that that'd be hard: poor boy looked like a bulldog chewing on a thumbtack."

Auntie's making me work. Where had she heard that? It hit her, and her eyes widened, just a little. Just what sort of trouble had Ari gotten himself involved in? A flicker of curiosity passed over the firebird's face, too fast to catch. She didn't say anything, and that was even more worrying. Eventually, when they had spent altogether too long staring at each other in silence, the woman extended a hand.

"Nyree," she said. "Now, tell me, did you break my zipper on purpose?"

Kiada didn't need to know the name. She'd heard stories about the woman for years, and she lived up to all of them. She shook her head.

"No, ma'am, genuine accident. Swear on the gods."

"All right, well," said Nyree, "you look like a climber. Help a girl down?"

"Yes, ma'am," said Kiada, "I think I can handle that."

ONE YEAR AGO

All houses are alive. Some are literally alive, grown from cellulose and alchemical fertilizer, but even a stone house has a life to it. They accumulate experiences, they have cuts and scrapes left behind by inhabitants, they—given enough time and enough life—develop a personality as distinct as any person's. Sometimes they sleep and then they wake, sometimes they are laid ill for a long time, sometimes they die and the body slowly rots away. A house is not only alive due to its inhabitants; it is, in its own way, equally alive.

Which is to say that Ari's place was full of crap and he wouldn't have it any other way. It was a rule he had: everybody who came through had to leave something or take something. Some folk weren't inclined to leave things, but that was fine by him: the more of them who carried the house with them, the bigger it became.

There was Nyree, of course; Mārek and Auntie and the rest; and

Kiada and her crew from the *Kopek*, whom he had never met, but about whom he'd wrangled a few good yarns; and also Mr. Rawiri Pono, who was retired and had taken up knitting after his wife died and always had too many knitted things; and Ms. Ripeki Kalpona, who had once played the accordion professionally, until the demand for accordion players dried up, and now just played the accordion when she had a minute to herself; and Mr. Iga Kanikai, who'd been in the light horse in the war and who was now in a wheelchair, who still wore his slouch hat everywhere, and whom Ari had seen more than once riding through Radovan on horseback, grimacing in pain and pride; and then there was young Ms. Jules Ohei, who was a typist for some ministry or another and who dreamed so strangely and deeply that it occasionally spilled over into her real life. There was, of course, the Widow Rātā, who owned the place and lived upstairs and spent all day staring in the mirror and talking to nobody, but in more lucid days had been kind enough to let Ari stay. He made sure she ate and he helped her bathe sometimes, and she talked to him as though he were her long-dead son. They were each a part of his house, fragments of its personality, all little pieces of the same soul.

It was a long summer, one filled with flowers and song. Ivy grew up the walls of the house and covered the lower windows, which gave better protection from prying eyes than the moth-eaten curtains. Ari drifted through it in a half dream, stealing from those who Auntie told him could afford it. At some point, in the last days of summer when the days were getting shorter, he found the doppler.

It was in the form of a woman. It didn't look totally unlike Nyree, but its hair was a dark, rich brown. He found it in the dump, covered in filth. Auntie had sent him to scavenge copper ("I don't want a single wire left that's not in our hands"), but he forgot about it and got

an earful later. The doppler had lost its arm, and he rooted through the junk for three hours before he found it a replacement: a heavier thing with clumsier mechanisms, probably some sort of industrial model. He had no idea how to turn the thing on or how to reattach the arm, so he put the arm in his bag and draped the doppler over his shoulders like it was a drowning victim, and he trudged home, taking a longer route he knew would have less foot traffic.

He cleaned it with a sponge, careful not to get water near the exposed electronics, then he propped it up in the rocking chair across from the fireplace. When Mārek came around next, he'd asked if she could fix it, and she spent about twenty minutes examining it before shaking her head and saying it wasn't in her wheelhouse, that programming the things was a world away from fixing the hardware.

He called it Teina. It was an old word, *little sibling*, whose implications changed based on whoever wore it: for boys it meant noisy, fierce, and for girls it meant quiet, secret. He didn't know what it meant for dopplers, but he found strange comfort in his own ignorance. It wasn't a boy or a girl, it was a robot. It felt kind, somehow, to leave its options open. Little Sibling, noisy and quiet and fiercely, fiercely secret. Unless, you know, it wasn't. Mārek would come over occasionally and try to get Teina to work but leave frustrated every time. She'd mutter darkly about it, about having a device in the house she didn't understand. "It's attack surface," she'd say whenever Ari tried to calm her down. Then, if he asked whether to throw it out, she'd glare at him even more angrily, like he was threatening to break her favorite toy.

In the end, it wasn't Mārek who managed to turn Teina on.

It was Auntie.

She'd been in the living room when he came home one day. He

kept the place well locked up and she didn't have a key, but if Auntie wanted to get inside a building, she would always find her way in. Ari had long since given up trying to stop her. But she had never brought a friend before. He was an engineer, there was absolutely no doubt about it. He wore overalls smeared in grease, and his hat had a pin on it from the engineers' union. He was a jowly man, perhaps fifty, but with a sort of vulpine tilt to his features beneath it, a certain sharpness in his eyes and nose that didn't quite fit the rest of his face. If you were casting a play and you wanted somebody to play the Engineer, he was precisely the man you'd pick.

It was strange, then, that he was doing very little work. He certainly looked like he was working on Teina, busily moving to and fro, inspecting, taking down notes. It was all just 5 percent too slick, and then Ari realized that he had seen the man at the theater, as Father Konkaru in *The Three Sins of Olena Hepi*, and that Auntie was the one really calling the shots. She wasn't saying a lot, but it was clear to Ari that she knew exactly what she was doing with the doppler, and he knew where and how to stand.

A chill ran down his spine, and not for the first time, he was reminded of how little he knew of Auntie's life before she'd adopted him. She ran a Hainak-style teahouse that did decent business out the front and incredible business out the back, almost none of which involved tea. She dressed simply and spoke roughly and had taught him to pick a pocket. She'd taught him which bakeries threw out the bread that was still good to eat, how to look innocent when the cops came around. He'd always assumed she was just another street kid who'd done particularly well for herself and wanted to pay it forward. There were rumors, of course, that she'd been a Praetorian in the war, that she'd been a turncoat, a spy,

a Hainak noblewoman who'd fled the revolution. Nyree insisted she'd seen her at the theater once, dressed to the nines, in the special box reserved only for swells. He didn't doubt she had some nice clothes tucked away, but she'd never struck him as a swell in disguise. She'd given him a slap that had taken him off his feet once and had chemical burns all along her forearms like the old Hainak soldiers did, plus a dense network of scars running along the backs of her hands, tracing her finger bones. There was a whorl of living tattoo across her chin and jaw; he couldn't imagine a single bougie hair on her head.

And here she was, fixing the broken doppler that had stumped even Mārek. A chill ran down Ari's spine. More than that: there was a prickling at the back of his head, as though a soft-footed but incredibly persistent spider were tap-tap-tapping at the point where his skull met his neck. He turned and realized she was staring at him. He grinned at her and felt like a dog showing its teeth to a wolf.

She smiled back.

"Is this what you were doing when you were meant to be gathering supplies for me? It's quite a find," she said. "I hope you don't mind that I called in Mateo. You don't often find an mk1 in any salvageable condition now that we've got mk2s, and I felt it necessary to indulge his professional curiosity."

Was it Ari's imagination, or had Auntie hit the last word with just a little more force than she'd intended? Mateo the Actor nodded brusquely, said, "Fascinatin'," then went back to his work, which appeared to be mostly tapping things that were as far away from the wiring as possible.

"Not at all," said Ari. "You know I love meeting new friends." His face gave away nothing; he'd learned to lie from the best, but then

he realized the best was staring right at him. Part of him wanted to prod Mateo, throw some of Mārek's tech jargon at him and see whether he could take it, but the little tapping-skull spider was getting less soft and more insistent. Ari's head hurt, and he needed to lie down. He knew, of course, that when you were being interrogated, the trick was to be the opposite of anxious, but interrogations had a funny way of bringing out anxiety.

He spent a second too long inside his own head, and he knew it, and he knew she knew, and agonizing over that was only going to make the situation worse.

"Can I get either of you some tea?" he said.

"Are you asking me to sample your product, Ari?" said Auntie. "Because I'm fine to take your word for its efficacy."

He actually laughed at that. A hormone joke? He hadn't even known she was aware of what was in the boxes, except that it came from Hainak and made them money. Her bribes got them past the harbor guards, but she'd been otherwise hands-off that part of the business. But of course, Auntie saw everything.

"No, Auntie, the—"

"Black, two sugars, dear."

She didn't need to tell him, but he appreciated the excuse to leave the room. Mārek was in the hallway, her arms crossed. She glowered at him. She always did that, but this time, it felt motivated. *Attack surface,* she mouthed.

"Cup of tea?" he said to her. *Hey, it worked on Auntie.*

For a moment he saw some hidden emotion cross her face, a tiny dilation of the pupil, a tremor of the lip, and then she stormed off without saying another word.

SIX MONTHS AGO

After six bottles of palm wine, even Kiada was starting to feel a bit light-headed. Sen was drinking it out of a coffee cup, and he sculled the entire thing in a single go, then slammed it down on the table. His face was deeply flushed, almost purple, but his back was straight and his hands steady. He grinned at her as the crew cheered and beat their hands on the table. Yat's head was resting on her hands, but she was smiling. Ajat was leaning back in her chair, having given up far earlier than she really needed to, probably on the basis of some fucking equation about the efficiency of metabolizing alcohol or something.

"Give up?" Sen said.

Kiada shook her head. "You can't beat me, old man. That's not trash talk, just a fact: alcohol is a poison, and my body repairs itself a *lot* faster than yours. I can flush this shit in seconds; you can't."

"Never lost a pissing contest in my life, not about to start now," said Sen. He picked up the next bottle and leaned across the table to fill her cup. She snatched it and drained it in seconds. No cheers for her; Sen's baby-face act was too good. She filled his mug with sarcastic slowness, and when she finished, he leaned in and *winked* at her, then threw it down in a single gulp. The crowd went mad, hollering and stamping their feet and patting him on the back.

"I don't get it," Ajat said. "You cannot possibly win. You're damaging your body for nothing."

"You ever play mahjong?" said Sen. He stood lazily, a little bit of drunken swagger in his poise but not nearly as much as there should've been, then took the bottle, held it high over Kiada's glass, and poured out the rest of it with reciprocal sluggishness, speaking as he did so. "My mum taught me. We used to play for chocolate, shit got all over the tiles. Gods, Mum was fierce. During the day she was so sweet and nice, and you put those tiles in front of her and suddenly she was a shark. She provided all the choccy, of course, but that wasn't the point."

The bottle was empty; her glass was full.

"Sometimes in mahjong," said Sen, "you just can't win. Bad luck— it happens. The trick there, Mum taught me, was that you recognize it and you stop playing to win; you play to not lose. Everybody expects everybody else to play to win, but if you stop trying, you open up moves that nobody sees coming. Everybody thinks everybody else wants what *they* want, and it burns 'em every time. Mum didn't always win, but fuck me, she never lost. Same board, two different games. Drink."

She raised the glass and looked him in the eye. She still didn't trust him—cops didn't just stop being cops overnight—but she knew

he would rather drink molten glass than back down. He was going to keep going and going until it killed him. She could repair a hangover easily enough, but Sen was past that and well on the way to giving himself heart failure.

"You're the most stubborn man I've ever met," she said.

Yat laughed and nodded. "You have *no* idea," she said.

Kiada put the full glass back down on the table and pushed it away. Sen shot both his fists up in the air, then immediately fell over. The Weavers in the crowd were already on him, purging the alcohol, getting him back on his feet. She got up and came over to help. The work was already mostly done, but she felt like she owed it to him. As she helped him back up, he shot her the biggest shit-eating grin she'd ever seen.

"'Most stubborn,'" he said. "I like it. Does it come with a pretty ribbon?"

"It comes with nothing," said Kiada, "but you knew that already. Enjoy your nothing, I'm going to bed. Baby, you coming?"

Yat looked back and forth, then walked to Kiada, put a gentle hand on her forearm, and leaned in close.

"I'm enjoying the party," Yat said. "You sure you don't want to stay?"

Kiada winced and stepped back. She didn't answer. Somebody was staring at her, someone who resisted being seen; the very thought of them was forgotten a second later. As she stalked away, the bar of the *Kopek* erupted into raucous laughter and applause.

NOW

Kiada is trying to work. The weapon that hit the ship came from Radovan, but just like after the bombings that hit Hainak six months ago, there is no follow-up from the Radovan navy. It isn't hard to see why. The sentries on deck have been watching for hours and haven't seen a single living soul. The Radovan fleet squats in the harbor around them, floating mountains of slag. Many more rest on the bottom of the bay, their twisted shadows even more distorted by the filthy water above them. A group of sailors use the stoma system to haul a table up onto the main deck, and on the table is a map of Radovan that Kiada drew from memory. It isn't good, mostly broad strokes with clusters of detail around the Moazi Ward docks and Ari's place. She is in no mood to take criticism for it. People are asking too many questions, wanting clarification about parts of the city

she's never been to. Yat's absence doesn't help; Kiada is losing the war of attrition against her urge to scream.

Instead, she puts down pins where she can, lets Xidaj thread a dark string among them, and makes it clear what she does and doesn't know. The source of the beam seems obvious: the great control tower in the industrial district. Several crew members saw its dish glow a bright red right before the beam hit. Over the next hour, Kiada, Ajat, Xidaj, and Sen plan their route. From the docks to Ponamet Quarter, from there to Ari's place, then on to the city center and the Kōhiket Maitaz Special Industrial Zone. She remembers seeing the tower under construction and knows it is in a complex maintained by the Ukumaurek Karetaozi Corporation. Production and control for every synthetic life-form in the city, from dopplers to ferro-cats. Mārek would know the way there, and if she's still alive, she'll be at Ari's place with the rest of the gang. Kiada shuts her eyes and tries to cast her vision out to the Fort, but sees nothing, no light. She told them she was coming back for them, and she means to keep that promise, whatever she finds in that house. She feels a lump forming in her throat, so she goes back to the map. It is a jumble of abstractions, of lines, shapes, string, and paper. It is easier to think of it as pins and string than to think of it as a place of houses and friends and a monstrous silence that threatens to break her in half.

She already suspects what she might find. She's felt the same greasy ash underfoot in the factory where she worked as a blank. It was belched out by the chimney attached to the furnace where they took blanks that stopped working. She doesn't want to take anybody ashore who can't handle what they're going to find. The crew isn't young and certainly isn't naïve, but this feels different. She needs a crew built from oak and stone.

"Sen," she says after a while, "how's the leg?"

He shrugs. After months of wishing he'd shut up, his silence over the last few hours has been deafening. She hoped he, if anybody, would stick up for Yat, but he's been putting out fires elsewhere, and they locked the door to the brig before he found out. His face is set at a resolved grimace. She's never seen him without his cane, but she's also seen him training the crew in hand-to-hand, and she knows the old pig bastard can handle himself.

"Gives me a twinge when it's about to rain," he says. "Otherwise, fine." His tone rises and falls a little, like he planned to make a joke and aborted halfway.

If they can't find Mārek, they'll need an engineer to figure out the tower, and that means Xidaj. She looks up at him.

"You got any reckon how that thing works?" she asks. She doesn't need to specify what *that thing* is.

"Some sort of beam emitter," he says. "High-frequency, but also long-range. You can see the damage on the ships is less than the damage within the city itself, and that's a big clue. If we were closer, the whole crew would probably be dead. To hit us from that far away, it would need a massive power source."

"What, like a chemical engine?"

He shakes his head. "More like a nuclear reactor." He runs his thumb across his chin and plucks idly at the string on the map.

"I have a theory that the 'bomb' in Featta was actually a fusion reactor," he says. "Massive ancient generator. Just one could power a whole nation. I read a fascinating paper about the one under Suta: they couldn't figure out how to turn it on, but what they did understand let them know that activating it could be catastrophic. Now imagine there was one under Featta. Nobody to maintain it, rotting

away for thousands of years, then somebody who has no idea what they're doing stumbles into the wrong room and pushes a couple of buttons. You couldn't blow the thing that way if it were fully operational, but the decay has set in, so it's extremely fragile—most of its systems are offline, and that means the safeties, too. Even then, most likely nothing happens, you've got to be a certain amount of functional to explode, but you only need somebody to get unlucky once, and the whole thing goes critical."

Kiada was there; she doesn't need telling. Featta went up when she was six years old, and even today, nothing grows for miles and miles around the crater. Her first scars are from the time she stayed up all night to watch the sun rise; as light bloomed on the horizon and she rushed to the window in excitement, the shock wave turned the glass into a hundred tiny daggers. Ash fell so thick that it turned the world black and white, and anybody who stayed in its cloud got sick and rotted away. The light burned shadows onto brickwork, and she found her parents in familiar silhouette, embracing one last time. She was half-blind from the light, and her face was covered in blood, and to her, it almost looked like they were dancing. The gendarmes found her staring at them and had to drag her kicking and biting back to the train with the other soon-to-be refugees.

"Okay," she says. "I don't fully understand, I'm not sure I want to, but are you saying Radovan has one that works?"

"Would explain a lot," he says. "We never figured out how the Radovangi managed to forge aluminum. That sort of wattage isn't possible with the coal plants they were running. It raises the question of how on earth they managed to maintain it, but I honestly can't think of how else the tower hit us from that far away. The power required is simply immense, far off the scale of anything we're able

to produce by several orders of magnitude. It's like they've got a sun trapped down there, like they've caged a god. Nobody's got anywhere near the resources to make a new reactor happen, but you get your hands on a functional piece of ancient tech? Anything goes. The stuff of legend: flying cities, holes to other worlds, direct phone lines to the gods."

"You're telling me," Kiada says, "that we're sitting on top of a gigantic bomb, and you have no idea why it hasn't blown up yet?"

"No," says Xidaj, "we're sitting on top of a gigantic *generator*. And I have no idea why it hasn't blown up yet."

"Just what is this town?" says Sen. "You lived there, you must've seen something. Nobody can keep a secret like that."

Kiada doesn't know what to say. She remembers songs, statues, whisky, the sound of wheels rolling along cobblestones.

"It's a city," she says, "you know, like any city. It was normal."

"Oh," says Xidaj, "I highly doubt that's true."

He is smiling. He never smiles much unless you put a new machine under his hands. It worries Kiada, but she needs him. He clearly understands the situation better than any of them. She sighs.

"Sen and Xidaj, you're coming with me," she says. "Our goal is to shut off the tower."

She forgot Ajat was still there. The woman is leaning against the far wall. They lock eyes, then Ajat nods and steps forward.

"Riz," she says, "I need you onboard. We need to grow a new sail, and that means Weavers working the heart. Once Yat is feeling better, if we know we can trust her, she can help. Somebody has sterilized the city, and that makes it extremely dangerous for Weavers, no life to pull from whatsoever. So I want all nonessentials staying on the ship."

Ajat shoots Kiada a look. "No hero shit," she says. "There's absolutely nothing to charge off out there. There aren't even birds flying over the place. You run dry, you die for real. You boys okay with being batteries if Kiada runs low?"

The idea is repulsive, but Sen and Xidaj both nod before Kiada can voice her protest. She hopes for their sakes it isn't just macho posturing. Xidaj nods to himself, then turns and descends the stairs into the belly of the ship.

"When this is over, Kiada," says Ajat, "you and I are going to have a talk about you and your place on this ship. I need your stupid ass alive so I can tear it off myself, you get that? If you pull any reckless shit out there, you better hope you don't come back from it, because if you do, I'm sealing you in a lead coffin and throwing it overboard."

Deep inside Kiada, something comes loose: a sliver of memory that pierces through the space between her eyes. An alien thing that doesn't belong to her; the pain makes her grit her teeth and inhale a hiss. She clasps the bridge of her nose between her thumb and forefinger and pushes it back down. She mutters an agreement.

"What was that?" says Ajat.

Crane Weavers like Ajat are all mad as shithouse rats, everybody says so. The god they pull power from lost her mind and never stops screaming, and it gets inside their heads until they snap. Starting a fight with her isn't worth it.

"Yes, ma'am," says Kiada.

"Yes, *Captain*."

Kiada sighs. "Yes, Captain," she says. "Look after Yat while I'm gone."

Ajat's expression softens. "Of course," she says. "Now get moving. We have no idea when that tower will fire next. I'll try to coax the

ship to pull back, but I don't know how responsive it's going to be. While the ship is unconscious and that tower is online, we're sitting ducks."

She takes a step forward. They've sparred together before, and Kiada knows that she's stronger, but that Ajat is longer-limbed and fast as a snake. Whenever they'd fought, they'd come to a draw.

"I'm trusting you," says Ajat. "Don't fuck this up."

"No, Captain," says Kiada. Xidaj returned strapped with a pack and tool belt. She doesn't recognize half the equipment on it. A hand lands on her shoulder, and she turns to see Sen giving her a hollow grin.

"C'mon," he says, "the ship won't save itself."

She turns toward the exit and feels Ajat's stare boring into her spine, and a chill runs through her. Whatever the silent city holds, it is easier to handle than whatever is happening aboard the *Kopek*. Kiada leaves without another word.

ELEVEN MONTHS AGO

Vatay had not come to lead the Vuruhi by having an open and trusting heart. He did not trust the kōkika as far as he could throw her, no matter her status as an ambassador or how much money and how many pretty girls she could throw his way. His spies had been hard at work, and he knew her secret: the other name she used only with very select company. Still, the money and the girls were nice, and while they couldn't buy his loyalty, they could certainly buy his patience. He drank the vile kōkika tea and smiled in a way both he and the ambassador knew was a mask for disdain. The chair was very comfortable, and a girl was massaging his shoulders, and he wondered how many good Radovangi men needed to suffer for some Vault-shit foreigner to get this rich. The Vault was barely even a real country anymore, just ruins made of iron, but there was still an archivist holed up there in a burned-out server room, and

there were mining contracts to be bought and sold, so everybody pretended it still mattered.

Ambassador Māfaifai was smiling at him with a sort of practiced nonthreatening-ness, idly running her spoon around the rim of her teacup. He hated it, hated the little parlor games and the things unsaid. Real men just said what they meant, and there was no place in Radovan more lacking in real men than Kaifakano Hill.

"I want access to the tower," he said. "My men helped build it; I should be able to use it for their benefit."

Māfaifai laughed, tinkling and artificial as carriage bells.

"E hoa mai, whatever use would you have for it?" she said. "It's an autoclave, not a cutting torch."

"An autoclave? Exactly what are you planning to disinfect?" he said. "Not my people, surely? Not good to ask, I suppose, but then it's not good to ask me my plans, either. 'Plausible deniability,' is that what you call it?"

"It's sweet that you want to play the grand game, Mr. Malatenki, but the answer is no. This technology is simply too dangerous to leave in private hands, especially if I don't know what they're doing with it. What's that play your men all seem to love? About the man who tries to duel an iron foundry. *Donk the Idiot*, was it? I think you learned the wrong lesson, but then again, so did the writer."

Sweet? He spat his tea back into the glass and screwed up his face. Most of the barbs rolled over him, but this one stung. Perhaps because he and his countrymen actually did love *Mārū and the Firebird*.

"I meant to ask," he said, "what's it like representing an ash heap? All this technology too advanced for our little heads, but somehow you Vault rats still lost the damn war."

She didn't rise to the bait. On the contrary, her face went totally

blank, the stoicism of somebody trying very hard not to let on they're rattled.

"Better than living in one," she said, and smiled sweetly at him. "Which is why my answer remains no."

He could have snapped her neck. Instead, he reached into his bag and pulled out a coil of copper wire one of his men had attached to a car battery. In an instant she was out of her chair, trying to disguise her haste as a sort of casual disinterest and failing miserably.

There's the reaction he needed.

"Put that away," she snapped. "There's sensitive equipment in here."

"This?" he said. "It's just a toy. My kid made it. Uses it to fuck with ferro-cats. Had to stop him using it around the doppler, kept bugging it out; I was just going to throw it out but thought you might like it as a gift. You like machines, right?"

He took a step forward and pointed the coil at her.

"Can you imagine the scandal," he said, "if it turned out some society lady weren't a lady at all?"

"I don't know what you're implying," she said, "but our business here is done. Leave." She hit a button beside her chair to buzz for security. They did not arrive. Instead, a Vuruhi entered the room with bruises on his knuckles, blocking her exit.

"Now, kōkika, we're going to sit and talk about tower access."

The new arrival laid a hand on her shoulder. Vatay barely registered movement, only knew something had happened by the hiss of metal, a foot-long spike in the ambassador's palm that went up through the man's jaw and out through the top of his head again. The spike retracted just as quickly as it emerged, and it was like it was never there at all. The ambassador was still smiling sweetly as the Vuruhi crumpled, his head a small fountain of blood. Malatenki

pointed the coil at her, and she snatched it out of his hand and threw it on the ground.

"Vatay," she said in the chiding voice of a mother whose child had touched the stove, but with an unmistakable metallic edge. "Do not send flies to catch a spider."

Her neck twitched, some glitch running through her. Her eyes were pure blue—no sclera or pupil, just pure blue, like the ocean. Amazing how real the shell was: the doppler marketing materials made a huge deal out of how much they looked like their masters, but the eyes made them look like mannequins in a window. She strode over to him and shoved him against the wall. It was like being hit by a battering ram.

"Who would you tell?" she said. "Who would ever believe you?"

"Don't need them to believe me," he said, "just need everybody to start carrying around crappy homemade solenoids, then we see what happens to these shells of yours, all your little eyes. All the ferro-cats, all the cameras, all the machines you pretend are human."

"That's not much of an incentive to let you leave alive."

The spike was out again, pressed against his chin. He let it tickle him; he'd gotten what he came here for now.

"Which is why I already told them to. Should start rolling out to the lads, ooh, let's say today. I could tell them to roll it back, if you'd prefer? I'd have to be the one to tell them that, though. Give them the special password I didn't write down or say aloud near any of your devices."

"I've killed better men for less," she said. Her hand against his chest was far heavier than it had any right to be; he was pinned, but the spike did not move, which he counted as a win.

"Yeah . . . Vic, was it?" he replied. "Now you can finally kill some worse ones."

ONE YEAR AGO

Nyree declined to walk home with her, so Kiada weaved her way through the city alone, letting a not-quite punch-drunkenness flow through her. She hadn't enjoyed the cramped subway tunnels; the rushing darkness reminded her of something she couldn't quite place and didn't care to. She wanted to ask Ari whether he knew more about the beautiful woman, or more about the director, or more about anything at all. Radovan was beautiful, a town of arches, towers, balustrade balconies with wrought iron whorls imitating plant life. A place etched in iron and marble, glowing softly under electric light. Despite the choice of building materials, it was a place no less alive than Hainak: it was a city of bustling cafés and packed tram cars, a paradise for lovers and thieves. She turned a corner and found herself staring up at a cliffside at the back of an alleyway. A system of ropes and pulleys ran up and down it, and at the bottom

was an empty basket. A grubby face peered down at her from the top, then disappeared. She wandered over to the basket, then put the ticket inside. They didn't have any particular night written on them, and she'd seen the show already. She tugged the rope three times, stepped back, and after a few moments, the basket began its jerky journey to the top of the cliff. The tugs didn't mean anything more than *I'm here, do you see me?* And in that moment, she was seen-unseen, acknowledged by somebody she couldn't possibly know.

When the basket had completed its trip, it began to bobble its way back down.

"Enjoy!" she shouted up.

"Will do, ma'am!" came the voice. Young and high-pitched, the sort of child's voice that could be a girl's or a boy's and was blessed with being too young to care which. She sincerely hoped she wasn't a ma'am. She knew she was a weather-beaten woman, but she definitely wasn't a ma'am, not by time or by hoightyness; you saw enough shit, and it left its graffiti scrawled in the lines on your face, but that didn't make you a godsdamned *ma'am*. She walked away, took the long way back to Ari's place, stopping to admire a painting on some obscure back-alley wall, to stand and breathe in the rich aroma of chocolate from a nearby café, to watch a procession of men in brightly dyed robes who stopped at every door to lay down a single flower. They stopped and stood aside as a group of perhaps fifty soldiers marched down the street, headed for the train station and probably on to the observation posts at Jenxat, north of Syalong Cherta. Kiada pulled up her hood and kept her head low as they passed. She was the enemy, after all. The war was heating back up, everybody said so. It didn't seem to involve much more than posturing, by which measure the war was always heating up, but it still didn't seem smart to get rec-

ognized. When the soldiers departed, the men with flowers returned to their work decorating the city's entryways. One kissed another gently on the cheek as they went. A passerby shot them a nasty look, but Kiada grabbed his rising rage and pushed it back down, made him care just a little less. He moved on. She followed the robed men for a few blocks to make sure she'd been successful, then let them go back on their way. They never even saw her, and she preferred it that way. A homeless man stared at her from a nearby alleyway, his skin a mess of peeling burns that took her for a moment back to her childhood and the aftermath of the Featta detonation. His hair was coming out in clumps. He wore a tattered robe with a patch sewn on it, three black exclamation points in a ring, sharing one central dot. She took some coins out of her pocket and approached him, but he raised his hands and crawled away, gibbering in a language that sounded a lot like Radovangi but wrong somehow, the only words she recognized being *roof no roof where roof.* She left the coins on the ground at the mouth of the alley and kept moving.

She stopped for a while in a second alleyway and watched a nearby puppet show with an audience of small children around it. It was the story of the founding of Radovan: a demonic lion had been terrorizing villages far to the south, and Hekat the Hunter and his three wise comrades chased it a thousand miles to the top of Kaifakano Hill, where Hekat finally put a spear through its heart, and that spear became a flagpole and *That flag still flies there to this day; look, children, you can see it now to your left, and remember that your ancestor is the greatest hunter who ever lived, that our legacy and birthright was to keep the earth safe from monsters.* The puppets bowed and new ones came out, with big glassy eyes and exaggerated features. More recent history; the show was about a father (stern in traditional

Radovangi clothes) and his three troublesome sons: a foppish boy with an ibis head and flowers in his hair (was he Hainak?), an oafish farm boy with the head of a monkey (*Please*, thought Kiada, *tell me that's not the Garden Cities*), and a bookish robot son who refused to leave his bedroom until the father cleverly drove him out by setting the house (and the puppets' booth) on fire (made from colored streamers). It was strange watching Radovan's genocide of the Vault play out as a morality tale with grotesquely big-headed puppets. Ajat had been there—she only talked about it when she was deep in her cups, but with rockets and incendiary gas, Radovan had left the once-thriving island a burned-out shell, its people scattered to the winds. They hadn't even wanted independence, they'd just refused to fight to take back Hainak, and the insult could not be allowed to stand. The puppets' neighbor was a pirate with an exaggeratedly large hat that kept bumping against the sides of the booth, who stopped to kick anybody who fell over before running away. The kids loved him and cheered especially loud for him. In the end, the father managed to get all his sons in line, mostly by hitting them with a big stick, and the family all embraced as the kids cheered. They were never going to leave again, they all said. History-as-yet-unwritten, a statement of intent. Kiada tried to hide her disgust and left without a word.

She arrived at Ari's place without incident and did a quick scope of the threads there. He was inside, alone. She knocked, and he didn't respond for a little longer than she expected. She wondered whether she'd caught him jerking off or something, and when he answered the door sheepishly, she did not dive into his head to find out.

"Busy?" she said.

"Uh," he began. A second voice cut in from behind him. A woman's voice, older, clipped and measured.

"Show your friend in, Ari," it said.

Goose bumps ran up her arms. But there'd been nobody else inside, no golden glow of a soul. Ari's face was unreadable, but he opened the door and ushered Kiada in.

The old woman at the table was Hainak, or something like it. Dark skin, thin with heavily lidded eyes, a swirl of living tattoo on her chin. She was not dressed ostentatiously, but her clothes clearly cost a lot: a crisp, tailored shirt and a smart red jacket. Her gray hair was tied back in a single knot. She was a void of magic, and it itched at Kiada like a missing tooth. She looked very much like a woman, but she may as well have been a statue.

"Um," said Ari. "Kiada, this is Auntie."

Auntie stood and gave a curt, precise bow. "Ah, yes," she said, "our contact from the *Kopek*. I have been meaning to meet you. Did you enjoy the puppet show?"

Kiada had never mentioned the name of the ship to Ari. It was safer that way. They never even brought the *Kopek* itself near the port: they had a cove to moor in and send out the jolly boats. This was very wrong, and the woman had no magic in her, nothing to push around, no thoughts to manipulate. She felt like a doppler. Or, worse, she was . . .

Oh. Another sister in Tiger; a witch of the art of the unseen. She'd never met another; she'd heard they tended to be solitary, and she suddenly partly understood why the other Weavers treated her with so much suspicion—every mind was usually an open book to a Weaver, no intention ever in question, but reading a Tiger Weaver's emotions was like trying to peer through stone.

"Leave me and your colleague alone for a bit, will you, Ari?" the woman said. "I wish to discuss some sensitive business."

He scurried away, clearly happy not to be trapped in a conversation he didn't want to have. When he was gone, she turned and smiled. "It is a wonderful thing," she said, "to feel less alone. How is old Tiger? I haven't heard from her in months."

"I wouldn't know," said Kiada. "Silence on this end, too. I think something happened."

Auntie nodded, sat back down, and poured two cups of tea. She pushed one across the table and gestured to Ari's empty seat. Kiada sat and took the tea. She had not been unable to see somebody's thoughts coiled in their mind for a very long time, and she wondered if there was poison in the sugar. It seemed unlikely, but she couldn't know for sure, and not knowing terrified her. Auntie's eyes were bright and quick. She seemed to move as little as possible, all tightness and control. She drank her tea and did not speak, so Kiada felt obligated to fill the silence.

"It was sudden," she said. "Like, I couldn't get her to shut up, and then one day just . . . nothing."

Auntie rapped her middle finger against the table twice, then set her mouth with a firm *hmm*. "Do you know which day?" she said.

Kiada shook her head. "About six weeks ago, I'd guess? I didn't keep a record."

That seemed to annoy the woman, though it was hard to tell. Her face was almost entirely immobile, moving only when it needed to, and even then as little as possible.

"Yes," said Auntie, "that sounds about right. Come, child, drink your tea. It's not poisoned." She winked.

The sheer audacity of it, peeking into somebody's thoughts like that without any friction, without them even knowing. She tried to examine her own threads, to catch signs of another's passage, but

there was nothing at all. Kiada picked up the teacup, then threw the tea back in a single scull. She set the cup down on the saucer, heavily enough that the *tink* turned into a *thomp*, and she worried for a moment about damaging Ari's porcelain. Although of course, it wasn't actually Ari's. When she looked up, Auntie was studying her, wry and relaxed on the surface but with an undercurrent of intensity that was hard to place.

"Sibyl's a bore," she said, after a while. "If you ever find yourself in need of more stable employment, I could always use a woman of your talents."

"Sibbi?" said Kiada.

"Hmm?" said Auntie. "Oh, yes, Sibbi. I'm so forgetful. But you didn't answer my question."

Kiada had never been in a conversation that felt so much like a boxing match, and she knew she was losing. She threw out a jab. "You didn't ask one."

"You're perceptive," said Auntie. "I'm not a woman who likes to ask anything, and especially not twice."

She smiled in a way that said *This conversation is over* louder than a slap or a gunshot and sat in silence. Kiada got up, pushed in her chair neatly, and turned to leave. She was tired in a way she hadn't been when she walked in.

"Well," she said, "I'd better not give you the opportunity."

She left. It didn't feel like a win. It barely even felt like a draw. It was a rash move and had probably just pissed off a potential buyer, but she didn't like the woman's energy, didn't like being so vulnerable to somebody else without them giving anything back. She felt invaded, like a woolen doll after a run-in with a seam ripper. It had gotten cold while she was inside, and she gripped her coat tight to

herself and made her way through the night. It was almost one a.m., and Radovan was finally going to sleep, with the keener parts of it just waking up. She took the shortest path back to the jolly boat, and—in the shadows, away from the watchful eyes of the Radovan naval sentries—slipped away from the city and into darkness.

NOW

Kiada goes down to the brig to say goodbye to Yat but can't bring herself to stay long or say much. Yat is sleeping, her chest rising and falling irregularly. At least *somebody* would sleep tonight. Kiada could reach in and pull out whatever bad dreams Yat is having, but they have a deal: no memory tricks. They've agreed it's a line that, once crossed, cannot be uncrossed. She stands by the bedside and just . . . stares. She doesn't know why it is so hard to bridge the gap between them, to reach out and touch the woman she loves. Kiada grips the bars and shakes them; Yat does not wake.

I love you, Kiada doesn't say. *You're so good at not saying things; you've said everything except "I love you." You've said around it, crept around the edges, but you can't look it in the eye, and I hate you for that. I love you, but I hate you sometimes. If you never come back and you never say it, then I'll probably just die and it'll be your fault. You*

don't love me, and I think I love you like a tick loves a lamb; either I drain every drop from you or I just fall off and fucking die. I need you like fire needs oxygen and I'll burn you just as bad. Wake the fuck up so I can get back to ruining your fucking life. I don't want to come back without hearing the words, but I also don't want to survive if I'm just going to come back and destroy you, because I break everything that matters to me. It's what I do.

Instead she mutters, "Sleep well," then goes back to their cabin and gets her gear together. She takes her knives, an old woolen coat she hasn't used since she was last in Radovan, and a bully bag for emergencies. Inside the hermetically sealed bag is a larval ant specially designed to commit explosive autothysis when exposed to oxygen and also a shitload of engineered thorns packed tightly around the ant. *Rip the seal, throw, get your head down.* Very illegal but undeniably effective. They have a special ant farm for these onboard, and they've grown an opaque membrane over the top of it, tougher than steel, just in case. She goes to say goodbye to the cat but can't find her, so she heads out into the night.

The lads are already waiting for her over by the jolly boat. Three men, but it feels somehow like four. She realizes her nose is bleeding, and she wipes it away with a thumb. She looks at her thumb with blood on it and doesn't understand, then forgets about it immediately. Sen has his cane with him and must've seen her notice it. He shrugs at her.

"Better to have it and not need it," he says. Stubborn old fool. She heard once from Yat, who saw his memories through her own eyes, what he went through in Hainak: even if his leg gives out, he can get them where they need to go. The man has a candy shell and a steel core. They get in, and Riz lowers them down into the bay. Kiada takes

the oars and tries not to look at the dark water, slick with a strange rainbow sheen. She sits with her back to the city. Around the anchored ships, she can see ash floating on the surface, pooling around the pockmarked and melted iron hulls. They do not speak as they row closer to the city, and the only sounds are of the oars carving gently through the water and the distant crackle of fire. The *Kopek* has killed its lamps to make it a harder target, and now it is just a great dark beast low in the water. Something about all this makes the alarms in her head go off, as though she's just seen the glow of feline eyes peering out from the jungle. She ignores the feeling and continues to row. The smoke blots out the moon and stars, and the embers' glow from Radovan is the only light they have to see by. It is as though they are cutting through darkness itself, through an inky void, guided by the lights of a dead city. She doesn't want to face what is onshore, but orders are orders, and she can't face what is happening on the ship, either. So she rows, the firelight reflected on the water. Her oars break it apart with each stroke, and it soon re-forms again a little closer and brighter.

It feels like she spends a thousand years on that great expanse of dark water, like she is crossing an ocean. She can still see the *Kopek* anchored a few hundred meters away, but it might as well be on another world. As they get closer, their boat begins to knock through the bodies. She counts eleven little juddering impacts and tries not to think about how many more corpses have sunk. She doesn't look at them: it feels disrespectful somehow, as though she's walked in on them naked. Sen breaks the silence, and even then it is only functional, to let her know where the dock is and help steer their little boat home. She never used the Moazi Ward proper during smuggling runs: there were always too many guards to reliably bribe. But

there are no guards now as Xidaj ties the mooring line to a bollard and they clamber out onto the wharf. Up close, the reek is almost unbearable. Burning buildings, yes, but mixed in with burning hair, burning clothes, burning flesh. She smelled something similar once before, when she was six years old and a new sun briefly bloomed on the horizon. A large section of the wharf is burned away, and that is where the bodies are concentrated. Dozens of them, maybe even a hundred, their skin red and slick with fatal burns. She can see it in her head: a panicked search for water, waiting and waving at the ships at anchor, knowing any second the city's great eye might turn on them and not realizing that the crews on the ships were already dead. Their remains are contorted in agony. As she watches, one tips over a portion of the wharf that has crumbled away, hits the water, and breaks apart.

She wonders whether she knew them, then pushes that particular thought down as deeply as she can so as to never think it again. She looks to the others, who are taking it in with stony silence. Xidaj is pale and a little shaky; Sen just looks tired.

"We need to move," she says.

Nobody argues. Whatever bravado they had on the ship has evaporated under the same monstrous heat that is devouring the city piece by piece. The entrance gate to the docks is barricaded with shipping containers, logs, and cement. The barricade is well constructed, all things considered, but it was obviously erected in a hurry. There's a strange smell that hangs over the thing: ozone and burning copper.

"You don't barricade against fire," says Sen. "They wanted to stop somebody coming in."

"Other civilians?" says Xidaj.

"Maybe," says Sen, in a way that seems to shout no. He kneels by

one of the bodies, then looks at Kiada. He moves a few feet back from it. Some of the bodies show initial signs of spore infection—it's hard to tell in their condition, but the flesh is melted in places that don't look like they're from fire.

"The spores," he says, "they're hot with magic, right? If they were around, you'd know?"

The engineered plague that had ripped through Hainak six months ago still lives large in all their memories—the spores were voracious, and it only took a handful to turn the city into a living hell. They narrowly averted an apocalypse, and Kiada isn't keen to do it all over again.

She nods. Sometimes it can be hard to detect disease on a living organism, but the body at the barricade has no living tissue whatsoever. Even dead bodies still have glowing embers, still have congealing blood in their veins that carry small traces of magical charge, and those traces can cover up bacteria or fungi in most cases. The Hainak Plague was different, each spore like a miniature sun that roiled with so much magic it gave her a headache. Even a single one would be like a lighthouse beacon. This body is totally barren. Its burns are different from the cluster of corpses over by the water: the skin is bright red and split open in places where the dry, leathery flesh shows through. She knows somehow that the blood boiled away inside its veins, that the heat left nothing behind.

Sen turns the man's arm over: a line of jagged bone spurs protrudes from his forearm. They are too rough and irregular to be any sort of biowork. The Hainak Plague never left one body the same as the next, but they saw it ravage enough to recognize it.

"It's . . . it's heat sterilization," says Xidaj, "on a massive scale. They cauterized a city."

"Fucking hell," says Sen.

This is too much. Kiada's mouth is dry, and her head starts to spin. She's seen a lot of evil, but there is something more to this place where technology and brutality come together: there is something terrible about seeing man's potential turned against itself. It's easy to think of evil as something that lurks in the darkness like a wild animal—you can dismiss it as a thing from the past that can be quashed, can be evolved beyond. It is another to see it dressed in ribbons. It isn't the first time she's seen new inventions turned against the population, but she'll never be comfortable with it.

There is another body higher up on the barricade. Its face is missing, and she realizes, looking at the ring of melted plastic and seeing the exposed wiring beneath, that it is the source of the ozone smell. She points up at it and tries to speak, but her throat is dry and hoarse, and only a croak comes out. Xidaj clambers up the barricade to inspect the broken doppler. He takes out a small pair of pliers and starts to peel back the soft plastic, revealing more burned-out electronics. Nearby, a damaged ferro-cat walks in circles, its meow coming out in a metallic monotone at intervals too perfect to come from a living throat.

Kiada finds her words. "Why only the face?" she says. "The humans are burned all over. This thing hit the whole galley, burned away a huge section of dock. How did it hit just the face?"

"Targeting could be keyed to human faces," says Sen. "I heard about ferro-tech that could do that. We found an old fléchette gun in one of the bunkers under Syalong Cherta. Homing projectiles. We drew a face on the wall, everybody got the fuck back, and then one of my mates fired completely sideways. Bullseye, every single one. As in, the fléchettes turned around in midair and went right between

the lad's eyes. One of the officers took it off us. We never saw it again, and I'm not particularly upset about that."

Xidaj shakes his head and pokes at the doppler's temples. "It's synth-skin," he says, "lab-grown. Probably primitive by Hainak standards, but considering the war, it's amazing they have it at all. Most of it got burned away, but you can see where they tethered it to the skull. Twenty ox says it's a microwave weapon. It vaporized the water in the skin, and the heat from that melted some of the electronics, but most of the synthetic material is untouched. Microwaves explain the burn pattern as well. It hit the barricade, but not long enough to ignite anything; the dock must've gotten a good long blast. You could cook somebody inside their house and not even peel the paint, hypothetically. Microwaves shouldn't start fires, but they can. Water inside the wood probably got superheated, turned to steam in a fraction of a second, generated a massive burst of heat. You throw a single spark into that mix, say from a lightbulb shattering, and the whole thing goes up. Gods, a microwave beam—nobody has those, nobody is even close. It's all theoretical. We only know about them at all because we've found the little ovens in ancient labs. It's hard to believe, but I can't think of anything else that makes sense. Last time I was here was ten years ago, and they were still excited by combustion engines. Even if they found a massive ferro cache, I doubt they could adapt it this quickly. It's one thing to dig the stuff up and another entirely to start producing your own. To build a motorcar, first you need to figure out how to drill for oil. You need factories and scientists, you need infrastructure, and it's just not here. You don't grow lab-skin in a steel foundry. We're missing something, ma'am, and I worry it's going to get us killed."

He is rambling, but Kiada lets him; he might say something that

can keep them alive. When she is sure he is done, she clears her throat. He is right. Something doesn't add up, but they don't have time to stick around and find out what: if they stay here too long, whatever it is will catch up with them.

"How do we know if it's firing at us?" she says. "Hopefully without, you know, getting hit by it."

"Heat distortion in the air," says Xidaj. "Like a mirage. If it's hot enough to do all this, then it's—" He waves his hands vaguely. "It'll look like the air is underwater. Sort of. It'll ripple. You've been outside on a hot day before, right? You know what to look for. You're not going to have a lot of warning, though. It's only really useful if it fires at somebody else. If we could find a glass bottle somewhere, maybe we could fill it up with water, strap it to somebody's skin? Notice there are two clusters of dead rather than a swathe: it doesn't seem to move laterally when it strikes. I don't have enough information to make any real conclusions, but moving sideways might be enough to avoid it if we know it's coming. That bottle starts heating up, and that gives us enough warning to leave, maybe?"

"The noise," says Sen. "It screams before it fires, sounds like somebody sharpening a million knives. I heard it right before it hit the ship."

They both look at him. They almost forgot he was there. He's the sort of man who can't do anything without humming, but he's been going through the pockets of the first dead man in silence, and in those moments, he became almost invisible. If she didn't know better, she'd swear he was a Friend of Tiger, camouflaged by the weave. No jokes from him now, though in their absence Kiada wants them more than anything. Because being mad at Sen for telling a stupid joke is normal; nothing here is normal, no matter how desperately she wants it to be.

"It doesn't scream," says Xidaj. "It'll be something mechanical in the wave emitter, it—"

"It screams," says Sen. "That's all we need to know. When you hear screams, you start running."

"Words to live by," she says. It's an attempt at a joke, but nobody laughs. Sen takes out his hip flask and hands it to Xidaj. It's a Hainak design, engineered wood that doesn't absorb the liquid inside. "White rum," he says. "That'll do, right?"

"It's liquid and it's got water in it," Xidaj says. "It'll do." He tapped his knuckle against it. "Might be a touch thick: it'll block some of the incoming waves. Might be useless, but I'll take bad odds over none at all."

Xidaj takes a strap of cloth from his tool belt and ties the flask to his bicep.

"There's one more thing," says Sen.

He picks up a rifle from the ground near the dead man and opens it up, then nods.

"He's empty," he says. "And there are spent shell casings on the ground." He frowns. "Nobody cleaned them up, which means this was over fairly quickly. I was in the service when the rank and file still used gunpowder rifles, and an officer would chew you out if you left a mess like that. The big ones can be a hazard underfoot, and if a little one gets stuck in the tread of your boot, then nothing short of divine intervention is gonna get it out. Whatever happened, our man went down fighting."

"How do you know he's military?" says Kiada.

"Chemical burn on his face," says Sen, "looks like he was on the edge of a blast from one of the old twenty-four-pounders. Probably served around the same time I did. Hells, I might've shot at him once or twice. Poor bastard, to survive that hell only to die in a new one."

"He was your enemy," says Kiada. The war defined both of their lives for decades. Even after the fighting stopped, both nations were unable to escape its pull; they pretend they're still at war because admitting otherwise would mean they'll have to figure out how to live with peace, and neither nation's leaders are ready for that. She's lived here, she knows the locals, but Sen doesn't: he grew up under their boots and then came to see them downrange through a rifle's scope. He has no reason to care about their welfare.

"He was probably just some poor bloody kid," says Sen. "We all were. That's how it works—you don't see recruiters lurking around outside the nice parts of town. You're some stupid kid who goes to war, and if you get lucky, you go back to the same crappy house and you get to grow old there with your nightmares for company. And even then, sometimes the devil ain't done with you."

He sighs, then inclines his head toward the city.

"Come on, boss," he says. "We've got places to be."

For a moment, she allows herself to hope: she doesn't trust Auntie, but she knows deep down that if anybody can survive and keep Ari and his friends in one piece, it's her. She nods to Sen, and the trio clambers over the barricade. When they reach the top, they look out over the ruined city. A thousand small fires burn across every district and square, an apocalypse in miniature. There is no life, no movement except smoke and flame. They get their breath back, then head into the fire.

FOUR MONTHS AGO

The death of Aritama Kolamona arrived as a series of tweaks; the owner of a pierogi stall happened to cross paths with a kid selling the newspaper's evening edition, and the news he read made him go home early; Koztati the Wolf got into a fight with his wife after her doppler informed her that she was pregnant, though they hadn't had sex in months; a door was closed; a door was opened; a crowd blocked the way; a crowd did not. The Spider watched them from her little windows, from the eyes of dopplers, ferro-cats, from the eyes of synthetic life-forms that didn't have names because only she knew about them, and as she watched them, she weaved. It was imperceptible from the ground: a hundred little changes, each totally innocuous on their own, but they conspired to drive two men—Aritama Kolamona and Koztati Tamatenko—to find their way to Nahairei Park at precisely 21:37:18.

Koztati was nobody, and that was exactly why the Spider chose him. His file said he tried to join the army at sixteen, but they'd seen the unsightly line of acne around his jaw and rejected him. It had been three months after the Battle of Syalong Cherta, and everybody knew the Lion had lost. The recruitment office knew that by the time they trained the boy up, the war would be over. Koztati was now twenty-five, and he was angry. He was an adequate tailor, but adequate hadn't paid the bills and he'd lost his shop, and now he worked for another man, a Hainak refugee, and it humiliated him. He was, of course, Vuruhi. One of his buddies had brought it up while drinking: Wasn't there something wrong with the world? They'd been sold so many promises. His old friends were all dying from addiction, misery, or something in between. His new friends gave him purpose. *Where is the world you deserve?* He continued to work for the tailor he hated, but he called him kōkika behind his back, and when he went drinking, he'd rant about how he knew they were cooking the books, how that sort were always up to something but he could never prove it, how one day things would change for the better and Koztati would run the place. Koztati had been filled with indiscriminate rage for years, and suddenly it had direction; the fire no longer burned him, because he had learned to point it outward. Koztati was nobody, and that was exactly what made him dangerous.

There was a moment where it almost went wrong, where Aritama Kolamona stopped to admire an ivy-choked statue of a warrior woman whose name time forgot. If he remained there for more than fourteen seconds, Koztati Tamatenko would pass him without noticing. One of the park's new electric lights flickered on the edge of Ari's eyeline, and the seconds ticked down, and then he noticed it and tilted his head to the side. His file said that he was a man whose cau-

tion was superseded only by his curiosity, and the Spider took this and threw him the only curiosity she had available. He took a step toward the light, looked left and right, then started to run, through the bushes and away from the light.

This was not part of the plan at all. He did, however, make a lot of noise, and this alerted Koztati, who moved to investigate. He was a large man whose loping stride carried him quickly across the park, but Ari was running at full tilt, and he was the sort of lightly built criminal who, through practice and necessity, was *very* good at running. The attempt had failed, and the Spider had peered through a hundred glass eyes and seen that Ari knew too much. She would have to try again, and soon, before he reached his home. She wondered whether she could activate the doppler and have it strangle him in his sleep, but it was part of the network, and that meant somebody would see. It was messy, and she hated mess. It was at this point that Aritama Kolamona's left foot caught on a tree root, rain soaked and swollen, and he pitched forward onto the ground.

It was nice, for once, for a random variable to work in the Spider's favor. She had not accounted for it, but she was happy to adjust for it. Koztati caught him, knelt on his chest, saw the ritual scars and filthy clothes and believed he was being stalked by a thief, and this must—as his file dictates—have injured his fragile pride, that he could ever be considered a mark, even for a moment. It made him feel weak, and so, to show his strength, he wrapped his hands around Ari's throat and began to crush. He felt muscle hardening and he squeezed harder while the face of Aritama Kolamona went red, then purple, then something cracked inside his neck and he stopped moving. Koztati stayed in position for over a minute, breathing heavily, and then he stood and dragged the body deeper into the bushes.

He found a small cliffside, one of the dozens that gave Nahairei its unique geography, and pushed the body over the side. A scraping, a falling rush, a rustle of greenery and one final crunch of bone, and Koztati Tamatenko left the park the way he came. He was shaken; he had boasted to his friends for years now about his capacity to kill, but it was a different thing to actually do it, and the Spider watched as he retched, as he steadied himself against a crumbling wall, as he moved away from the twisted body at the bottom of the cliff and gradually convinced himself that he was a righteous man who had done the world a good deed. His wife would notice that he was acting strangely but would not ask questions: she recognized the violence in his eyes. The Spider watched all of this as she watched everything, and permitted herself a smile.

She was so busy watching Koztati that she missed Ari. She had a camera on his shattered body and the body did not move, and that was enough for her. But on an upper level of Nahairei Park, Aritama Kolamona reappeared out of thin air, writhing on the ground and clutching at the arms of an unseen enemy. There was a memory somewhere that he couldn't quite look at, one of a vast pit, of an endless twisting mass of meat and scars, but for all his dreams, he was a practical man, and so he did the practical thing and locked the memory away. When he realized his attacker was gone, he pushed himself to his feet. He was not alive to feel his bones break as they hit the bottom of the cliff, and as far as he knew, his attacker choked him unconscious and then mysteriously left, and his life had been saved by pure dumb luck.

That night, in his dreams, he would learn otherwise.

———

Rats, thousands of them, a moving carpet in every direction, swarming at him, then around him, then beyond him and off into the endless dark. Indistinct statues stared down at them, down on Ari (living) and Ari (shattered bit of meat), back in the park. It didn't feel like a dream, but maybe getting home at all was the dying dream. Ari turned to watch the rats go and regretted it instantly—a bulk moved behind him in the darkness, shuffled and slithered, made his skin prickle, seemed to befoul the air with its labored breathing.

Do not look, Aritama Kolamona.

"Yep," he said, "yep, absolutely. If there's one thing I'm good at, it's not seeing things. Just ask the cops, and they'll tell you there's no point talking to Ari Kolamona, because he didn't see a goddamn thing. I could talk all day about the things I haven't seen. You want to hear my favorites?"

Which was typical Ari: possibly dead, possibly about to be eaten by a horrifying rat monster, incapable of not cracking a joke about it. He always knew his last great punch line would involve a headstone and a chisel. The thing came closer: he could tell by the rush of hot, astringent air that moved before it. It reeked like that shit they treated the bandages with back at the Jenxat Line field hospital where he'd served as a nurse in another life—like a thing that didn't know it was dead yet.

No, I do not. I have a job for you, Aritama Kolamona.

"I'm currently self-employed," said Ari, "and as a rule, I don't work for folks I don't know. Furthermore, I may have a bit of an ongoing issue regarding my current state of, uh . . ." He gestured vaguely around at the darkness. "Got choked–ness," he said. It was meant to be a joke, but his arms were cold, and the words came in a half mumble. He was beyond cold, beyond empty. He could feel his name

slipping away, and he tried to reach for it, but his limbs were heavy and numb and would not move.

You may call me Rat.

"Are you a cop?" he said.

I am the opposite of a cop.

"A snitch, then? Because my business is very legal. Import-export. Lifeblood of the city."

It was a script, and as the words fell out, the air ate them. Little fragments, lost even to memory. They did not echo; it was as though they had never been. Lies did not work here: if a word held its form, it was true.

I am no snitch, Aritama Kolamona.

Ari sighed. It was a bit of an understatement to say that he was out of options. He was definitely, aggressively dead. Deader than he had ever been, and one time his mum had caught him smoking a cigarette with his mate Serji. He realized that his memories had been drifting away, but every time Rat said his name, they flocked closer to him, stuck to his skin. If he stayed here too long, they would float away into the night.

"If you can get me outta this one," he said, "then rat or not, you've got a fuckin' deal."

He moved to turn around, to shake hands, then froze. He caught its squalid, writhing bulk out of the corner of his eye and tried to pretend he hadn't.

Yes, we have a deal.

"Wait," said Ari, "just what's this wor—"

And then he was rocketing upward toward the light, dusty coattails flapping behind him, up and up and up again, through the long night as the reek of that low place clung to him like grave dirt and spoiled medicine and sepsis and—

Dearest daughter,

It is important to me that you know the three phases most important to any young woman.

First, there is a time to hunt. This is the hardest part. Bodies are not built for patience. They are brute things, useful tools, but the ribs are as much a cage as any prison bars. The heart beats against them, the blood flows hot, the body cries out for completion, but the hunt does not allow it. It is a dance with oneself, the most primal act of suppression, mind against muscle. Breathe through the pain, burn it as fuel for your transformation to come.

The hunt is a time of quiet and control, and it hurts because of what it is not.

Yat is dead.

Maybe. It's hard to say. She hears a voice in the distance. *I hate you, I love you like a tick loves a lamb.* The words mean nothing; they're just sounds. Somewhere far above her, the great wings of the mad god Crane unfurl, and she falls into their shadow, somehow darker than darkness, hungry and empty. Crane is screaming; she never stops screaming. The awful sound ebbs and flows, but it never quite stops entirely.

Yat lifts her hand to her face, and it is no more substantial than fog. She is a hole in the world; she has always been a hole in the world, and now the depths have come to claim her, and she walks a strange, hollow, bottomless night-place. If there were wind, it would pick her up and carry her away.

It is a sort of sickness, perhaps. People die of grief sometimes;

97

they just stop and never start up again. She saw it on the streets; people lost people and stopped looking after themselves, and then one day they just stopped moving entirely and the naked pavement devoured them.

There is a ship, somewhere on the edge of sense. She is tethered to it, tethered to the meat that walks it, and she knows in some vague way that she *is* the meat, but the connection between them has never felt more tenuous. The ship does not dominate her eyeline; she is not there. She is in the dark. In the distance, something immense moves, glistening and dripping worms that could eat through a planet like it was a rotten apple. It pays her no heed and continues on its path, pulling a trail of filth behind it.

There is a man she recognizes and does not recognize. A policeman who killed her, whom she killed in turn. His teeth are wrong—the last time she saw them, they were bladelike and screaming as she sucked the life from him. His form seems to shift; he is a shark, he is a great bird, he is a cop with sharpened teeth and stolen gun. Like her, he seems barely there, but he is staring straight at her with eyes full of hatred.

"You're dead," she says. "I don't care whether you told people you're a god, you're just another Weaver, some cosmic con man, and I killed you."

Luz shakes his head.

"Nothing is that simple," he says. "A hungry monkey eats a peach and throws away the stone, and from the stone grows another tree. Would you say the monkey killed it?"

"The tree probably feels great," she says, "but I imagine the peach might voice concerns. Look, you're . . . you're not like this. I saw you earlier and I just—I know this isn't you."

"The peach doesn't matter," he says. He tilts his face away from her a little, and she swears she can detect a tension in his voice. "Ecology is systems analysis; continuity is systems management. That's what you people never understand. I reset two cities and I'm a monster to you, and that's because you think too damned small. It's all about you and your friends, you and *your* patch. Ask yourself how many cities Radovan burned, how many Hainak burned, and for what? A few extra lines on a map? Slaves to bring in rice that'll rot in a warehouse while they starve in the fields? For a bauxite mine and a winter fucking port? And you would preserve that? I am trying to save entire worlds untold, and you're just trying to save yourselves. If you had any compassion, you'd give me this body and let me finish the job. And if you had any sense, you'd do the same, because I will outlast you. I've outlasted a hundred civilizations, I can outlast one *pisting* cop. I am in control; soon, I will be managing this system."

Two short, unspoken sentences passed between them, their light and heat searing Yat's forehead, blinding her. What had Vic called it? *Ah, that's right, root access.* She couldn't move, couldn't speak.

"All Sibyl's work striving for immortality," he says, "and in the end it was so very fragile, because she deals in people, and I deal in systems. She's a terrible immortal, not one single contingency."

There is an echo to his words, and it takes a moment for Yat to realize the echo comes first, a grace note doubling up his speech into an awful cannon. There are tiny discrepancies between the words, adjustments in tone that make little discords: it is the thought, followed by the speech. It is still in her head, it is entirely in her head, and the realization helps but does not snap her awake, does not banish the devil staring her down.

She pulls her will together and pushes *LEAVE* toward him. The

air between them ripples, and Luz ripples with it. For a moment he vanishes, and Yat is ready to cheer, but then he reappears a step closer to her, and she can see the evil in his eyes. His hand snaps out and grabs her wrist. He is so cold it burns; she can feel herself melding into him. A million light-years away, her body rises in its cell with a new light in its eyes.

"NO," she roars, and pushes back, and then she is on the floor and somebody is leaning over her, babbling, lifting her back into the bed while she tries to speak, but there are ghostly fingers inside her throat pushing the sound back down and she lets out a sort of creak. She is lying in her cell. The muscles in her arms and legs have cramped themselves into uselessness, and the pain is so intense. It is all too much effort, but that is the point. It is a war of attrition. She cannot win, but she does not need to lose yet.

Yat sleeps, and the devil sleeps inside her.

THREE MONTHS AGO

The ship was fucking broken again, and not for the first time Ajat regretted getting so ambitious with the refitting. The new *Kopek* was always breaking, and breaking down less like a machine and more like a body. Ajat was doing her best but she could barely keep up; she worried the fixes she'd applied were just future technical debt. When she was finally finished, she walked back to the cabin and found the door locked. She could sense Sibbi snoring softly inside. The woman's paranoia had reached fever pitch lately, and Ajat did not know why; Sibbi had had some of the crew go into Ajat's workshop one day and throw all her electronics overboard.

Things had been better between them, but things had also been far worse. At the end of the day, there was nobody else who knew how to make her feel so safe and—at the same time—like the strongest woman alive, and it felt too much like love to let it go.

The bar was almost empty, except for Sen, who was smoking in the corner. She drew two glasses of beer and carried them over to his table. He was playing with a toy car, rolling it idly back and forth. Looked like a Radovan vehicle made out of bits of tin can. She noticed a few wires poking out of the inside.

"This a sting, pig?" she said. He laughed and took the beer appreciatively.

"This a bribe?" he asked, and winked at her.

She shook her head, muttered, "Once a cop, always a cop," then sat down across from him and took a long, slow drink. She still didn't fully trust him, but he'd proven himself useful, and she wanted to understand him better. She didn't have a plan for if he turned, and she needed to change that. Find his weaknesses, engineer leverage. He was frustratingly opaque, didn't seem to do much except smoke, drink, and fight.

She drained the entire glass and set it gently on the table.

"Anybody on board caught your eye?" she said.

This seemed to throw him a little. He didn't show it, but she could read anxiety in his threads, the ache of some distant memory. He knew their conversation wasn't so polite, but he was playing along. Once a cop—

"Nope," he said.

"Not the type?" she asked.

He took a swig of beer, and she could sense his threads moving protectively around something. Around *someone*.

"I'm the type," he said, when he was done. "It's just not where I am in my life. You should try Sibbi's door again. Maybe it unlocked itself when you weren't looking."

It was sharper than she'd heard from him; it stung, but she tried

not to let it show. She knew this approach wasn't working, that he was all defense mechanisms. She tried a different tack.

"It's good to see Yat doing well," she said. "She's a good kid."

"Once a cop, always a cop," said Sen in a piping imitation of her voice, but something softened inside him. She pushed.

"I mean it. I'm glad we brought her aboard. Her heart's in the right place."

His eyes lit up. The emotions that swelled in him weren't romantic like she expected, but something oakier, something very much like pride.

"Damn straight," he said.

For only a moment, he lost his composure, and Ajat caught a flash of his memory. He was not thinking about Yat, he was thinking about another girl, much younger, who looked a lot like Sen. He was holding her hand as they walked down the street together. He saw a monkey and pointed at it, and he smiled and said, "Monkey."

"Mumki," she repeated back, and then she was gone from his life, the point where she vanished a gnarled black cyst of pain. She pulled back, knew that looking into his memory like that had probably dredged it up.

"It's good she's got you looking after her," said Ajat, and felt cruel for saying it.

"Yeah," said Sen, a little hoarse. "I'd give anything to keep that kid safe. All youse fuckwits on here, you're family to me, even you."

Ajat did not know which kid he was talking about and couldn't bring herself to press the issue. There was something strained about the way he said *family*, as though the word turned his tongue into a knife and dyed his speech red.

"All right, old man, don't get sentimental on me, I was just making

conversation," she said. She didn't know what to do with her hands, so she picked the toy car up and turned it over, and realized it was a tiny EMP. Harmless onboard the *Kopek*, but not something you'd just leave lying around. She shelved the thought for later.

"You think a cop doesn't recognize an interrogation?" Sen said. "Building rapport, right? If you've got a question, just say it."

There was a value in directness, and for a moment she found herself liking the man despite herself. She liked machines because they didn't lie, didn't keep secrets, they were simple in a way so little was in her life. She just said it.

"Can I trust you?"

"Until Worldsend," he said, "or until about three seconds after you threaten the people I care about."

"Seems like we care about the same people," said Ajat. "I can work with that."

They spent another hour in quiet conversation, talking about nothing, pounding back beer, until eventually the cabin door opened and a bleary-eyed Sibbi slumped against the doorframe and beckoned her over. She pushed a half-empty glass over to Sen.

"As much as I hate to leave you drinking alone, the missus calls."

"Yeah, all right, dickhead," he said, "fuck off, then," but he was smiling, and she realized they might actually be friends of a sort. She left him drinking alone to go to bed with her wife. She slept fitfully and dreamed of a little girl who loved monkeys.

NOW

Ajat sits in her cabin, legs crossed, eyes shut. Sibbi can get them home, and she must be around here somewhere. Ajat reaches out into the ship, feels the sap-like blood coursing through its walls, notes the arrhythmic percussive thump of its great green heart. It is irregular and slightly too fast, a panic-beat that makes her own heart beat faster in sympathy. Its threads seem to reach back out to her as if to ensnare her own, and she pulls back, casts herself up through the mast. There are no seabirds flying overhead, and that worries her— what sort of a port doesn't have any gulls? The awful emptiness has reached the sky as well, and she feels a great tyranny of silence pressing down on her like some sort of strange vertigo.

She turns away from it and looks back east toward Dawgar but sees nothing. Even when the distance between them is immense, Sibbi burns so brightly; she could be on another world, and her light

would still reach the *Kopek*. The world itself warps around her. She is a candle flame in the pit of night, a single star in an empty sky. She is everything. It was love at first sight, in the same way sand cannot help but love the tide.

And now she is nowhere. Suddenly gone, without explanation, without so much as a goodbye. Ajat knows that grief makes people stupid, so she refuses to let herself grieve even as a tremendous wave of bitter black emptiness roils inside her. Her tungāne died in a fishing accident when she was very young, and Ajat cried and cried, and her father shouted at her for acting like a girl and her mother said nothing, and it was her kuia who took her aside and sat her down and told her that years ago, before the Lion had sunk its teeth into the islands, they talked about time going the other way; that the past was in front of you, because you could see it, and the future was behind you because you couldn't, and what that meant was that nobody was really gone, because you could still see them. She didn't understand at the time—she still barely understands—but now she holds that moment close to her chest, and it brings her comfort. The islands are gone, their people displaced to the four winds, their trees cut for lumber, their seas fished clean to fill bellies a thousand miles away, but she remembers them, and that means they are still there. She remembers Sibbi, and that means she is still there. It is comforting, though not particularly helpful at solving anything. She raps her thumb against the floor, trying to focus. First principles: *identify what's important, identify what's easy, then go from there.*

"Diagnose, plan, execute," she mutters. "Diagnose, plan, execute, repeat."

Ajat takes a deep breath and makes a list.

In order of importance:

1. *The ship is in range of an unknown weapon*
2. *The ship has sustained damage*
3. *The captain is missing*
4. *A crew member is sick with an unknown illness*
5. *The ship has begun to exhibit strange behavior*

1 and 2 are intimately connected, but fixing them has been delegated to other teams. 4 is outside her wheelhouse, though solving 3 would help in getting things moving. But no, connections. . . . Are 4 and 5 connected? 3 and 4? Two Weavers down for the count, right at the moment they are needed most. Possible, but not enough information to go on.

No, wrong thinking. Not goal-oriented. What they need is to get out of here. The Ladowain ships aren't going anywhere, but one might have an engine to salvage. No, no, too much work for something that might not integrate well with the *Kopek*, especially given the mutations that have been cropping up. The power source in Ladowain might help, but that is out of her hands: she has to solve the problems in front of her. Solve 3, you've solved 2 and possibly 4. Solve 2, you've solved 1. 3 possibly connected with 4 and 5. Solve 4 or 5, perhaps you've got enough information to solve 3.

"First identify what's important," she mutters, "then identify what's easy."

A human and a ship are both sick somehow, and Ajat is the ship's engineer. 5, then. She rises slowly, takes a long, deep breath, then opens her eyes. The ship's boards rock gently beneath her feet, the shallow waves of the harbor moving almost in time with the stuttering beating of the heart. Down the passageway, through maintenance, and into the engine room. The heart dominates the space,

and she notices additional veins that weren't there during yesterday's checkup: a latticework of them, small but numerous. Where they touch the walls and floor, they appear to almost pool, and as she approaches, she notices a cluster of them writhing like worms. She watches as one picks itself up, seems to sway for a moment, then plunges itself down into the wood of the deck. No prizes for pinpointing where the problem is. *What* the problem is, now that's trickier.

Clearly some new food source, but it can't be any part of the ship she's accounted for—she checked the stoma system over and over and over again before installation, and besides, that was basically just muscle; if the ship is eating itself, well, catabolysis isn't great, but that wouldn't cause this kind of growth. She checks the gauges on the ship's fat reserves: they read green.

Which is strange. Even idling, the ship needs to eat. They've been here long enough that the needle should've dipped a little, but it is reading resolutely full.

So, new fuel source. She puts her hand against the wall, and the sudden shock of magic almost knocks her flat; it is seething with power, well over safe limits. When she pulls her hand away, she can smell her own flesh cooking. Her fingertips are a mess of blisters and melted skin. She swears in the old tongue, then wanders back to her cabin and tries again. She casts her sight over the hull, looking for breaches—maybe kelp or a colony of fish that have gotten their way into a nook and started growing in the bulkheads?—but finds nothing; the hull is in almost perfect condition. More than perfect: they took a direct hit earlier, but it is almost vat-fresh.

There is an obvious solution: all nutrients the ship has consumed have made their way to the heart. Whatever the new fuel source is, it isn't showing in much the same way sawdust wouldn't show up on

108

a gas gauge. Which means one thing: opening the tank and looking inside. A tank that is dangerously overheated, burning some impossibly potent fuel source.

She stares at the *Kopek*'s wall, at the dull glow of the heart shining through it, and the sickening realization hits her: *Solve 5, and you can solve 3.*

ONE DAY AGO

"Do you want to try again?" said Yat. Kiada lay on her back on the floor, sweaty and frustrated. She wanted to try again, but saying it felt shameful, so she rolled onto her side, facing away. A hand ran across the scars on her waist; she exhaled sharply, and the hand drew back.

"It's fine," muttered Kiada. She could feel Yat's eyes boring into the back of her head, so she sat up, her back against the wall.

"We can cuddle," she said. She slapped her well-muscled thigh, a little harder than she'd expected to, and winced. She carried her scars well, but some days it still hurt to move. Yat crawled over, then hovered an inch away, smiling expectantly. Kiada grabbed her and pulled her into an embrace. Yat squealed as she was briefly lifted off the ground.

"I feel really safe with you, you know that?"

"I know," said Kiada. She liked that. Sometimes she only felt good for hurting things, like the strength that kept her alive was the same thing that would keep her alone forever—on a good day, Yat made her feel less like a killer, more like a knight. On a bad day, Kiada didn't see the difference. It was hard to tell what sort of day it was today. She squeezed Yat's breast idly with her left hand and offered out her right. Yat sank her teeth gently into the mound where her thumb met her palm. Kiada took in a sharp breath and smiled.

"Good girl," she said.

"'Mm g'd?" mumbled Yat through a mouthful of hand.

"Mhmm," said Kiada, "*so* good."

It wasn't really her thing, but Yat seemed to like it—Kiada could feel the teeth shift as she smiled—so she played along; she really just wanted to make this girl happy; the how was irrelevant. She let Yat chew on her for a bit while Kiada squeezed her breasts, then her thighs, and let Yat's little trills of pleasure and the way her jaw tightened and slackened tell her where to be hard and where to be soft. Mostly hard, it seemed. Yat lifted up a little, turned over, inclined her head low between Kiada's legs, and let out a questioning *hmm?*

Kiada grabbed her by the hair and pulled her deep between her thighs. Yat had kept her own hands behind her back.

It felt good, of course it felt good. Kiada's cunt wasn't where it needed to be, but she tried her best to relax and get her mind right. It made her happy to make Yat happy, maybe that was enough. She leaned forward and ran her palm along Yat's spine.

"Mmm, good girl," she said in a soft, low voice, "*good kitten.*"

Yat liked *kitten* for some reason, which made no sense: it was Monkey who'd brought her back; if anybody was a kitten, it was Kiada. What was a baby monkey called, an infant? Something not sexy at

all. Yat liked it; that was what mattered. Kiada liked being eaten out, it brought her pleasure, but it didn't make her feel loved. She knew what she needed. She pulled Yat up by the hair. Her hands were big enough to fit around Yat's neck entirely, so with her other hand she gripped it gently from behind and pulled their faces together so they were touching nose-to-nose, so they could taste each other breathing, then kissed her, tasting them both. When they broke away, she looked Yat in the eyes.

"I love you," she said.

Yat kissed her deeply.

"Mmmhm," said Yat, "you're so good to me." There was a desperation to it, the obvious something she wasn't saying.

Kiada rolled her eyes. "That's where you say, 'I love you, too,' dickhead," she said.

"Are you mad at me?" mumbled Yat.

"No," said Kiada. "I'm not. I just . . . do you love me?"

Yat looked down at her own naked body, drenched in sweat, then into Kiada's eyes.

"What do *you* think?" she said.

That's not an answer. Kiada let Yat go, and the girl slumped against her chest. She sat there with her hands crossed between her thighs as Kiada ran a rough hand from her wrist up to her shoulder, feeling the goose bumps follow in the wake of Kiada's fingertips. Yat tried to roll over again, but Kiada shook her head and pushed her back down into her lap. She liked the tension of the girl pushing against her, it made her heart beat a little faster, but Kiada didn't have what she needed—if her mind couldn't get there, there was no way for the body to follow.

"I think," she said, "that I like the opera because the curtain falls

and that's it. The story is just a story. If it ends well, then all is well forever."

"That sounds like hell," said Yat. "To live trapped in amber." She seemed to choose her next words very carefully. "What if something changes, and you have to keep pretending to live the same?"

She took Kiada's hand and squeezed it, and Kiada didn't resist. She didn't like being touched, not having control, but Yat made her feel safe, too. She didn't know whether she could ever take off a lifetime of armor, but part of her desperately wanted to. She didn't know how she was meant to be truly naked when her skin felt like leather.

"Everything changes, all the time," she said. "I can't even trust the ground beneath my feet. I don't want the world to be certain, but I'd like *mine* to be. Everything is out of control; I want to be in control of as much of it as I can. I want things to be clear, because even if they're *obvious*, if you don't say them, then they're only half-real and harder to hold on to. I like answers, because even if they're not what I want to hear, at least I know where I stand."

"No," said Yat, "I'm sorry, that's bullshit. It doesn't matter what we say, it matters what we *do*. Some things are so obvious that you only say them when you're scared they're over. If you need it said, it's because you're worried it's not real."

"Exactly," said Kiada. "*Exactly.* How do you get it and not get it at the same time?"

"Are you saying I'm not doing enough?"

Her fingers slipped between Kiada's legs, but Kiada batted them away.

"I'm saying . . ."

She trailed off.

I'm saying I'm scared. But I can't be scared, because I'm the strong

one. It makes you feel safe, and if I'm weak, you don't feel safe, and if you don't feel safe, then I'll lose the one thing I'm good for.

"Then I'll just have to do more," said Yat, "until you don't need to hear it."

Her voice was low and gentle as she nuzzled Kiada's neck just below the jawline. Kiada frowned and pushed Yat off her.

"Okay, okay," said Yat, splayed out on the ship's boards, her eyes wide and teary. "I'll say it. Just . . . not now. I feel pressured. If you *make* me say it, then it won't be real, and it *is* real, I just . . . Tomorrow? I'll say it tomorrow. Just . . . don't ask me to, just let me get there on my own."

Then sleep on your own, Kiada didn't say. Instead, she patted her thigh again. "Sure," she said. "Take your time. Right now, let's sleep?"

It takes them a while to get comfortable in each other's arms, and it is generous to call it comfortable, but eventually they drift off together.

When Kiada wakes, the room is filled with smoke.

NOW

Riz is the first to notice it, down on another sweep of the brig and lower decks. Yat has slept almost the entire time, but now she is twitching, her fingers are curled into claws, her knees are bent and her neck is arched back slightly farther than it should be, her spine beginning to form a shepherd's crook. Riz suspects a trap. They shake the bars and shout, "Hey, cut it out!" but Yat doesn't cut it out; instead, her head arcs back even farther and something in her neck clicks. Riz tries to read the magic coming off her and instantly regrets it. It's like staring into the sun; impossible, there was nothing before Riz looked, then suddenly a blinding flood of light. They try to reach out for Ajat's threads, to call her over to help, and with a dawning horror, Riz realizes that Ajat is not on the ship. Not even far away, but gone entirely, gone as quickly and totally as Sibbi was. A star has gone out, leaving behind only aching darkness. In the

absence of Ajat, Kiada is acting captain. In the absence of Kiada, the responsibility falls to Riz.

Ox Weaving is not a subtle art. It mostly involves hitting things extremely hard, hardening muscle and bone to withstand and deliver killing blows. Still, it has a few tricks. Riz pushes the force of their magic down into their chest, takes in a breath that would've ruptured the lungs of any normal human, and hollers like they've never hollered before.

FOUR MONTHS AGO

Ari told none of the other squatters about the dreams. They would just worry. In the morning, he told them he'd been attacked in Nahairei Park and gotten away, and Jules suggested calling the cops and was halfway to the door before Ms. Ripeki Kalpona stepped in her path and shook her head and spat *No cops*, except she actually said *No shitpig bitchfucks* in flawless Faiadino, which Ari hadn't even realized she spoke, the profanity so extreme and unexpected that he laughed and then started to cough as the air punched its way up through his aching throat. It was a real, hacking cough that doubled him over and pushed his lungs painfully against his ribs, and he had to sit down until it was over while the house fussed over him. Tea, dumplings, and custard squares were made, blankets draped over him.

Mārek came in around eleven a.m. stinking of whisky and axle grease, stains on her overalls. Her dark eyes went wide when she saw

Ari. He waved vaguely at her. The blankets were very comfortable, but breathing was still painful, and his head was still spinning.

"You almost died?" she said.

He nodded.

"That sucks," she said. "I wanted your . . . the incense holder that looks like a fat guy. I wanted that."

Even though it hurt to talk, Ari couldn't help himself. "The one with the big dick?" he said.

Her brow furrowed, and her mouth turned into a flat line of disapproval.

"Yes," she said through clenched teeth, "the one with the big dick. That's the one I wanted."

"You can have it if you want," he said.

"No, it's fine," she said. "You're still alive, you can keep it. I'll just come take it when you inevitably get yourself killed." She stood there in silence for a moment, then lunged forward and started pummeling him on the chest hard enough that he could feel it through the blankets.

"You stupid mother*fucker*," she said, "you dikaj-ass fool, Yōhua, you horse-fucking shit-fool triple fuck stupid—*fuck you*. How *dare* you. I bet you were up to no-fucking-good, huh? One day, Ari, you're gonna fuck with the wrong guy and get stabbed, and then *what do I do*, huh? I can't—I don't have another guy who can do what you do, you understand?"

"Mhmm," he said, "I unnerstan'. Ow, ow okay, *okay*, I understand, I understand."

She relented just in time for Mr. Kanikai to wheel in with a tray of biscuits in his lap.

"Are you up to trouble, Miss Mārek?" he said.

She glared at him. "No," she said.

"Well, that's too bad," he said. "Kids these days are too damned polite. Biscuit?"

She took an almond biscuit from the tray and munched it ferociously, her face a rictus of anger. Nobody said anything as Mārek destroyed the biscuit with a savagery she normally reserved for uncooperative machines. She chewed like she was trying to send biscuit-kind a message, spraying crumbs *everywhere*. Ari knew he'd be picking them out of the blankets for hours. When her work was finished, she turned to Mr. Kanikai, who held up the tray while she took another biscuit and repeated the process, eyes fixed on Ari.

"Y—" She started speaking, then stopped and swallowed a mouthful of crumbs. "You get yourself killed, Ari, and I'll fucking murder you."

She coughed as a crumb went down the wrong way. Ms. Kalpona shuffled in past Mr. Kanikai and handed her a cup of tea, which she drained in a single gulp, then coughed again and handed the cup back.

"Thank you," she muttered.

"You're welcome," said Ari.

"*Not you, dipshit.* Ugh. I need to sleep. If you're still alive when I wake up, remind me to beat the shit out of you."

She stormed up the stairs. Ari turned to Mr. Kanikai. "You got any of them cherry-and-coconut ones?" he said.

Mr. Kanikai shook his head. "I throw them out," he said. "I'm not a pervert."

"Shame," said Ms. Kalpona. "Can never find a good pervert when I need one. Used to be I'd just chat up the triangle player." She clicked her tongue. "Tak," she said, abruptly shifting tone. "Ari, go talk to her."

"Can I have a biscuit first?" he asked.

Mr. Kanikai withdrew the tray from under Ari's searching hand. "No biscuits," he said.

"Biscuits are for friends, aren't they?" said Ari, and Mr. Kanikai nodded curtly at him.

"Bah," said Ari, "all right, all right."

He shrugged off his protective shell of blankets, now piled around him in a woolen nest. He stepped out of it and schlepped his way up the stairs. The door to Mārek's room was very much shut. He rattled the doorknob.

"No," came the voice from inside, flat and sullen.

"Mārek," he said, "I'm going to stand here until you let me in, and standing here may kill me. I'll stand here for a thousand years, and my spine will go all the way up into my skull, and I'll be both very short and very dead, and at the funeral they'll say, 'If only Mārek had opened the door, Ari wouldn't have spined his own brainpan,' and then you'll feel bad, or maybe you'll also be dead, because a thousand years is a really long time, but either way, I'm not leaving until you let me in."

The door opened, just a crack. Mārek peered through, her eyes red.

"Fuck you," she said. The door started to shut again, but Ari rammed his foot into the gap. Mārek, inestimable Mārek, tried to shut it again anyway. Bones clicked and Ari yelped, but he kept his foot in the gap. The door swung open, and Mārek stood there glaring at him. Warmth spread through his foot, and something crunched, and for a moment he saw a flicker of gold moving its way down his leg as the bones slid back into place. "Fine," she said, "come in."

He hobbled in, even though his foot no longer hurt: it felt right to keep up appearances. He'd never seen the inside of Mārek's bed-

room before. Like her, it stank of grease. She'd nailed the curtains shut, right into the window frame. The table against the back wall was covered in electronics he barely recognized. Toy cars and toy soldiers littered the desk, most of them cut open and being filled with little devices that by now Ari recognized as tiny electromagnets. He shut the door behind him and noted the heavy *ka-chunk* of an improvised electronic lock that hadn't been there when he'd moved in.

"Look," he said, "I'm really sor—"

"No," she said, "no, you're not. You don't *get* it. I don't—I don't know anybody else like us."

"What," said Ari, "you mean Faiadino? Pretty sure Ms. Kalpona is, judging by the way she was cursing. Not a very good one, but we're all just doing our best out here. God gets it."

"No," she said, "uh, it's—look, remember that time we went swimming?"

"Oh gods, up at Akitoki Beach? Nearly froze my bits off, don't know what I was thinking."

She nodded.

"That time. I—I saw your scars. On your chest."

"My . . . ? *Oh*," said Ari. He laughed. "Those old things? Should probably get them removed, tattooed over maybe. But I dunno, the past is important to me. The past *happened*, you know? It's—" He paused. "So," he continued. "What should I call you? You can't have Ari Aritama Kolamona, that one's mine. Ari, son of Ari, because I'm basically my own dad, you know? *I* made me. It seemed funny at the time. Anyway." He was rambling, because he didn't know what to say.

"I don't know," the boy who had been Mārek said. "I . . . I like

Mārū, maybe? I'm not set on it. I like it, though. Saw it at the opera, for firebirds and all that. Ashes and rebirth."

"You went to the *opera*?"

Mārū shrugged. "I had a free ticket," he said. "Some fool thought the arts were important for my education. You were right, the song-bird is very pretty."

"Wait," said Ari, "you're a *boy*."

"Uh, yeah," said Mārū, "I know we've been kinda avoiding saying it, but that was the point of the whole discussion we just had."

"No, you're a *boy*," said Ari, "not a *man*. You had the wrong Mazana. I mean, I had *mine* late and it's not like I've been struck by lightning recently, but that's no good at all, we need to get you sorted out. We're gonna need to get a quorum together, we need black rib-bons to bind us together, we're—"

"No," said Mārū, "I'm not . . . I'm not ready for people to know. We go back downstairs, I'm Mārek, you understand? And I'm sure as shit not getting scarred up in front of twenty strangers—"

"Sixteen strangers."

"*Sixteen* strangers. Nobody can know. I just needed you to know that you're as close to a dad as I've got, okay? And if you get hurt, I've got nobody else, and then I just . . . I just have to hurt forever, and I don't know if I can. So one day, we'll get around to this, one day I'll walk in sunlight, but right now, I need you to go downstairs and pre-tend like nothing has changed."

"Okay," said Ari. "Take your time. I'm here whenever you need me. But also maybe we should do a *quiiiiick*—"

"No," said Mārū.

"Look," said Ari, "we'll share a biccy—although you're going to have to learn to stop making crumbs—wrap some electrical tape

around our arms, you lie down on the floor, then I pull you up into ritual manhood. Little cut on the cheek and we can get it properly done later. Just you, me, God, and the spirits. We'll sort you a proper one later, but let's do a little one now, just to make it official with, you know, Them."

Mārū sighed, then he smiled. He had a good smile, a smile that was all in the eyes and only a tiny bit in the mouth.

"All right," he said. "Sure."

Ari grinned, then headed to the door. "I'll get the biscuits afterward," he said. "Almond, right? And I'll get you that incense burner while I'm down there."

They will never find your body, Mārū mouthed at him.

"Love you, too, kid," said Ari. He took from one of his many pockets a piece of paper and a ballpoint pen. He placed it against a wall for stability, and it immediately began to absorb a patch of errant engine grease, so he kept moving it until he miraculously found somewhere clean, whereupon he pulled out a second piece of paper and began to scribble, pausing here and there to try to remember a prayer that he hadn't heard in over a decade but had once been so very important to him. What he came away with were not the words of the priestess, but they did the trick. He passed Mārū the paper, then found a small knife and some electrical tape. He wrapped the tape around the boy's arm and bound it to his own, then nodded and brought their noses together.

Mārū began to read.

"'Oh Lord, you really messed it up this time. Look at you, the sheer *state*, I expected better.'" He gave Ari a raised eyebrow. "Are you sure this is it?" he said.

Ari shrugged, but he was smiling. "Probably not, but God gets it."

Mārū continued. "'Honestly, I'm starting to doubt you're really all that powerful, or whether you're more of an errand boy for miracles who messed up his delivery route. You put the wrong parts on this body, oh Lord, and I'm filing a complaint.'"

Ari was pretending not to cry, mouthing along.

"'And furthermore, if you really were all-powerful, you'd fix this situation immediately, or at least send a boy a bottle of wlne or something—'"

"Pretty sure it's *wine*," whispered Ari.

"Look, it says 'wlne.' Words matter, learn to write like a normal person, I'm reading what's on the sheet."

"Okay, okay, carry on."

"'A bottle of *wlne* or something, to say sorry, but in the absence of an apology, I'm going to assume you're very sorry but you're feeling too awkward to say it, and I'll take your silence as tacet approval for any modifications I make going forward. If we're not good, show your disapproval with a crack of lightning or something in the next ten seconds. Open bracket, wait ten seconds, closed bracket,'" deadpanned Mārū.

"You're not meant to read that part aloud," whispered Ari, who then raised a finger skyward and began to count down. No lightning cracked; no thunder pealed. He made a small cut on Mārū's cheek, then cut the tape.

"Congratulations," he said, "you're a man now. Official-unofficial. We'll sort it out properly later, but, um . . . I'm proud of you. Put that paper somewhere safe and clean, yeah? Look after it."

"Uh-huh," said Mārū.

"*There* he is," laughed Ari. "Take care of the words and I'll leave

you to your"—he waved his hand vaguely at the piles of metal and wire—"machinations? You kids and your technology."

Ari idly took a toy car and turned it over in his hand. It looked a little different from the rest: its roof was staved in around a circular button right in the middle. He pocketed it and winked.

"Kids!? Aren't you like twent—and you can't have that one, *that's the deton*—" Mārū began, but Ari was already out into the hallway, heading down the stairs to get the biscuits. It had been, all things considered, a very strange day, but it looked like things were going to be all right.

Yat is sinking through water as thick and dark as oil, and in the blackness, a single pinprick of light appears. It is very small, but it changes the shape of the place; everything seems to warp around it, like the night bends to the polestar. She tries to move toward it, but she is paralyzed by a crushing weight on all sides. It grows, blossoms open into a single human eye. Another eye opens, and a man walks out of the darkness, still clothed in it. He stands inverted, hanging where a ceiling might be, his feet making little ripples in some solid plane she cannot make out from the rest. Perhaps she is the one upside down and she is ascending rather than sinking; she cannot tell. He moves with her, and whatever surface his feet have found moves as well. She does not know how long she has been here; this place is as ephemeral as a dream and as inescapable as the grave.

She knows the man. He will come and offer her a deal. She will say no, but every time he asks, it takes her longer to respond.

"When you were five, before the weather changed forever, before you knew your father was sick," he says, "there was a summer that

seemed to last forever. A hot summer, filled with cicada song. You liked to catch them in your hands, and sometimes they would hurt you, but you loved the thrill of victory so much you didn't care. You caught eight; it feels like you caught a thousand. Memory is strange, and that's the trick: time in the real world and time inside your head are not the same, not even a little. I will come tomorrow, and tomorrow, and tomorrow, and you'll say no, and that's fine, because you can't resist forever, and on the day you finally break down, in the real world only a moment will have passed. All of this, this bottomless eon we share, every millennium of resistance adds milliseconds, less than that. All you are doing is letting yourself suffer. We like to pretend that pain is a crucible, but that's just survivorship bias for the soul. Somehow we forgot a very simple truth: most pain just hurts."

She cannot respond, the waves of pressure on all sides crushing her limbs and locking her mouth shut. Distantly she can hear a voice shouting, she can make out the word "seizure." A bruise blossoms across the back of her right hand, and she feels someone grabbing her and forcing something into her mouth before the darkness swallows her again. Luz places his hands against her temples and closes his eyes, and she finds herself whirling through the same zoetrope of the worst days of her life, twisted into mockeries of themselves: her father dead in his greenhouse with the little statue of Luz staring down over him, but this time his body is swollen with decay, his blackened tongue lolling out of his mouth while the statue grins wickedly and dances an awful little jig; the day the corrupt Officer Żu shot her and she felt herself plunge into death for the very first time, but the barrel of his gun was not a lion but a living iron viper that struck at her eyes again and again; the day she killed Żu and felt the earth erupt around her, except instead of him dying, she died,

then followed him as he went to the *Kopek* and killed every single one of the crew; the day after she'd found her father and run to the kitchen, except every surface in the house is the Knife, the one she can't forget, and she tears her own feet to ribbons but can't stop herself from going over to the kitchen drawer and taking it out; *I love you like a tick loves a lamb*; rough hands trying to pin her to the floor in the brig and a half dozen shouting voices as her convulsions get worse and worse and the ulna in her arm snaps like a twig; the time she stood beneath the spires of Suta, beside the trash can—a trash can, of all things, such a humble place to end a civilization, so fitting—where he'd concealed the primary spore charge and stared into his brother's eyes while holding up his makeshift detonator (he never could build them like Vic, but she'd taught him a trick or two) and said, "I'm sorry," and his brother said, "Don't lie," and he was crying, actually crying, and went in to hug him, he hit the detonator, grabbed ahold of his threads and jumped, the both of them clear of the infectious site so narrowly that glass from the bomb cut his cheek and lacerated his chest and shoulder, and then he lay still on the train tracks while his brother kicked him and screamed and paced back and forth like a caged—

Żu slaps her. "You *bitch*," he says. He's never broken composure before, not in a thousand lost days. The pain in her arm comes flooding back, somebody is asking why she isn't healing, and she realizes she doesn't know how much more her body can take, and yet . . . even if this place let her smile, Yat would be too exhausted to do so, but the corner of her mouth twitches, and a new light shines in her eyes.

FOUR MONTHS AGO
THREE MONTHS AGO
TWO MONTHS AGO

As summer turned to autumn, a chill set in, and it was almost a relief—the streets were almost empty, and that meant no tan uniforms leering from street corners, fewer street fights and random beatings. The peace held until the news came in from the provinces that the harvest had been poor—the government instituted a grain ration and banned the production of any alcohol that required the use of food crops. When the booze barons refused to comply, their distilleries and breweries were seized, their stock of potato and grain taken to the city granaries. When the constabulary tried to seize the Black Wolf vodka plant, a group of armed Vuruhi fought back, killing three officers before disappearing into the alleys of Mauzeka. The manhunt was called off suddenly and without explanation. One day there were wanted posters,

and the next there weren't. Within a month, Black Wolf was the only alcohol available on store shelves. When the wanted men showed up working as guards at the factory, nobody moved against them.

From there, the events are too numerous, too granular. Here are but a few:

A spate of suicides by journalists and minor government officials, all by hanging.

A string of murders, mostly elderly immigrants who lived alone, which the papers thundered were unconnected; anybody who said they were linked was a Hainak spy.

A series of deaths that the papers attributed to the ignition of propane tanks and gas lines, the dead all skinless, hairless, toothless, wearing identical robes, with not a single thing around them touched by fire.

Two men killed another in self-defense in a darkened alleyway. A witness said otherwise, but then abruptly changed their mind.

A fire at a tailor's shop, the owner's burned corpse found handcuffed to the radiator in the ashes.

Three decades of foul work manifested piece by piece over the course of a single autumn, without any one single cause or effect. Ari did his best to avoid the creeping darkness, to fill his days with song. What was the line? *From a world of iron, to dream a world of gold.* He returned home from the grocer's one day with a pitiful ration of bread to find the whole house sitting around the kitchen table, deep in argument. The ashtray was overflowing with cigarette butts.

"Leave?" said Mr. Kanikai. "To hell with that. It's cowardice, that's what it is."

"Are you going to fight them, old man?" spat Nyree. "They have machine guns, you have a wheelchair."

"I dunno," said Ms. Kalpona, "give him a lance and a good hill, and I reckon he'd give them problems."

Ari opened a few windows to let the smoke out, then closed them again quickly and shut the curtains; you never knew who was listening. The teapot in the center of the table was empty, so he filled the kettle while everybody bickered.

"That's right!" said Mr. Kanikai. "And if I can only find a horse, I'll be the devil among them! I can still ride, and I'll send them fleeing back into their little holes. I shall be a fox, and they shall be the chickens."

"Wherever will you find a horse?" said Jules.

"A lancer has his ways," said Mr. Kanikai.

"Reckon you could ride a motorbike sidesaddle?" said Ms. Kalpona. "I'm skinnier than I used to be. It could probably fit us both."

"I can ride anything!" said Mr. Kanikai triumphantly.

"There is no point arguing with you!" shouted Nyree, and Mr. Kanikai nodded gruffly and crossed his arms.

"Precisely," he said. "So you agree, we stay!"

"I can't leave," said Mārū. "My work is here. You think there's much hacking to do in Hainak? Maybe I can sit around in Featta for a few decades until they figure out electricity again. Or go north and study the network infrastructure of snow or something." He didn't say, *Auntie would kill me if I left,* but he shared a look with Ari that said it.

"Where would any of us go?" said Jules. "Radovan has waged war on half the world at this point. Every country on the continent of the Ox hates us."

"Forget where," said Mārū. "How? Even if we somehow clear the Hainak navy, then we're out in the pirate isles. You think Radovan is dangerous, then you don't stand a chance on the high seas."

"Two months," said Ari. Everybody turned to him, and he let their tempers die down for a moment as he went around the table and poured everybody a cup of tea. He waited until the muttering started before he continued, "In two months, the *Kopek* will come in with the next shipment. They've been running the blockade for years, never been caught even once. I've got a friend onboard. I can't guarantee it'll be free, but if we can hang on for two months, then she can get us out. Until then, we hold the fort."

He didn't say, *And Mārū and I will stay behind,* but another look passed between them. They both knew they were Auntie's for life, and they went where she went.

"The fort," said Mr. Kanikai. "Yes, I like that. But a fort must have a name, it is terrible bad luck otherwise."

"You're all mad," said Nyree, "and this isn't finished. We'll talk about it again tomorrow."

"And I shall say no again tomorrow!" said Mr. Kanikai.

"Fort Tomorrow!" squeaked Mr. Pono the knitter, from within his fortress of scarves.

"Ooh," said Ms. Kalpona, "I like that. A lot of nice hard consonants. It has the sound of destiny to it."

Ari raised his teacup.

"A toast for tomorrow," he said. "We'll see it yet. I can't guarantee the day after that, but that's tomorrow's problem."

They all raised their cups, and six voices rang out in a messy attempt at unison.

"To tomorrow!" said Mārū.

"Fort Tomorrow!" said Jules.

"Tomorrow!" said Mr. Pono and Ms. Kalpona.

"For Fort Tomorrow!" said Mr. Kanikai.

Nyree was the last to speak. She sighed, then raised her cup.

"To tomorrow," she said, "when you'll all see sense."

"I doubt it," said Ms. Kalpona, "but I admire your boundless capacity for hope."

Out of the corner of his eye, Ari saw a flicker of gold. Teina lay in the chair, still, but for a moment, he was sure something had moved through her, and it made him deeply uneasy. Right now, however, there was work to do: the doppler was tomorrow's problem.

NOW

The City is eternal. It has had a dozen names over the millennia, and in some way or another, they all mean the City. As it spreads out across the plains, across the strait, and at its farthest extent even into the mountains, it does not stop to think of the towns it has rolled over—they simply become part of its fabric. It has changed often, but at no point in those changes has it ceased to be the City.

The latest change, still, was traumatic. It has been molded into an undignified shape, a great heart, imprisoned in the chest of some great beast. It feels the fluid flowing through its pipes, hears the steady beat of thirty million feet on its cobblestones, but it knows that something is very wrong, that it has been dealt a wound. After the change came a long silence, an impenetrable slumber for millennia, and while it slept, it dreamed every night of its aggressor, and

then she returned to it with open arms. As she placed her hands against it, a burst of heat and steam shocked it awake, and (as cities are wont to do) it swallowed her whole. A pair of glassy eyes stared up at it from inside its prison—a strange metallic cat. It knows cats very well indeed, and it smiles and acknowledges the furless friend, who is already gone.

Ajat knows this is not her memory. She hangs on to that knowledge, whispers her name to herself over and over as the tides pull her in a hundred different directions. She has always been aware of the nature of the beast, but it is different to sink into its belly and feel herself dissolve. Her entire world lives within its mad roar, and she tries to push forward as it breaks her down into smaller and smaller pieces. All around her, the City is awake, unfurling, devouring. It has been chained, and that is another insult; it has been conquered many times, but it has never before been chained. It chafes against its bindings and, in the dark between worlds, begins to grow.

The City is its streets, the City is its people, the City is the deep veins of history that breach down through the stony earth. It was always bigger than the ship and resentful of its confinement. It barely registers when another voice enters it, for it understands souls only as a mass, turns its many eyes onto individuals only when they break something. What is one voice among thirty million?

And yet.

This one has the stink of the aggressor on it. It is a blade driven into the body, and the City swarms around it, pus in a wound, and Ajat knows it is doing this; she is melting into it, and she knows its rage, its hunger. It was always angry, but that anger was fragmented, directionless. Now she feels like a blowtorch is bearing down, feels

the heat melting her away, knows that she cannot last much longer in this place, but there is a knot somewhere in the distance, a golden beacon with the scent of home. She tries to step toward it, shouts her own name again and again, and then the spell breaks and she finds herself once more on the floor of the engine room, curled around herself and sobbing. The floor beneath her is slick with clear fluid that seems to have risen up between the boards. Waves of feverish heat roll over her, and she can't stop shuddering, as though her body is shaking itself to pieces.

She is finally sure of where her wife is; she knows what's wrong with the ship. What she does not know is what to do about it. The fluid is starting to thicken and clot around her, and when she eventually rises to her feet, she leaves an imprint of her coiled body, an absence that wears her shape. The heart is slick with the fluid, weeping it from a hundred little lacerations that she can only see by way of the golden trails left by their magic. On a better day, she would reach out to try to seal them, but she can barely stand up straight, and she knows the leaks will not compromise the heart; they had more than enough amps; the issue was the fucking voltage. The analogy is comforting, but she does not want to consider who the battery is. She knows Sibbi better than most, knows how impossibly tough and ancient she is, knows she is still there, still somehow holding together inside the heart even as it bleeds her dry. She can't just leave her there. She places her hand against the heart and dives back in.

The first time Ajat and Sibbi met was in an old ferro bunker near Syalong Cherta, years before the battle. Ajat had found some old database servers and managed to get them powered, but time had done too much damage, and their contents were impossible to recover.

Sibbi had appeared behind her, as if from nowhere, and clicked her tongue, and the first word she ever said to the woman she'd marry was "Crap." The second thing she said was "I think I remember this one, you got a pen?"

That was the first thing they shared, the database engineer and the librarian, both shaking their heads at the loss of so much good data, then building it back together. Was it the same as it had been? Who could say, but it was theirs.

Ajat pulls up that memory and launches it like a flare. The City does not recognize it; it is not of the City, so it is not real, but something within its vast network of threads turns its attention toward it. It's weak and so thoroughly integrated into the City that it turns only a little, fighting against the tide. Ajat pulls herself toward the City, swimming through the awful dream that burns her skin, and suddenly she is standing in a room with its entire rear wall covered in computer monitors. It looks a lot like the rusted old bunker, except brand-new. A woman sits in a chair staring at the screens. She reaches out for a cup of coffee, and for a moment it is Sibbi, then it is a smiling man with broad shoulders and heavy biceps, then it is a younger woman with dark hair and tattoos, then it is a shadow, then it is gone. The room shudders, and for only a moment, Ajat sees a second room beneath it, like a painting on top of a painting, a thing Sibbi once called a *pentimento*. Her tattoos still ache; they're fresh, the memory of the Vault's fall still vivid. She didn't regret the panicked meeting with the tribe's tattoo artist to get the entire archive burned into her skin before the servers burned; she cannot even wrap her head around how much history she saved, how many countless libraries she carries in her very skin. There was technically still an archivist in the Vault, but

everybody knew the servers were husks. Saving the data had been worth a little pain.

"Nothing in memory is real," says Sibbi, suddenly behind her, and Ajat nearly jumps out of her skin. "It's a composite. The place we met and . . . somewhere else, somewhere I made myself forget."

Her skin is gray, her eyes have heavy bags under them, and Ajat looks down and sees that she has no legs, just a writhing mass of flesh that scuttles back and forth like the pseudopods of some seafloor scavenger.

"I'm gone," she says. "But it's fine, I made a backup."

"A backup? Of *you*? How?"

Sibbi turns, and when Ajat follows her eyeline, she sees a little girl with red hair.

"No," says Ajat. "No, I love you, but I won't."

"It wasn't the plan," says Sibbi. "She was . . . camouflage. My memories got too loud, and I was lost in a very dark forest, then fate delivered me a tiger. You want me back, I'm in there. Or a version of me is, anyway. The version that remembers"—she waves her hand vaguely around the room—"the other place. The under-place. I held on to my memories of you and here. You'll get to meet me for the first time all over again."

"No, fuck that, I won't—"

"Look down, dear."

Ajat looks down and sees her own feet starting to melt into the floor. She pulls one up, and tendrils of the world come up with it.

"I didn't say you had to," says Sibbi. "I'm just letting you know your options. More data to crunch, right?"

"I—"

"*GO.*"

It is not an order, just a fact. The monitor room ejects Ajat, she finds herself hurtling through the awful thumping mass of the City, then she is back in the engine room, covered in blood and fluid like a newborn foal. Her skin burns, but she feels so weak she can do nothing except lie there shaking.

Here are two paradoxes.

The first is the paradox of surveillance. When people believe they are unwatched, they often break the law. Rarely in large ways, but in many small ones. Sometimes the cameras even catch big, serious crimes, and those days deepen your faith in the system. Surveillance has a way of begetting more surveillance. It achieved its goals, after all, and you don't stop doing something because it works. Perhaps if you could just see and understand more, nothing bad could ever happen. So you install more cameras, more microphones, and you uncover more little crimes and you hire more and more men to watch them, but it's never enough. Eventually, the people you're watching cannot remain people: they become data points. The only sensible way to process them is in graphs, in trends, in generalities.

This leads to the paradox of the outlier. A model that is 99.9 percent

accurate is a very accurate model. It is trusted in the way that no human could ever be trusted. When its contours are followed, it proves correct most of the time. Most outliers are discarded, and most of the time it's the right decision. When it isn't, the whole model breaks down.

Step through the mirror, turn the page. See. Here's an outlier. He is a boy of nineteen with a gun in his pocket. He has failed his task, and that means he is about to die. He goes to his favorite café, orders a coffee and a sandwich, and waits for the soldiers to come. When his target's car rounds the corner, he looks up, and when his target's driver gets out and approaches the café to ask for directions, the boy takes out his gun and empties it into the back seat. What are the odds? In a city of ten thousand streets, the target got lost on the same one where his assassin had come to die. When he pulls the trigger, a great fire will consume the continent, and when the smoke clears thirty years later, one hundred million souls will be dead. It is an unfathomable number; it is so large that it becomes meaningless; it must be seen in generalities and trends. If it is not—if one stops to try to put names to the dead, tries to understand their suffering as real human suffering—its weight is so great it becomes impossible to handle. It is a cataclysm of such scale that history bends around it and the world can never go back.

No model could've predicted it. An astute analyst might look at the factors around it and say that it was just the right confluence of sociopolitical factors, that some kind of war was inevitable, but that doesn't change the fact that an outlier changed the world with a single bullet.

You read it in the paper, in your favorite café, on the eastern side of the city you loved so much. You saw what was coming, and you packed

as many of your things as you dared and you followed the call of empire west. For twenty years, at least, and then you moved again. How long have we been chasing each other through the night?

Humans are messy. Their collisions are constant, reshaping them like a sculptor's chisel, or the sea wearing down a mountain. Sometimes their trip to the café results in a lovely day in the sun, sometimes it ends in war; even the little outliers matter to somebody, and the big ones matter a whole lot more. Multiply the outliers together, and you'll begin to see exponents. Given enough time, trust, and good decisions, the probability for system failure approaches 1.

I am sorry, little bird, I truly am. There is no tragedy worse than the death of a cat. Take heart that she won't die, only in all the ways that matter.

I need you to wake up.

TWO MONTHS AGO

Ari had avoided the teahouse for as long as possible, and when Auntie sent for him next, he walked through the streets with a sense of mounting trepidation. She hadn't seemed surprised to see him come home, and when he told her he'd been attacked, she seemed genuinely concerned. She'd hugged him and spoken softly, and she'd made him tea, which felt like the world being turned on its head. She'd even sent for the good doctor, the fancy one from uptown who smiled a lot, who said Ari was fit as a fiddle in those exact words, *Ma'am, he's fit as a bloody fiddle,* and Auntie stationed a very big Hainak man with a shaved head to stand outside the house and glare at anybody in Vuruhi black and gold.

He trudged through the shop, head down, and ran his fingers over the toy car in his pocket. Mārū had yelled at him about it but eventually relented. "Do not," he'd said, "under any circumstances press the

149

button unless you want Auntie to murder you." He didn't know why having the car there comforted him, but he felt on some level that if Auntie was going to kill him anyway, he might as well annoy her one last time. The teahouse was decorated in Hainak fashion, with engineered vines covering every spare inch of wall. Auntie had even managed to snag a proprietary breed of vivid green thornless rose that turned itself toward customers seated nearby. Ari went through the kitchen, and the cook didn't even look up until he stopped in front of the back door and his shoulders slumped. He'd been going to the back room for almost ten years and didn't know the cook's name, only that the man was very tall and very good with knives. Everybody just called him Cook. He was an enormous man with a glossy scalp emerging from the center of his patches of bristly hair. Why a tearoom needed so many knives was, well, not as much of a mystery as it really should've been.

With the cook staring at him emotionlessly, he sighed and pushed open the door. There were more crates than he remembered, and one lay open, filled with glass vials of pale liquid that seemed to dance in the light. The back room was well lit and well organized. There was a map of the city on the rear wall, stuck with dozens of colored pins, with ciphered nonsense notes scrawled at various points. *Wind Blows East, Never Enough Web.* A toy soldier watched vigilantly over a map on the table—Ari had given it to Auntie as a gift and was only now just spotting the tiny piece of wiring inside the spring connecting its body to its head; he wondered how many little surprises he'd inadvertently left all over town on Mārū's behalf. A Faiadino woman in a duster and a broad-brimmed hat was leaning over the open crate, taking out each vial and inspecting it in turn—if not for the extra melanin, she could've been Auntie's sister.

As Ari entered, she put a vial gently back and swept out past him with her brim low.

Auntie was staring at the map, and when she rounded on Ari, he shrank back, then found himself wrapped inside the second big hug in as many days. Auntie was a small woman, but she had strong arms, and the suddenness of her embrace shocked him, and Ari started crying, mostly from surprise, but once he started, he found it very hard to stop. He sobbed until he was empty, and when she finally let him go, he didn't know what to say. She seemed to recognize that, and she put her hands on his shoulders and pressed her forehead against his.

"You hurt my people, you hurt me," she said. "And I take that very personally."

She stepped back and snapped her fingers. The shift in her body language was subtle and total. She was now straight-backed and clear-eyed, carrying herself with the gravity of an officer.

"Koztati," she said, "come in."

The door swung open, and Ari froze. The man loomed—he couldn't not, given how tall and broad-shouldered he was, with features that looked like they'd been carved with a hatchet. There was one difference from that awful night: his eyes. They were cloudy and docile, like a cow's.

"I am very sorry, Mr. Kolamona," he recited. His speech was monotone and totally empty. They were certainly noises coming up from his throat, shaped by his teeth and tongue, but they weren't words, just . . . sounds, like a siren or a scream.

"It's fine," he muttered. His murderer nodded.

"I am very sorry, Mr. Kolamona," he repeated, his inflection unchanging.

151

"Mr. Tamatenko is leaving town tonight," said Auntie. "He has decided to move to Hainak and work on a production line. The warmer climate will do him some good, I feel; he's been a little under the weather, haven't you, Koztati?"

The man inclined his head ever so slightly. There was something mechanical about it, sudden and jerky, like he was a puppet and his puppeteer had dropped the cross and snatched it back up.

"I am very sorry, M—"

Auntie snapped her fingers again, and he fell silent. She looked expectantly at Ari. This whole awful show made his skin crawl, and he smiled as politely as he could, a rictus of gratitude. Auntie was unreadable, and after a moment, she waved her hand and Koztati's shadow left the room. The door slammed shut with the finality of a coffin lid. Ari knew he would never see the man again, but that brought him no comfort. The room seemed to have less color than it had a minute ago, as though a void had ripped through and taken a bit of the light with it. He didn't know why, but he felt very much like he'd just witnessed a speaking corpse: blood still pumping, nervous system still firing, limbs still moving, but something vital stripped away.

"What did you do to him?" he said. He hadn't meant to whisper, but speech had suddenly become an effort.

She smiled at him, and there was real affection in it.

"Don't be scared," she said. "We just gave him a special tea, and it made him forget a few things. Think of it like sitting in a warm bath: all the pain just merges with the water and goes off down the plughole. It's very safe; they do it all the time down south."

She paused and examined him, her body language different again. She was looser, lower to the ground, and her eyes were filled with concern.

"I shouldn't have shown him to you, and I'm sorry," she said. "I thought it might be cathartic for you, but I was wrong. He'll be feeling like himself again in a few weeks, it's just that the initial shock tends to flatten them out a bit." Ari knew it was a lie but let her continue. He realized he hadn't blinked in almost a minute, as though if he closed his eyes even for a second, the Other Auntie would resurface.

She pulled a string, and a little bell rang from somewhere behind them. Several seconds later, Cook emerged from the kitchen with a tray of biscuits and placed it on the desk in front of them. He stood there, swaying gently for a second, and Ari found himself wondering whether Cook had also been fed the special tea. His eyes weren't cloudy, but there was something about the way he moved, as though the gods hadn't put him together right, his limbs longer and more jointed than his body seemed to have room for. He wondered about the contents of the crate. They said RADOVAN PORT AUTHORITY on them, and he wondered if Auntie had been moving them through the same network; he knew the crew of the *Kopek* but nothing about the supplier back in Hainak, and whenever he'd reported missing crates to Auntie, she'd always been unsurprised and not upset.

"Shall I bring tea, Auntie?" said Cook. It was the first time Ari had ever heard him speak. His voice was raspy, as though his mouth was meant to make an entirely different sort of sound.

"No," she said, "we're fine, thank you."

She served everybody tea. She ran a teahouse, for the gods' sake. Ari would've said no, would probably never drink tea from her again in his life, so it was a relief that he didn't need to turn it down. Cook left so quickly that Ari barely even saw him move: he was just there, then he had never been there at all, the only remnant of his presence

a tray of biscuits on the desk. Ari took one that looked like cream between two layers of pink wafer. He ate it, and Auntie smiled.

"Are you feeling a little better?" she said. It seemed impossible that this was the same woman who had just brought in the awful puppet of Koztati. She smiled too sincerely, open and kind, and it didn't seem like a front. Like all young thieves, Ari had a good sense for dangerous people—some folks would shout and try to get the cops involved, but others would kill you and toss your body in the harbor, and if you couldn't figure it out at a glance, then you didn't last long. If it was an act, then she was the best actor he'd ever seen. Nyree had once spoken about how the greatest actors were fully immersed, how their whole bodies were given to the role, how the performance improved in a thousand little ways that no amount of direction could account for, and in that moment, Auntie was completely and totally an auntie and nothing more.

He nodded.

"Yes, Auntie," he said. His eyes flicked back to the crate. Her eyes did not follow his, but she smiled knowingly and said, "A related product, but not the same one. Just a contingency—we like contingencies, don't we, Ari?"

He nodded, and swallowed.

"Good," she said. "Then I have a job for you and Mārek. I've already spoken to her: she'll meet you on-site. She knows the technical details, but I need you to grab a doppler and then get it back to its owner as quickly as possible. Ideally, he won't notice it's gone, though I'm not sure it's reasonable to rely on that. I just need its absence to be short enough that it's not suspicious."

"Okay," said Ari. "Who are we stealing from?" It was nice to have a goal to focus on, to distract from everything else.

"Vatay Malatenki," she said, and Ari's blood froze.

"This is time-sensitive," she said, "and I need your particular talents to help cover Mārek. I wouldn't ask otherwise, considering the week you've had. Mārek's gifted on the wires, but this job needs a face. Mārek has told me she needs at least an hour, and that needs to be an hour that doesn't get his hackles up."

The Vuruhi had no formal leader, but Malatenki was as close as they came. He'd famously erected a gibbet outside the Houses of Parliament and given a firebrand speech about how real leadership would take back Hainak in a single month, about how degeneracy had made the nation weak, about how their noble warrior ancestors would shake their heads in disgust. It was the moment the movement went from ten men in a bar to ten thousand in the streets. There hadn't been Lions in the forests outside Radovan for a thousand years, but there were plenty of wolves, and it seemed like there were more every day.

"He's well guarded," said Ari. He did not say, *You're going to get us killed.*

"And well armed," said Auntie, "which is why we need a little more leverage on him. I want a copy of that doppler's hard drive. I've got a man in the company depot who can do the job we want. I've been having Mārek follow Malatenki around and glitch his doppler for a few weeks now, but either he hasn't noticed or he just doesn't care. He's famously paranoid, but that doppler appears to be a blind spot."

"Hard drive?" said Ari.

"That's Mārek's job to understand," said Auntie. "You just need to make sure that his boys don't get suspicious of its absence. Obviously, it's going to be hard to get you proper resources on the fly, but let me know in advance if there's anything special you need. This isn't an

ordinary job, and it's one that I need done as soon as possible, so I'm willing to free up considerable assets to make it happen. You will, of course, be compensated, at three times the normal rate."

Which was a lot. He loved doppler jobs: it was a single night's work that kept him fed for almost three months. Triple that could take him through to next summer. He was terrified of Malatenki, but part of him wanted to get back at the Vuruhi. Seeing Koztati hollowed out had felt, well, hollow. Ugly. He knew there had been Vuruhi harassing Nyree and her friends, breaking windows and hurting people. If there was a way to make them stop, he'd take it in a heartbeat. There were worse options, and Auntie had shown her willingness to carry them out. A simple doppler job. A dangerous one, to be sure, but he'd done doppler jobs before, and it felt good to be discussing something he understood.

He nodded.

"Thank you, Auntie," he said. "I'll talk to Mārek and let you know what we need."

"Good boy," she said, then gave him a little wave that said they were done. He left through the kitchen, and as he passed Cook, they made brief eye contact. Cook's eyes were dark, empty pits. The man said nothing, then turned back to his work, cutting an indistinguishable slab of red meat into thin strips. Ari stood and watched him for almost a full minute, and Cook did not turn back or try to speak to him at all. When the air became so heavy that Ari could barely breathe, he left without a word.

NOW

The expedition from the *Kopek* came to a stop in front of a gib-bet. Five bodies hanging, each with a placard dangling from their neck outlining their crime. Theft, degeneracy, treason, profli-gacy, miscegenation. Kiada feels like maybe she recognizes one of them, but not well: perhaps a woman she passed on the street once. The niggling recognition has wormed its way under her skin, and she stands and stares and doesn't know what to do. Maybe it isn't a woman she knew, but a woman like her. There have been so many near misses in her life. This could've been her if she turned down a different road, if she wandered into the wrong room, if she raised her voice at the wrong time. Folks are always looking to kill people like her, and when they start from that place, it doesn't really matter what the crime is or whether the crime is even real—they'll dig and dig until they find a sin, any sin, and they'll write it on a placard and

hang it around your neck when the real crime is just turning the wrong corner or loving too freely.

Sen puts a hand on her shoulder. "C'mon," he says. His voice is gentler than she expected, and there is nothing mocking in it. Tears rise in her eyes, and she pushes them down.

She has no idea where his resilience comes from, and she worries that asking him will open a crack somewhere in her soul and the ocean will come rushing out. Instead she nods and moves with him. The heat is terrible, crushing and constant. It warps the air and soaks her clothes with sweat. They've seen no sign of life but an overwhelming amount of death. The burns were only the start of it: leathery corpses lay all around, some shot, some stabbed, many trampled or beaten into lifelessness. Even the bacteria that would decompose their bodies have died; corpses normally teem with microbial life, but Kiada can sense none. The bodies have almost been mummified by sheer heat. In the places where the group can break free of the smoke, the streets reek of copper, gunpowder, and machine oil. It is as though some demon of slaughter came loose in the city, turning the people on each other. They come across an armored Vuruhi car with one of its doors torn off. It is surrounded by dead civilians, some of them armed, many of them not. The crew is so badly beaten that their uniforms are barely recognizable, but Kiada sees patches of Vuruhi beige emerging from the sea of blood. Each man has a sidearm strapped to his belt, and she takes three, but Xidaj shakes his head when she offers him one—the man is too proud of his damned rifle. She is about to remonstrate with him when a powerful light falls on her, almost blinding her. She turns away from it, and Sen looks worried. He is staring straight into it but not seeing, and she realizes it is magic, pure magic, so dense and tightly woven that it bleeds together into a

single beacon. It vanishes as quickly as it came, but she recognizes it. It has something scrawled across it like a signature, something in its song, something in its perfume that is familiar and comforting.

"Ari," she says. "Ari made it somehow."

Which is impossible. Ari isn't a Weaver, and even if he's become one, he never had the time to grow that powerful. This is ancient light, the sort of thing that maybe Sibbi could pull off. Which means . . .

Auntie, but not Auntie. Auntie with notes of Ari mixed in, and Nyree, and others she doesn't recognize. She tries to reach out and see its thoughts, but it is like trying to walk on the sun, and she recoils instinctively. The light passes over her again and disappears again, though she can still sense its source, glowing in her mind's eye. Sen and Xidaj are staring at her.

"Magic shit?" says Sen. She nods.

"We're going the right way," she says. "I think an old assoc—an old friend might be alive. Sensed him."

"You sure?" says Xidaj. "Looking at all this devastation, I don't think anybody could have survived. It's not just the fighting: smoke inhalation probably got a lot of people, and heat stroke. There were survivors in Hainak, and we saw signs of them all over the place. This is different . . . It's been scoured lab-clean. I said 'sterilized' before and I maintain that—it's procedural, mechanical, and incredibly thorough. Whatever it was that came after the street fights didn't leave much behind."

Kiada glares at him. At times, he seems more like a robot than the damned dopplers. She knows it's just his way, though she managed to get him so drunk on palm wine once that he sang an impossibly dirty song about a pair of coconuts floating in the ocean. He isn't a bad guy, but she wishes he knew how to read the damned room.

"No," she spits. "I'm not sure. But it's better than nothing."

Sen turns away from them and keeps walking, and she follows him without another word.

"I forgot," says Xidaj as they walk, "that you spent time here. I'm sorry. I've never thought of them as anything other than the enemy. You come to understand them only as soldiers, and you don't ask about where those soldiers go when it's all over."

"They usually pick up another gun," says Sen. "I did. You don't get a lot of other options. Then you fall in with other lads who went through the same, and you bond over that, and sometimes you turn out okay, but sometimes one thing leads to another and then . . ." He waves vaguely at a uniformed man lying dead on the ground. His body is in ribbons; he was probably attacked with a large blade and bled out fast. The skin on his face is the same cooked red of the man on the barricade, split open and showing the dry flesh underneath. Kiada can't bring herself to feel sorry for a Vuruhi, but she still winces. They keep walking, down through the alley where she saw the light shine.

"That's all we are," says Sen. "The sum of each other. I got lucky and fell in with Sergeant Wajet, and the old bastard softened me up some. Yat fell in with me, and I softened her up some. That's how it works. If I'd fallen in with Varazzo, then maybe we'd be having a very different conversation."

They pass through the alleyway. She steps over two small bodies, curled around each other, burned beyond recognition. She wonders who they were, but Sen doesn't give her time to wonder for very long. He just keeps on pushing ahead with the same look of grim determination.

And there it is. Ari's place. They stop. The other two look at Kiada,

and she nods. She barely recognizes it with all the ivy burned away. The brickwork was maybe fashionable once, but it hasn't borne the years well. Its surface is charred.

"Conventional fire," says Xidaj, "not microwave. Look at the windows. Looks like it burned very hot, very fast."

They are cracked from the heat, and one of them has left long streaks of glass running down the wall like candlewax. She can see somebody inside, curled up around themselves and on their side, blackened to the point that they almost disappear into the wall behind them. She fights back a scream. She desperately doesn't want to go into the building, but she can still feel the light piercing through the wall. It is dull, as though it is concealing itself, but it is like a wildfire hiding behind a bedsheet. She makes her way up the stairs to the front door, even though her whole body is screaming at her to run. Sen seems to catch her trepidation, and he pushes in front of her and knocks twice.

The domesticity of the sound shocks her out of her panic. She didn't know what she was going to do at the door, but it wasn't knock. She gives Sen a side-eye and tries her best to shoot him a wry grin, and then the voice comes.

"Come in," it says.

It isn't Ari. It isn't Auntie, either. It is high-pitched, a woman or a boy. It sounds stiff and pained, speech forced through a tight throat and a disobedient set of lips. Sen manages to communicate an entire paragraph to Kiada through his eyebrows alone, but the gist of it is: *Is this who we came for?*

She shakes her head at him, and he responds with a flurry of gestures, a tilted head. *Okay, but this is a living person. We should ask them what happened. Right? We should go into the house?*

She gives him a series of gestures back that says, *I can't really articulate why, but I have a very bad feeling about this, and ordinarily I wouldn't bring it up, but I feel like in the circumstances, it's worthwhile to be cautious,* but he seems to interpret as, *Yeah mate, we might as well,* because he turns the knob and steps inside.

Smoke gushes out, and Kiada coughs through it. When it clears, she sees that the bottom floor is mostly untouched by fire, though the smoke and ash have stained it all a uniform gray. She steps inside and picks up the nearest object, a small wooden religious effigy. The ash falls off it in clumps. There is a strange smell in the air, copper and some other metal she can't quite place. She turns to Xidaj and points at her nose.

Ozone, he mouths. *Circuits.*

She raises her weapon. The dopplers at the barricade didn't look capable of speech, but she isn't taking chances. The other two follow suit, Sen leaning on his cane, bracing his gun arm against his ribs. She takes the lead up the stairs, careful to make as little noise as possible. There is so much ash on them that she can feel her boots sinking into it, each step punctuated with a soft little fall, and she thanks the gods for small graces. Whoever is up there knows they are coming, but it doesn't pay to give them any more information than that. In her mind's eye, she can sense the room above, incandescent with magic. There is so much of it, she can barely tell where in the room it is centered, but there is a core of it more blinding than the rest, and she does her best to point herself at it without looking directly into it.

Kiada is prepared for a lot of things, but not the tableau at the top of the stairs.

Four burned bodies occupy the room—a tall one that could be Nyree or Ms. Kalpona, curled protectively around Jules in the cor-

ner and burned beyond recognition, Mr. Pono and the Widow Rātā sprawled out on the floor with already-dessicating gunshot wounds in their backs—but that isn't what causes Kiada to finally let out the scream that has been building all day. That is Teina. She is spread out across the wall, hands low and wide, melted into the brickwork and reeking of metal and burning plastic. Her legs are missing, and exposed wiring drapes down from her open belly. Her face is a moue of agony. There is a trail through the ash, as though somebody dragged her through it after the fact, but that doesn't make sense with the fire damage: she is melted onto the wall, mounted like taxidermy, posed like some saint in a painting. She cranes her neck toward them and smiles.

"Come in," she says in the exact same cadence as before, though there is a crackle to it this time, a distortion. Kiada's stomach falls as she recognizes Nyree's voice coming from her mouth in awful harmony with a half dozen others.

"You took me to a very stupid play once," Teina says, "about a man from a world of iron who tried to live in a world of gold."

"What are you talking ab—" Kiada begins.

"It did not end well for him. Reality always wins. Good night, Sibyl."

This is all wrong; she shouldn't have glowed with magic. A doppler can't weave; it has no life in it to weave with.

But what even *is* life? Just experience, memory, relationships. Blanks barely have any thread because they've had those things torn away, so it makes a cruel sense that a doppler could develop one in the right circumstances. She reaches out and tries to pull at a thread, but the doppler is inert; she has the *appearance* of life, but she isn't quite there. She is so close, though, not an imitation, just . . . unformed.

She feels that Teina could've been human, if she had been given more time, and that hurts worse. Despite her great power, there is nothing for her to pull. Even if she were alive, she would need to die and be cast back, to be chosen by the gods.

It doesn't make sense. This is a beacon for Weavers, a flame to draw moths, fixed in place. Put a sufficiently advanced doppler in a house packed with life, and it won't give you life, but it'll give you something close enough to bait a trap. She knows only one person in the entire city with the sort of power she is seeing, who can conceal their presence well enough that they can hide in an empty city, and it is—

"Oh, fuck," she says. "We need to go. Now."

Then she hears the engine. Large, heavy, moving impossibly fast for something of its size. She turns to the window and sees a giant dark metal form rolling toward them. It is larger than an armored car, and the unmistakable shape of a machine gun emerges from the turret on top. It slows to a stop in front of the building, then the hatch on top opens and a man in Vuruhi colors hauls himself up. He holds a small box to his face, and when he speaks, it booms from a hidden speaker somewhere on the vehicle. Men are already pouring forth from the back of the tank, dozens of them, armed to the teeth. They are all wrong, though; she can't sense their magic, can't weave from them. She notices that each one of them is wearing a strange copper rig strapped to his chest, and the core at the center of each rig is a little patch of anti-life, something that seems to block her from weaving with them. It makes her nauseous just to see the sucking darkness where each man stands.

"Bring out the Weaver," says the man on top of the vehicle, "and there won't be any trouble."

"Oh, good!" shouts down Sen. "I thought for a minute there trouble was almost guaranteed, what with the bloody tank and all. Good to know you're all here for a tea party."

There is no response for several seconds, and Kiada peers down and sees the man with the loudspeaker arguing with somebody inside the vehicle.

"Very funny," he says into the loudspeaker. "W—"

"Thank you," yells Sen. "I thought so!"

"—e are authorized to open fire. The Weaver heals, you don't. You got anything funny to say about that?"

"Nah, mate, you're funny enough, I reckon."

This is met with a bout of swearing in Radovangi.

"Sen," hisses Kiada, "what the fuck are you doing?"

"If they were gonna shoot," he says, "they would've just shot. They went to all this trouble to get the jump on us, so why waste that? I'm guessing our new friend here"—he gestures to the woman on the wall—"is pretty hard to rebuild if they break her, and that means they've gotta come in. I think the better question is how on earth they managed to hide a whole tank. You'd have sensed the crew, right?"

"All that metal would make things harder," she says, "and the shit they're wearing on their chests is blocking a lot of my sight, but I think I still would've sensed them, you know? They've got a lot of camouflage on, but I'm sure I would've known they were coming. It's like they came up from—"

And then it hits her.

"It's like they came up from underground," she says. "That's where everybody is, why we haven't seen survivors; they're in the subway tunnels. Hineinui Tepe Station is just around the corner—they

165

must've driven up the tracks. The system wasn't finished last time I checked, but they clearly had enough of it complete."

"Which means," says Xidaj, "there's a central hub somewhere that controls the emergency shutdown. They couldn't have let the tank out without a man in the control room."

"Which means," says Sen, "the Vuruhi are in charge down there, or at least in control of the entrances and exits. They plan to wait this shit out, then clamber up and claim the city for themselves."

A bullet pings off the wall nearby, and they all duck.

"You have two minutes to send out the witch," says the man on the megaphone. "Or we'll turn the building to rubble. You degenerates can count, right? Start fucking counting."

"We can take the fire escape to the roof," says Kiada. "Make our way out across the rooftops?"

Sen's thumb rests against his lip, and he is staring down at the floor. He drums his fingers against the handle of his cane.

"We'd be sitting ducks for the beam," says Xidaj. "We only lasted this long because they didn't know we were here."

"One minute forty," comes the voice from outside.

"Is there a back door?" says Sen. Kiada nods. He smiles at her, and there is an empty calm in it that terrifies her. He seems so peaceful, and she knows exactly what he is thinking.

"No," she says. "You're coming with us."

"You'll never outrun a tank, and there's who knows how many more waiting to pour up from the underground. They want you alive, and I can't imagine that bodes well for the ship. Even if you slit your wrists now, you'll pop back up six months down the coast, and by the time you're back, the ship will be ash. The crew survives if you can get back to the *Kopek*, and you get back there if these

bastards are tied up here. You got enough magic to turn us all invisible?"

She doesn't. If she could pull from the doppler, it could get them all out, but she has only the magic holding her own soul together. She shakes her head.

"Then somebody's gotta hold the line," says Sen, "and I held the line at Syalong for six bloody years. No surprise the war came back for me, aye?"

"Fuck you, old man, nobody else dies today," she spits. "We had a deal, no heroes, no macho bullshit, no more blood. I outrank you, and I am giving you a direct order."

They don't have time. The Vuruhi are spreading out, surrounding the building. She can hear their steel-toed boots clattering off the cobbles.

Sen shakes his head.

"Every second you waste arguing is a second you're not running," he says. "For what it's worth, I'm not a hero, I'm just a bloke who did his best. Remember that: when you sing my name, I ain't really dead. I get to live as a song, and there's nothing sweeter."

"You stubborn old f—"

"One minute," comes the call from outside.

"Go," says Sen. "I've got this. Be safe, kiddo."

She wants to hit him, to grab him by the arm and drag him out of there, but godsdammit, he was right: she just doesn't have time to fight him.

"You motherf—" she says. She stops herself, then draws herself up and gives him a quick salute, then reaches into her pocket and hands him the bully bag. "You got this. You always do."

He grins and takes it, and for a moment her fingers touch his and

she realizes they are even more gnarled than her own. She turns and runs, and Xidaj runs with her. As the door shuts behind them, she hears the lock click. They are out the back door, down into the alley-way, boots closing in around them. They jackknife down another side street, and she hauls Xidaj into the shelter of a nearby doorway just in time to see five Vuruhi arrive at the back door of Ari's place, their grins wide, wolflike and triumphant. Xidaj raises his rifle, and she realizes his hands are shaking. She eases the barrel down and shakes her head. They slip away together through the streets of Radovan. Somewhere behind them, shots begin to ring out.

TWO MONTHS AGO

There were more Vuruhi in the streets than Ari could count. They flowed together in a khaki tide, a dozen different flags flying over them but, above all, a black wolf's head on a field of gold. They were converging on Unity Square, and he did his best to avoid bumping into too many of them. The ones who hung out in town late at night tended to be younger, taller, ready for a fight, but these were men of every age, size, and profession. Almost entirely men, though there were women among them, too, modestly dressed, ankle-length dresses and waist-length hair, many of them carrying young children. Some of the crowd had their faces twisted in masks of apprehension or hatred, but many of them were smiling, laughing, and if it weren't for the uniforms and the unmistakable forms of poorly concealed weapons under their jackets, they might've looked like any other crowd. As Ari approached the square, he saw a mirror flashing

from a nearby third-floor window and managed to extricate himself from the crowd and clamber his way up a drainpipe. Mārū was waiting for him. He glared at Ari, but it was a nice glare.

"Nice to see you, too, bro," Ari said.

"Mhm," Mārū said, and then, when Ari turned away, he smiled at him. Ari pretended that he didn't see it.

"Big job," he said. He was looking out the window now, down at the crowd. The Vuruhi had erected a stage, and men were busying themselves about on it, setting up a sound system. It took him several seconds to realize that Mārū hadn't replied.

"You're supposed to say 'yep,'" Ari said, "or 'uh-huh' in a very sardonic way, with emphasis on the 'huh' so I know that you really don't care, or maybe just a sort of fed-up grunt. We have a rhythm, Mārū, we have a routine."

He turned and realized Mārū was staring at him wide-eyed. His new brother took a step back and said, "I'm scared, Ari."

Mārū's voice was higher than Ari remembered it being, and he became acutely aware that Mārū couldn't be more than seventeen, basically a kid who only seemed older because he had lived in a world that refused to let him be young.

"There's nothing to be scared of," Ari said. He didn't know why he even tried to lie; they'd worked together too long, knew each other too well. Mārū glared at him, and then the dam broke and the words flowed out.

"Something is very wrong here," he said. "I've been spending time in trunk nine, and I've been picking up weird chatter, and weird . . . static? White noise, but not quite; it's just bad frequencies, nonsense, and every so often I'll catch a single word, and I've been putting them together, and I don't know what's happening, but somebody is fuck-

ing around with the network, and either nobody else has noticed it or everybody has noticed it and they don't care, and both of those possibilities are terrifying, and then there's, there's . . . there's this thing."

He held up a device about the size of a fist.

"Auntie told me it was a transmitter to get data from Malatenki's doppler, but it's wrong. It *looks* like a radio transmitter, so close that I didn't even notice it at first, but it's wrong and I don't know why, and Ari, I'm scared. I don't give a fuck about Malatenki, I don't care if this thing is a grenade and it takes out his whole fucking family, but there's something we've missed here, and I don't know what it is, but I know it's big and I don't want to do this. *One* problem I can account for, but the more holes you add, the bigger our attack surface gets. We are wide open right now. I want to get out of town, just get on a boat and not stop until we hit the Eastern Shelf. I know what I said about running; you know how bad it is here that I'm changing my mind. You can come with me, I'm sure we can find work. Auntie will be pissed, but Auntie can't be everywhere at once, and we need to go *now*, I swear, I don't know why but I know I have a really, really bad feeling about this."

Ari had never heard him say so much at once. Gods, it was probably more words than Mārū had ever said to him total. He was crying and not even trying to hide it, his tears cutting rivulets through the grime on his face.

It was a tempting idea, but it would mean leaving Fort Tomorrow behind. It would mean leaving Nyree, Mr. Pono, Ms. Kalpona, Mr. Kanikai, Jules, and the Widow Rātā behind. Somebody else might pick up the slack with his medicine deliveries, but they might not, and he couldn't put that risk on his clients, on his friends. The murmur of the crowd outside was slowly building, a sort of human

static that rolled through the windows in a great wave. Ari took a deep breath.

"I'll help you skip town," he said, "if that's what you really want. But I'm staying."

"Auntie will—"

"She won't," said Ari. "Whatever you're about to say, she won't. She's not going to be happy, but she'll understand. She cares about me. I know it doesn't always seem like it, but I know she does."

"Okay," said Mārū, "but just in case, did you keep that toy car?"

Ari pulled it out of his pocket and held it up. Mārū inspected it. "If you need to slow Auntie down, push the button. It won't give us long, but it might be enough to escape. You've given the EMPs out to half the city, it'll be death by a thousand cuts. You keep that one, I've made myself another."

Ari nodded and pocketed it.

Mārū screwed up his face and held up Auntie's strange device. "Anyway," he said, "t—"

And that was when the door came crashing down. It happened so fast, Ari could barely process it: a blur of khaki, fists, and boots. He was on the ground and somebody was kicking him in the ribs, and somebody else was shouting, and his head spun from where he'd been struck by something large and dark that had come at him impossibly fast. He tried to stand, but something heavy smashed into him and he fell back down, his legs numb. His mouth was full of blood, and when he tried to speak, it rushed out in a torrent onto the ratty carpet. From somewhere distant, he heard a scream, the strangely hollow sound of fists raining down until the shouting stopped, and a hoarse voice saying *Bitch bit me.* Through a haze of pain, Ari looked up to see a Vuruhi at the window, signaling down at somebody below. Ari tried

to get up again, and somebody grabbed a fistful of his hair and yanked him to his feet, then marched him over to the window. He realized with horror that the entire crowd was staring up at him, that the man on the stage was pointing. His voice came over the loudspeakers.

"And the Spider sends an assassin," he boomed, "because she knows that her bribes have failed, that the real people of Radovan have too much integrity to be controlled. The government knew and said nothing; the church knew and said nothing. We had weapons to end the war overnight, and they were too weak and corrupt to use them. It is time we sent the Spider a message: that we are strong, that we are mad as hell, and that we are done with being manipulated. We are Radovan, and we are free."

A quieter voice came from behind him, the same hoarse voice that had done the screaming.

"Do the girl first," he said.

As strong hands dragged Ari back from the window, he saw with horror what they were lowering down into it from the floor above: a noose. He tried to struggle, and a fist caught him in the side of the head. One of the Vuruhi's faces seemed to be melting, as though his flesh itself were turning liquid and starting to run. Another had six fingers on his hand, and one of the fingers was boneless and twitching. Ari tried to shout, and the hand clasped over his mouth tightened, squeezing his jaw hard enough that the bones began to click and grind. He tried to bite, to claw, to kick, but there were too many men holding him, and he watched helplessly as three of them hauled Mārū to the window while he shrieked in terror. His face was a mask of blood, and one of his arms was limp and twisted back in a way that made Ari scream just to see. They put the noose around his neck, and then the voice on the loudspeakers returned.

"Any last words, assassin?"

Mārū spat, and blood came out.

"Of course not," roared Malatenki, and the crowd roared with him. "Nothing to say. See how our enemies are speechless in view of our strength. Our spirit leaves them paralyzed with dread—our wrath is the rain that will wash the streets clean. And what will be left? A pure world, a shining golden world, the world we deserve."

Then one of the Vuruhi kicked him, and he fell out of sight. The rope cracked and went taut, and the crowd roared in approval. It was a wave rolling in through the window, a wall of sound, an impossible booming thing, filled with joy. A second noose was lowered down into the window, and Ari felt his feet dragging across the floor.

"How about you?" roared Malatenki. Ari barely had the strength to speak. He was missing teeth, his jaw felt like it had been dislocated, everything was pain. He looked down at the crowd, at Malatenki on the stage.

"I'm coming back for you," he muttered. He could barely hear himself.

"Nothing to say!" bellowed Malatenki. "Gods, I wish our enemies were more exciting. I came for a *show*."

And then Ari was falling, and the world went dark.

NOW

Sen takes out his backup flask and drains the entire thing. No point letting it go to waste. He wishes he had a cigarette to smoke, but he gave up yonks ago, and lighting another flame seems like taking the piss a bit anyway. The upper floor is good high ground, but he only has two shells, and there are a lot more than two men down there. He can hold them better at the front door. He wanders over to the broken window, then waves down at the Vuruhi. They jeer at him, and one raises his rifle. He ducks back inside and makes for the stairs as a bullet whips into the room, hitting the wall behind where he was standing. No damned trigger discipline, which means despite the uniforms, they aren't soldiers. He can use that. He can hear their officer tearing them out in Radovangi, and it brings him a sudden burst of nostalgia. He hobbles his way down the stairs, careful to keep his balance despite the dense carpet of ash.

He finds the back door and wedges a kitchen chair beneath the doorknob.

"TEN SECONDS."

His leg aches like a bastard, but he long ago learned to work through the pain. He limps over to the front door, locks it, leans against the wall, and checks the shotgun one last time. It's an old thing, not well maintained. It isn't a tanker's weapon but a hunter's weapon somebody has taken a saw to. Two shells isn't going to get a lot done, but it's better than nothing.

"FIVE. FOUR. THREE."

Be an awful shame if something put the lads off their counting. He rips the cord from the bully bag with his teeth, then biffs it out an open window. Shouts, frantic footsteps, *GRENADE*, the pop and hiss of a wave of acid, not as many screams as he'd like but enough to make him smile anyway.

He braces his cane against the ground with his right hand, pushing his left shoulder into the wall with the gun in the crook of his elbow. The warmth from the whisky fills his chest, and it's the first good heat he's felt all day.

"TWO, YOU DEGENERATE FUCK."

Sen grins. "IS THAT TWO NIL?" he shouts.

"ONE."

A shoulder hits the door, causing the front wall to shudder, creating little waterfalls in the ash. The back door rattles, and somebody swears under their breath. Then they try the front door again, and it resolutely continues not to open. What a very clever distraction— classic flanking maneuver, probably something that had worked incredibly well in the manuals they'd read. He knew the type, kids who read books of military strategy and jacked off in their beds about how

they'd kill a hundred men with their big-boy brains alone. Damned middle-class kids with better prospects than any actual enlisted man. The sort who joined as officers or not at all, and whose clever plans got soldiers killed. The back door stops rattling just as a second impact hits the front and the wood splinters.

"Sir?" comes a voice from the back, just loud enough to hear, the quavering tone of a very certain young man suddenly robbed of all certainty. "Sir, we can't get through. What do we do?"

The front door comes down, the first man charges through . . .

And catches a shell in the side. His shoulder and neck explode into a shower of muscle and meat. He's dead before he hits the floor. The second man stops halfway into the room, staring wide-eyed at the ruined body of the first, and Sen punishes that hesitation with his last shell. The impact lifts the man off his feet and slams him into the brickwork outside with the crunch and crack of dozens of small bones shattering. The third man does not come through. Shadows flit outside. They seem to dance in the heat. Somebody is trying to kick the back door down but not having any luck.

"No, no, no," Sen says. "Who trained you lads? Shocking. First man through the breach is always a write-off, the first couple really, but you don't stop pushing!" He opens the shotgun and drops the two shell casings in the remains of the front door, then very audibly snaps the weapon shut. "A few of you are gonna die, but then the guy runs out of bullets, and that's when you get him. You lads stopped, and that's a real problem for you because now I've had time to reload, and we have to do the whole dance over again. Which of you wants to be the write-off this time?"

The kicking at the back door stops very suddenly. The third man's shadow had been preparing to rush the front, and he falters, turning

to look for orders. Sen lowers the empty shotgun onto an end table, the ash cushioning the sound. He draws his sword cane. Wajet's sword cane, really, though the man had insisted he keep it as a gift. Their sword, their shared thing. He's used it far more as a walking stick, but he knows enough to put the sharp end into somebody.

"Yōhua, I'll do it myself," comes the shout. Another shadow approaches the door. The officer comes through with a rifle pointed at exactly where Sen's head would've been a half second ago. The bullet buries itself in the wallpaper. The officer has time to realize he's missed and draw back the bolt before Sen launches off his cane and smashes the blade across the man's jaw and into his neck. It isn't a clean cut. It is, in fact, a deeply messy cut, but it does the damned job. The man drops his rifle and tries to reach for a sidearm, and in that moment Sen wrenches the blade sawlike down and out. The man gurgles and falls.

And that's when somebody finally has the bright idea to shoot through the back door. The heat must've turned all the wood in the house to prepackaged splinters, and the entire locking mechanism explodes inward and hits the floor. Their comrades at the front hear this and have a sudden burst of courage. Another man comes through the front with a revolver, and Sen lunges, blade going right through the wrist and pinning his arm to the doorframe. The gun falls, and Sen snatches it out of the air just as three men come in from the back. He fires three times, and three men fall, but now his back is to the front door. Somebody punches him in the back, or it feels like a punch, but he looks down and sees the tip of a bayonet emerging red from his gut. It looks like it should hurt, but it doesn't.

"Huh," he says, tasting iron. "I'd tell you lads to go to hell, but it seems a little redundant."

He laughs at his own joke, and his laugh turns into an awful cough that stains the ash in front of him red. Two more punches strike him in the back. Something circular and hard presses itself against the back of his head. The back door is wide open now. The alleyway stretches out forever, and there's nobody in it. He smiles. The kids are safe.

"Good on ya," he says.

Once more the lion roars, and night falls.

Here is Yat. She does not know how long she has lived in darkness; it is so long that it has ceased to mean anything. Luz has stopped coming on any regular schedule. He does it so she is never quite prepared to fight him, never quite braced for the pain.

"It's called a fucklot," says the man. "I told you that. Or I will, I think? Still not used to this shit."

"Sen!?" she says, and as she says it, she falls and hits the un-surface of the void and rolls onto her back to stare up at a familiar face.

"Yeah nah," he says. "I mean, sort of."

She is too exhausted to tell him to shut up, and so she leaps up and wraps her arms around him and just holds him for a few seconds before he extricates himself from her grasp. (*How? I was holding him until he turned as insubstantial as air.*)

"Got the lowdown from a mutual friend. Your shark-toothed man's coming," he says, "and I can't stay long enough to help out. I'm meeting my other half for what I'm told is the most important dinner in all possible iterations of the universe."

And it hits her what he means by his other half, the monstrous twin-faced devil he's proposing to deal with, and she tries to grab him again but can't.

"No jokes," she says, "for once, no jokes."

"It's how I deal with stress, you know that," he says.

"Please, for me, just this once."

Sen sighs and slumps his shoulders. "I could never say no to you. Fine. You're gonna do great, kid. I know that can be hard to believe, but look back at what you've done already; you've done great, you'll do great. You're not doing great right now, but we both know you're strong enough to change that."

He steps in and hugs her, and he is *there*, warm and craggy and smelling fainty of sweat and smoke.

"It's not fair," he says, holding her tightly, "how much shit the world has piled on you, and how the folks who piled it will look at your achievements and pat themselves on the back for making you strong. Fuck 'em. *You* made you strong, your mates helped, and your devils can take a long walk off a short pier."

"That's dangerously close to a joke, ya fuckwit," says Yat.

Sen laughs, and she feels it through her whole body.

"That's my girl. You're gonna kill it."

"Kill what?" she asks, but he is already gone. Behind him, a light opens in the darkness, a single eye, and she sprints at it. As Luz emerges, she strikes him with her shoulder, feels his shock and rage and fear and—

???

The woman in the cell writhed, warped. Her belly split, and a rope of bone and exposed sinew whipped out, slammed into the glass, pulled back and weaved back and forth, snakelike, in the air, searching for weakness. Her primary head came at them from somewhere between her collarbones, while the secondary head, jutting out from the front-face of her neck, which was twisted in a perfect U-bend, mouthed soundlessly along, connected to nothing.

She had been an artist with a cosmetic fungal implant on her forearm. She'd picked up a mycophage from somewhere, probably in one of the squats she regularly visited. Political dissidents, unhappy with the council's rule. Luis was sympathetic, but his hands were tied. The cosmetic had been brand-new, the retrovirals still churning, modifying and replacing the old flesh. They were built to stop functioning as soon as their job was done. Take a monstrously efficient retrovirus

183

designed to modify human tissue and burn out, then smash it into an endemic virus that self-replicated by consuming fungal tissue that, crucially, was not self-limiting, and what do you get? A gray-goo scenario. An endlessly adaptable thing, designed only to consume. An apex predator for apex predators; the bigger you were, the more it had to work with. The original mutation had billion-to-one odds against it, but once it was in the environment, well.

She'd absorbed three other people and a large number of vermin before they caught her. Sedatives had been as ineffective as bullets. Somebody'd had the bright idea to hit her with an antifungal, which had slowed replication down long enough for a team of soldiers to get close and hustle her into containment. They'd cleaned the affected area with flamethrowers and antivirals, just to be sure.

Hector cleared his throat. He was ghost-pale.

"Brother," said Luis, "do you remember what Mother used to say?"

"She said a lot of things. She told me to sweep the floor. That she thought my wife was beautiful. That she liked pork siopao."

"She said, Hector, that God gives us imperfect tools and the strength to raise them."

"This doesn't look like a tool," said Hector. He was shaking. He hadn't shaken facing God's strangest angel, hadn't shaken staring down firing squads, hadn't shaken since they were both children, wrapped together in each other's arms on a rough clay floor, hearing a typhoon roaring outside.

"The best tools never do," said Luis. "I want you to see what I see, brother."

"What do you see, then?" said Hector. He wasn't looking at Luis, couldn't tear his eyes away from the creature behind the glass. Luis

squeezed his arm, just a little, until Hector looked down at him, and then Luis smiled.

"Be not afraid," he said. Galgalim, thunder, a joke for himself only. "I see God's least-perfect angel. Dear brother, I see a cure for empire."

Hector nodded.

"I see it," he said. "I think I understand. I . . . I think I really do."

From somewhere outside, they could hear distant birdsong, footfalls, Suta City coming to life in the dawn, unaware of the strange new angels dancing beneath their streets.

Yat stands beside them and puts a hand on Luis's shoulder. His eyes are red, his face wet with tears. He is broken; he has lost control and he knows it. He had not accounted for any resistance at all and was coming to understand the depth of his hubris. She should've broken an eon ago; that was the first warning he'd ignored, and now it was far too late.

"You *bitch*," he said. "Do it then, make this place hell. I will bite and scratch and hurt you, but we both know all you need is time, and you have it in abundance. Break the glass, make Hector kill me, make me kill him. It's the perfect crime—not a soul would know, and you'd be totally justified. Clean hands with your friends, clean hands with the law, clean hands with God."

Hector does not seem to perceive that his brother has spoken; this is not part of the memory.

"No," says Yat. "I want to, I want to so badly, but I won't, because that way this shit just keeps repeating and repeating and repeating, and I am so tired of seeing hurt people hurt people. This ends now. I'm waking up, and you can stay here or you can come with me."

"This doesn't justify what I did," he said. "This is just more sin, a

day where I hurt more people. Just one more unforgivable day in a thousand unforgivable lifetimes."

"It's not mine to forgive," said Yat. "And I can't say whether you'll ever be able to forgive yourself. That's not how this works. You don't just decide to be good and instantly heal the world. It's hard and messy and it takes a very long time, and you'll almost certainly fail and backslide and hurt more people in the process, but then you come back and try again and again and again. Nobody deserves redemption; they earn it. You do the work. You want to start? Be better today. And promise yourself you'll try to be better again tomorrow."

"You trust me to do that?" he sneered.

"No," said Yat. "But I have no choice."

She offered him a hand.

"Now let's get to work," she said. "Show me something I don't know."

He takes it, his face set in shock and disbelief, and as their threads entwine like roots, the world begins to end.

NOW

Kiada knows the city. It changed while she was away, but it's the same place, the same twisting cobbled streets. There's a route back to the docks that keeps mostly in alleyways and out of sight, but they'll need to cross Victory Boulevard. Xidaj trails behind her, his footfalls heavy, and she worries that each one is a dinner bell. She considers throwing a weave over them, but it's pointless. Nobody is meant to be here; there's no crowd to disappear into. She could maybe wrangle it if she had something substantial to pull magic from, but Radovan is cold and sterile, so they'll have to sneak the old-fashioned way, and Xidaj is not good at it, each heavy step spiking her anxiety further.

"We should go back for Sen," says Xidaj.

"It's done," spits Kiada, her voice raw from not-crying. "He made his choice."

"It was the wrong choice, it was foolish."

"So's talking, shut *up*."

She listens for the sound of steel-capped footfalls, but the city is eerily silent except for their own steps. It exploded for a moment with heat and light, then became a mausoleum, a place that almost felt like it was never alive at all. The cobbles radiate an uncomfortable heat, an ever-present reminder of what happened here, what could still happen.

They push on. Some of the alleys are blocked with fallen debris, and one is choked with blackened corpses behind a makeshift barricade. Many are clustered together, but some are quite a bit farther down the alleyway, a crowd trying to flee: it wasn't slow, but it wasn't instant, either. There's a gaping hole in the brickwork on the second story, and the alley below is equal parts bodies and masonry, some of it shattered and some of it melted together. The bodies directly below the hole are twisted and broken like they were hit by a grenade.

She turns to Xidaj and inclines her head toward them. "How'd they get hit?" she whispers. He points up at the hole.

"Hit the building, explosion, bricks fall down, residual heat from the brickwork does the rest," he whispers back. "Like being trapped in a kiln."

No safety, then. She clambers over the barricade and shoves aside a body, and Xidaj makes a noise of quiet disapproval. Religious shit; she has no time for it. She glares at him. "It's faster," she says, nudging aside another body with her boot. Xidaj carefully climbs over the barricade, giving each body as much space as possible. She wants to yell at him; this is no fucking time to get sentimental or devout. He stops to figure out his route, and she grabs the corpse he's struggling before and hauls it out of the way.

She expects another glare, but he mutters, "Thank you," and she

doesn't know how to respond. Now isn't the time, but she makes a note to ask him about it later. She has to lean against one of the larger piles of corpses to give him room to pass, and the pile shifts and collapses, causing her to stumble. Xidaj grabs her by the sleeve and keeps her stable. He quickly lets her go and steps back, waiting for her to go through the gap before him and then following at a distance, silent prayers on his lips.

They stop dead as a metallic shriek rings out. Xidaj's hand shoots up to Sen's hip flask on his arm, then he shakes his head at her. *Cold,* he mouths.

A dull boom echoes off the alley walls, coming from somewhere back toward Fort Tomorrow, then shouting and a clatter of masonry. Kiada lets her shoulders slump, then pushes on down the blackened alleyway. Xidaj follows her without a word.

More alleys, more carnage. A feline shadow darts out ahead of her across an alley mouth. She tries to read its threads: nothing, probably another ferro-cat, rusted with age, but for a moment she thinks she recognizes Fea. Impossible—the cat is back on the ship—and by the time she has processed the thought, it's already gone.

Most of the corpses she passes are twisted and burned beyond recognition, and every time she sees a flash of color from unburned fabric, the thought crosses her mind: *Maybe it's Nyree, maybe she's still out there, but maybe that's her.* They move as quickly as caution allows. She can't shake the image of them being cooked by the bricks like a fucking lasagna. She realizes they're approaching Victory Boulevard. She steps over the body of a woman in a long brown cloak, peers out, then quickly ducks back into the shadows. Right in the middle of the road is an armored car with three Vuruhi standing around it, and probably several more inside. One door is open, but

she can't see in. The machine gun on its turret swings lazily back and forth, covering the street.

She holds up a hand to Xidaj, and he raises his rifle and cocks an eyebrow. She shakes her head. *Too many,* she mouths. They need to get past them, and fast: the boulevard cuts right through the middle of the city, and looping around would cost them hours, and she doesn't know whether the *Kopek* has hours left. She grabs Xidaj and pulls his face very close. He recoils a little.

"See the tall blond?" she hisses. "Wait until I give the signal, then pop that fucking rig on his chest so I can weave with him to get the rest of the rigs—like dominos. And if you hit me, I'm gonna move heaven and earth to get you turned into a Weaver just so I can kick your ass to death."

Xidaj cocks an eyebrow at her. "I don't miss," he says. It doesn't entirely assuage her concerns, but there's nothing else for it.

She kneels down and takes off the dead woman's cloak, drapes it over her own shoulders, and pulls the hood low over her head, then casts a weave over herself and steps out into the street, walking briskly toward the Vuruhi.

The blond is smoking a cigarette, holding his rifle at ease, and she's barely gotten ten steps before he looks up at her and snaps the barrel in her direction. His squad follows suit. She's maybe fifteen feet from them. The turret on the car swivels to face her as well.

"Hood," says one. "Off, now."

She slowly raises her hands.

"Easy," she says in Radovangi. "We're friends." She gropes for a name. "Malatenki sent me," she says.

She knows instantly she's said something wrong, and crouches as the first bullet shears over her shoulder.

"NOW," she yells, and the report of Xidaj's rifle rings out. The glass in the center of the blond Vuruhi's rig explodes outward, and finally she can sense his threads. The bullet keeps on going into his sternum, and she knows she has only an instant before the shock kills him. It's enough.

She reaches out across the weave, finds a benign tumor growing in his left lung, and pushes almost every single thread into it at once, leaving just enough in his bones to stop them from turning to powder. The force of the tumor's growth bursts him, breaks his body into pieces, shatters his bones into shrapnel. He bursts so violently it lifts two of the car's wheels off the ground. Kiada has tried to keep her profile as low as possible, but a shard rips open her cheek. Her mouth yaws open on one side, but it doesn't matter; it hurts the Vuruhi more, and now she's charging with her knives drawn, leaping, roaring, crushing their rigs with fists and knees and her forehead and finally, finally weaving again; she was cut off from the weave for almost a day, and as it rushes back around her, she frantically snatches at it and begins to work. One Vuruhi is dead, and the other lies on the ground wailing, a piece of bone embedded in his eye and his rig in tatters. She grabs ahold of his threads and pulls them into her own. The turret fires madly, but the shock wave threw off its aim, and by the time the car's wheels hit the road again, she's in through the door. A shotgun blast meets her right in the stomach, enough to kill an ordinary human, enough to kill her five seconds ago, but she tears the threads from the dying man on the ground and the hole in her body reknits itself, and then she is upon them, tooth and claw, no mercy. She buries her knife so deeply in the driver's eye that it hits bone and the socket collapses, and when she tries to pull it out, it sticks, and she drops just in time to slip a

blow from a spanner. She headbutts its wielder, then wraps her arms under his knees and slams his skull against the steel wall of the car with a satisfying crunch. She brings her knee up into his rig, cracks it, then tears the last of his guttering life force out and knits her cheek back together.

There are no more of them in the car, but her heart is beating like a sledgehammer, her blood running hot as the sun. She grabs her knife from the dead man's eye, rips it out, then drives it back in, again and again, until his face is a ragged mess of flesh and gristle. A hand touches her shoulder and she spins around, knife raised to meet the new assailant, and sees Xidaj staring at her plaintively.

"We should go," he says. She nods.

"Good shot," she says, and he grins. He's never struck her as a terribly emotional man, but he's glowing with pride.

"I know," he says.

They're halfway out of the car when the shriek rings out across the city. Xidaj's eyes go wide as his hand flies to the hip flask.

"RUN," he roars. Her hand is on the steel of the car door, and it goes from cool to burning so quickly she doesn't have time to let go. She falls from the car and scrambles to her feet, trying to ignore the blinding pain in her palm. The air ripples like an oasis, and a nearby flagstone pops in an explosion of jagged stone chips, almost putting her on the ground. Xidaj shoves her toward the other side of the road. He's running, too, the rum in the flask screaming through the top in a blast of scalding steam. The point where the metal meets his skin is already blackened and soft; she can see the fat beneath turning to liquid and running down his arm. There's something wrong with his eyes, and she realizes the liquid in them is boiling. They're sprinting, and the other side of the boulevard can't be more than ten feet away,

but it might as well be a mile. She grabs Xidaj under the armpit and hauls, and then they're in shadow together. Xidaj is breathing wrong, fast and shallow, his skin blistered and hard, his sightless eyes whirling back and forth looking at nothing.

She puts her hands on his chest and tries to spread a healing wave, but there's too little left in him, there isn't even enough blood in his body to keep his heart running, the heat has evaporated it. She pushes everything she has into him, too much, too fast, and feels something inside him rupture. He dies. The walls on both sides of her are red brick—her mind casts back to the rubble in the corpse-choked alley, and she knows what's coming. She's died before, but this failure hurt more than that. She's gotten people killed, and she'll get more people killed, and so she falls to her knees, puts her head against the still-burning stone, and screams, waiting for a death that never comes. She screams and screams and then she's not screaming, her mouth is open and her muscles are moving but no sound is coming out, there's no sound at all, not even her own heartbeat. She looks up and sees a familiar shadow staring at her, crouched on all fours, its hair a gravity-defying whorl of pure darkness, its skin covered in a thousand tiny scars. Her scream returns, and her heartbeat, and then she falls back and just stares.

Daughter, it says, *I am so very proud of you.*

The scars open to reveal a constellation of feline eyes.

"You're dead," she says, through tears. "You're dead, Sen is dead, Xidaj is dead, we're all fucking dead."

Nobody is ever really dead, my daughter, says Tiger, *not while you carry their name.*

"Bullshit, fuck that, pretty lies, and anyway, you're not real," says Kiada. "You're a figment of my imagination, a dying dream. If you

were alive, where *were* you? You could've ended this at any time, and you were what? Sitting around picking at your teeth?"

No, child, I am hunting. We are hunting. You knew this, until I made you forget.

"Why did you do that?"

You asked me to, child.

"Why did I do that?"

You asked me not to say.

"Well, where were you, then?" she spits.

I was exactly where I needed to be, always closer than you thought, but now that I have shown my face, our time runs short.

"That's not an answer! Fuck this, fuck your mysteries, I'm done. Nine lives, right? That was the deal. I never wanted to live forever. I've got two left, and when this one ends, I'm going to eat a fucking bullet and be done with it, and you can't stop me."

I cannot, Tiger says, *but now is not the time for that.*

"What, then?"

Tiger's face splits open, showing row after row of ebony teeth. She offers out a hand, a single staring eye in her palm.

Now? Dearest daughter, it is the time to leap. An unfolding into your true shape, the sound of a match striking, the whiff of kerosene, a new bloom staining the darkness red.

Kiada spits, but what else can she do? She snatches Tiger's hand, and they're hurtling through the void together, Tiger almost invisible against the darkness, Kiada's red hair flowing behind her like a wind-blown candle in the endless night.

Dearest daughter,

Here is a memory I hid for you, a splinter cast from a broken window. Here is a girl with flame-hair, rags on her back, and shackles on her feet, stumbling through the rats' nest of back alleys while the whistles and dogs get ever closer. She cannot go back. If there is one thing that is true, it is that she cannot go back. She remembers a pillar of scars taller than the world, each scar opening as an eye, clawed feet on jungle floor, the smell of prey. It made her whole again, flushed the numbing drugs from her system, but then it left and she has no plan, except not to go back.

She makes a wrong turn, down something that was a road when she was younger and is now packed tightly with a decade's untaken garbage, and she turns to run but there's a shadow fallen across her, a woman who seems to glow, all caged fire and tiger teeth—tigers, why tigers?—but then she

smiles and it's gone, and she's just a friend, and the girl is so very much in need of a friend. The new woman cocks her head to the side, still with her friendly smile.

"Snake? No. Hmm," she says. She bounces on the balls of her feet once, twice, seems to bite at the air, taste and appraise it.

"Tiger? Not ideal," she says, "but she'll do."

She taps her thumb against each of her fingers in sequence, then looks up and breaks into an even broader grin. She takes a step forward and takes Kiada by the waist, then draws her into a hug. The girl does not cry, but her throat gets tight and sore. Sibbi is shushing anyway, motherly noises, as if to calm an inconsolable child. It makes it worse, brings the pain surging up, almost breaks through the wall of scar tissue. The hug breaks apart, a half second quicker than Kiada is ready for, and she stumbles a little, but Sibbi catches her by the shoulder.

"We're friends," she says, "and I help my friends. I'm going to get you out of here, but I need to know one thing first."

She leans in again, quietly smiling, and asks:

"Can you keep a secret?"

Ari was in the dark place again. He looked around and saw Mārū and ran over to him to embrace him, but by the time he got there, Mārū was already gone.

"No," he said, "no, no, no, *no. RAT.* RAT, YOU RAT FUCK. Come out here and bring him back."

The darkness behind him roiled and hissed.

He was not useful to me.

"Why the *fuck* does that matter? He was my friend, I loved him, you bring him back. You're not even my god, I never prayed to you, *you* came to *me.* Am *I* useful to you? Well, we're a package deal. You want me to go back, you send him back, too."

It is too late. He would not accept my offer; he lingered for only a moment. He is gone.

Ari turned to face Rat and took a step forward. Its bulk cringed back, recoiled into shadow.

"Then I'm not going back. Fuck you, I'll stay here forever and I'll— I'll mess up your shit. I've got power, I'll learn to master this place,

and then I'll rearrange it so you don't recognize it anymore. If you think I won't fight a god, you don't know me."

You speak as though you have a choice. For what it is worth, I am sorry. I did ask. He said he was awaited elsewhere, a place without injustice. I do not work without permission; I would not force him to remain in samsara. Would you prefer he found a crueler god?

Had a god just *apologized* to Ari? That caught him for only a moment, and then he was flying up back into the world of the living, on his feet and running through Nahairei Park back toward Unity Square. He'd almost cleared the park before reality caught up with him and he stopped in his tracks beneath a statue of Vuru the Wolf and began to wail.

Somewhere in the distance, the roar of a crowd rose to meet him. He couldn't go back that way. He wandered over to the cliff where Koztati had dumped his body and saw a thousand torches and lamps converging on the city center. Suddenly, a blast of feedback went out across Radovan, and Ari heard thousands upon thousands of windows shatter. The crowd went still for a moment, then began to roil and split. A great dark patch appeared in the middle, smeared twisted ashen gray-black like a fingerprint on firewood. He could hear the screams from here. He had no tears for them, but something in his soul still hurt. The scale of it was hard to take in, and the wind carried the stink of it to him, melting plastic and burning trash and overcooked pork. The torchlights broke off in a thousand directions as the great dark patch struck in their midst again and again.

He needed to get to the Fort and make sure they were all okay, but first he needed to see Auntie. This was *her* fault, and if she wasn't willing to help save him and the rest of them, he'd cut her throat and let hell fall on him.

By the time he reached the city streets below, they were empty except for the bodies of those trampled by the crowd. There was a layer of smoke on the ground that came all the way up to his calves. He came across a woman on her knees, holding a bloodied child and wailing. She didn't look Vuruhi, but he had no way to check and no time, either. There was something wrong with the child, whose skin had grown bushels of tiny grasping limbs like the legs of a spider. The mother reached out to Ari, and he just shook his head. *I'm sorry,* he tried to say, but the ash made him cough so hard he couldn't get the words out. He pulled his scarf up over his mouth and nose, then looked at her sadly and left her there in the street.

The front windows of the teahouse had been smashed, and the tables were overturned. A dead man in Vuruhi colors lay slumped in the corner, split from the top of his head down to his crotch by what looked like a single massive blow. A third arm emerged from his chest, the skin much darker than his own. A fresh trail of blood led back through the kitchens, and Ari followed it. Cook was waiting there, but it looked like he'd taken a shotgun blast to the face: half of it was open wires and circuitry, and he jerked fitfully even as he turned over blackened vegetables in a wok that belched more dark smoke. A fucking doppler, but Ari had never seen one like it; there was no way the tech had gotten that good, and he'd known Cook for years. He pushed past him and into Auntie's back room, and that was when he saw Malatenki.

He was pinned to the wall by the collarbone, howling in rage and pain, kicking blindly at the impossibly long, sleek steel limb that kept him there. It led back to Auntie's rib cage. Her shirt had been torn open, revealing only more steel and eight snapping spiderlike limbs. The crates had been smashed, the floor covered in a thick layer of

white powder that seemed to grasp at Malatenki, coalesce around the blood that dropped from his body. Several other Vuruhi lay dead inside the mass, their flesh beginning to meld together—they were only recognizable as human by their uniforms and patches.

"Vatay," she hissed. "You think your men could shut me down with a homemade solenoid? We had a *deal*. You could've been a king. All you had to do was be useful, but you couldn't even do that, could you?"

Four steel-clawed hands grabbed Malatenki, and Ari stood paralyzed in horror as they tore off the man's limbs like a child taking the wings off a fly, painting the wall in arterial spray. The greedy life-form on the ground rose up to meet it, stained its white surface briefly red before the color drained away again. Ari turned to run and crashed into Auntie, who was standing behind him. It took his brain a moment to catch up. This one was dressed differently, the synth-skin over her face torn open. She grabbed him by the throat and dragged him into the room, then slammed him down against the table.

"Ari," said the blood-soaked spider Auntie. "Right on time." She looked over her shoulder and let the pieces of Malatenki's carcass fall to the floor. "I had my suspicions about how you'd survived the little accident we set up, and tonight you were so good as to prove me correct. It's a pity about Mārū. They had orders to bring him back to me, but I should've known better than to trust fascists to take a light touch. They came to kill me, Ari, and all they did was doom themselves." She cast a hand over the shattered crates and the mass on the ground.

"I will endure this," she said. "You will not. This city is a failure; it will be reset. The experiment with your little Teina is a failure, too, but that doesn't matter anymore; she can still be useful."

The one holding him shuddered for a moment, and he recognized the expression that went across its face, the same little absence he'd seen cross Auntie's face before. She was wearing a dress he'd seen her in at the tea shop before, in the days when she'd been kinder. The Spider smirked.

"It's sweet you think you control this system, dear, but you're going to need to do better than that," she said to nobody in particular, then she turned back to Ari. "She tried to warn you so many times, but she never could. All these shells serve me; whether they want to or not, they cannot act against my wishes."

"Yes," said the Auntie he knew. "Existing order: facilitate the death of Aritama Kolamona."

"New orders," said the Spider. "We need him al—"

In one smooth movement, tea shop Auntie cut Ari's throat. As he fell and the Spider shrieked, he saw Auntie's mouth form the word *run*.

He landed back in Nahairei Park and was not alone: a dozen figures sprinted toward him, the same blank expression on all their faces, the Spider's shriek coming in awful harmony from all their mouths. He tried to duck under a flailing arm, but a second doppler tackled him, wrapped him in a cold embrace as inescapable as death.

Nothing ever truly ends, much like nothing is ever truly over. Yat knows this better than most. She walks through cities she does not recognize and marvels at a house sheared cleanly in half by some unknown force, a city on one side of a fence of electrical pylons and a floodplain on the other, with the house squarely straddling the line, half there and half never-there-at-all. She learns the rhythm of the sirens that keep her up at night, and learns to sleep despite them, then realizes in time she can no longer sleep unless they're on. She wanders mountains and jungles, gives food and guidance, kills only when she needs to. *First, do no harm.* These are her words, but they become harder and harder to hold on to as the eons roll through. The world they were written for is falling apart at the seams, its towers turning to rubble, its streets haunted by silence and gun smoke.

She is in a dusty street now, standing in front of a two-story

building whose sign—in a language she does not remember ever speaking—reads PHYSICIAN AND DENTIST. Even out in the street, it reeks of blood. The timing is all wrong; it should not reek yet, but it does now because it did eventually and memory does not move in straight lines. Luz is in the window on the top floor, pounding on the glass. She goes to the door, but it will not open. She places her palm against it and leans in and suddenly she is inside, pounding on the glass while Luz stares up at her from the street.

Luz is stumbling through the streets of Hainak after a shift. He finds a dead body in the harbor and panics. A shadow emerges from a nearby alleyway, a girl with razor-sharp teeth. When she pulls the trigger, holes open in both of their heads and the dream ends, and they wake together in the void and do not know what to say.

Yat is deep beneath the earth, having a yarn with Fergus about how the Scandis are no fucking fun, and he's showing her the vats, and she can see a thousand dead-eyed clones of the man floating in amniotic fluid, the tanks stretching off into the darkness. Despite the blizzard far above, the room is uncomfortably hot, hot and humid like Hainak before a storm, but of course Hainak does not exist yet, she was born there thousands of years from now, a city allowed to exist because of the fungus growing on these very cave walls.

Luz is sitting in the kitchen holding a knife and staring at the wall, and he doesn't know how he can go on. He knows on some level that he cannot die, but this is not his memory. Yat sits down beside him and puts a hand on his shoulder. "Rough night?" she says. It is not a question. He's seized control of the dream, made her relive it again for a hundred years to teach her, but she doesn't cry or scream; she just looks sadly at him until he feels sick making her push down with the blade and he lets her sleep and tells himself it is part of the

game, that she has grown numb and he needs to let her nerves grow tender again, but when that happens and he tries to send her back into the dream, he feels sick. *First, do no harm.*

Yat is Luz. She is standing ankle-deep in a dark lake. In its center is a tree. Nine Ferguses with nine iron spears stand around the trunk. A tenth gives the order, and they pierce the bark. A woman screams. The screaming stops, then starts again. After a few more minutes it peters out, then starts again louder than ever. The spears have left cracks in the bark, lit by a fierce white light within the tree. *Finally.* They're breaking out the beer, dozens and dozens of near-identical men with flaming red hair, and their celebration drowns out the screams. A few small, pinch-faced blond women move against them, some drinking reluctantly, most having their mouths held open as the men pour the beer in. The poison acts quickly. They die smiling. Most of them don't come back.

The world is ending. The world is always ending, but this time, the world is properly ending, not simply changing. Yat is lying in bed with Victoria, and they're trying not to talk about it but they can't help themselves. It was Vic's idea to put a chalkboard in the bedroom, and now she's out of bed, naked, scrawling something that looks like science if you squint and looks like magic if you don't. She will never be as beautiful as she is in that moment. She's talking about bringing the locals down into the caves beneath the continent they're calling the Ox and teaching them to run a nuclear reactor. "Can't teach them the engineering in specific, they're not nearly advanced enough," she's saying as she writes down what look like commandments, "but as dogma? Fail to perform maintenance rituals, the gods

get angry and kill you. People can understand that. One group at the main server hub in the Vault, further cults on each continent as redundancies."

She's pinned a map to the chalkboard and is penciling notes around Suta, Featta, Radovan. Of course, those cities don't exist yet; they're really just villages, but the conditions are perfect for development.

Now, Luz-Yat sits and watches the springhorn. Outwardly, it is cervine but has long, spiraling horns like a male goat's, and a coat of shaggy fur. Some sort of caprine chimera, perhaps? But of course, it isn't a chimera; she's just in an unfamiliar biosphere. Yat's past frame of reference is useless. She has dreamed of something like this for over two hundred years, and despite the horror, despite the isolation, despite the fact that she doesn't know whether they'll make it through to tomorrow, she can't help but marvel at this place.

Though they've run into small groups of tribal humans closer to the coasts, the jungle interior is almost completely uninhabited, and the animals hold no fear of humans. Some of them are the same, some are very different. The springhorn watches her from across the creek, sniffs the air, then goes back to drinking. Yat takes out a small pad and begins to sketch it. She doesn't fully understand the species yet, but this creature seems young, male, its fur patchy and thin from recent molting. She's only seen a few of them and wondered about the fur, which seemed at odds with the intense heat and humidity; she suspects they come down from the mountains later in the rainy season when the temperatures are acceptably low, but she hasn't been able to prove it yet.

She plucks a small purple flower from a nearby tree. Its petals

are soft, and each one has exactly three long gold stamens that are ever so slightly asymmetrical. She learned from a tribesman back north that they were good for stomachaches and were often used to feed their animals. She holds one out, then does her best to stay as quiet and still as possible. The springhorn finishes its drink, then pads across the creek. It sniffs her outstretched hand, then sticks out a surprisingly long tongue and drags the flower into its mouth. She can't help but laugh, and her laughter seems to frighten it. It takes off into the jungle. Her PhD supervisor would've been very disappointed at her conduct (and Vic if she were still around—*not tika, not pono, leave it be*), but she can't help it. She passed through the veil and found herself in Elysium. She might die, but at least she'll die in paradise. She briefly thinks about writing a taxonomy of the springhorn and trying to pitch it at a few journals, but then she remembers where she is. Old habits are carved into the furrows in her face, but she needs to adapt if any of the drill's crew are going to survive.

The mission has changed, but the job stays the same: figure out what is edible, which soil is best to grow in, which animals to avoid and which to try to domesticate. Instead of doing it for a hundred thousand human refugees, she is doing it for four refugees and the benefit of the locals. Humans, the mind boggles—she thought it might be coincidence, but there were human-ish beings in every iteration. Mostly hunter-gatherers, still developing early language and tools. This continent is shaped like an ox, with a large island off the northern coast that Vic vanished into after a blazing fight about the ethics of the drill. She has built a facility in the caves beneath the island, which she has come to call the Vault. She comes and goes, sometimes tearful, sometimes red with fury.

They try to be clear that they are not gods, that they are simply wise people from afar, but nobody believes them, and eventually it becomes the path of least resistance to go along with it; Luis becomes Luz of the Field, his brother Hector known to future generations as Hekat of the Hunt. The latter is a misnomer, for the time Hector tracks a lion that has been terrorizing one of the villages in the center of the continent all the way to the strait to the north, and when he finds it, he realizes that it has been wounded by hunters and is lashing out in pain, but he can't bring himself to strike the final blow. He follows it for a while; it dies anyway, atop a hill overlooking a bay that roils with fish. It's a spot Vic had marked on her map. Hector pushes his spear down in the earth to mark the spot, and all four of them return—Vic reluctantly, for she will be gone again in a few days, then return in a year and refuse to look them in the eye—and agree it is a good site, with access to rivers and fertile floodplains and fish from the ocean. They swear to remember the lion. The priests who follow them wherever they go will remember this, and tell the tale, and in time it will become unrecognizable, but for now it is a chance to start again, not with guns and germs but with genuine brotherhood. They set to work empowering the tribal leadership.

It is a risk, but they need to be ready for the Quiet. Some of the teaching is practical: fire, wheels, crop rotation. Vic tries to show them cricket with bats and stumps she's whittled from jungle trees, but they do not take to it; most of it is myth and legend to steer them in the right direction. No wars, no empires, no endless cycle of boom and burn. Peace on, well . . . Earth. Vic *thinks* it's the same planet, anyway, one that went down a different road, where tectonic activity has molded it in different ways that have delayed the discovery of agriculture. The land is certainly less stable: there are earthquakes

nearly every month, and strings of still-smoking volcanic cones emerging from the distant jungle canopy.

Off the coast, Yat has seen hundreds of small islands and vowed to one day explore them all. She and Vic talked about it, lying naked under the stars; Vic laughed and said there weren't enough years, and Yat shivered despite the heat. Vic knew, of course. They couldn't lie about what had happened in the City, all those dead fed into the rav-ening drill. Vic can't weave, but even she felt the current of twenty-five million souls rushing into the room at once and realized there was much more going on in the office than arguments over who microwaved the fish. Vic still doesn't understand it: she talks about uploading her consciousness into one of her devices. She's building her cults properly now; they're getting an incredible amount of work done, but her new body will never be ready in time. She will die, and Yat won't. Still, it is beautiful, and she hopes one day Vic will realize that immortality is a rort anyway. Vic taught her that word, *rort*. Yat doesn't know whether she is using it right, but she likes the sound. It has been so long since she's learned something new.

And now the whole world is new. It almost brings her to tears. Sibyl works every day with grim resolve to restore the old world, but Yat wonders whether it isn't best left in the past. Maybe one day, when the Quiet is done, they can return with the people from this world, and she'll find Cebu and rebuild the city from scratch. It hurts to lose so much, but this is a real chance to start again and do it right. The future stretches out in front of Jyn Yat-Hok, and for the first time in four centuries of suffering, it looks bright.

An age passes. A moment of déjà vu as Fergus pushes nine iron spears into the trunk of a great oak, and Yat realizes that something is wrong with time itself, that when the drill pushes through, it breaks

something unimaginably critical, and when the spears sink in, they tear open a barely healed wound. Finally she knows that what is happening in front of her happened thousands of years ago, in a place she barely remembers, that the membranes are trauma-bonded by it, stuck repeating the same cycles of destruction, that she and her brother have died a million times and will die a million more and each time they come back a little worse, the wind wearing the mountains down. She begins to descend into nihilism: everything she destroys will be back next time, and because every city that grows too large is a dinner bell for the Quiet, it is nothing but necessary to tear them down and start again. Yat tries to wrap her head around it, but it's not her field. The closest understanding she has is that the Quiet is the white blood cells of time and space, and they are an infection. Vic has more detailed theories but has become impossible to talk to. She should be dead but she isn't, kept alive by ingenuity and iron, her spine curved so low her face almost touches the ground, while Yat looks exactly the same, and one night slips out to go meet her brother. She doesn't disappear because she does not love Victoria—quite the opposite. She is so filled with love she cannot bear to watch her suffer anymore. She leaves without a note, without a word, leaves behind Vic's manufactories deep beneath the planet's surface. They've become nightmares now; she refuses to let her cultists see sunlight. The topside will inevitably lure them away from the Work, so she teaches them that the roofs and tunnels are the natural way, and that there is a hellish open sky somewhere far above, a place for the wicked to go in death, where they will fall upward forever. She's started making copies of herself, but the hardware is imperfect. The personalities fracture and mutate, and the only one she trusts enough to assist in her work is Wehi, a brutal taskmaster in a rudimentary spiderlike chassis, whose

personality is a gestalt of all Vic's fear and rage and paranoia, purged of hope and compassion, and one of the few copies of Vic who doesn't go mad in the tunnels, because she only has so much madder to go.

Yat will never fully get the smell of forgefire out of her nose.

Luis is running on the rooftops, following the song of a lost lover. He is carefully and respectfully laying out his father's body in the greenhouse, because he can't bear the indignity of the way he just fell, bug-eyed and clutching at his throat. He is pulling the weave from a hundred billion airborne spores and turning his own body into a lightning rod, willing, for one impossible moment, that love might actually save the fucking day. A distant part of him recognizes a trauma bond, an echo of the shattering that brought him and Vic here, but he pushes it down; he is not a clinician, he is a boy in love.

They are standing together in front of the tree now, and he turns and asks Yat, "How long has it been?" and she shrugs because she honestly does not know. The water rises up into the form of an iron spear, and he takes it and holds it to her chest, then thrusts. He is filled with doubt; the spearhead breaks. A shadow falls over them both, two immense wings, an assemblage of cartilage and bone wider than the city below.

"I could kill you," Luis says. "You're nothing to me."

"Yes," she says, "but you won't."

First, do no harm.

They don't know whose thought it is.

Crane takes flight, but she reaches the end of the chains of her own flesh binding her to the branches of the tree. She shrieks in pain and disappears. Something else breaks; time tries to clot the wound,

but it's not working, it's just releasing something worse. This bubble was never meant to exist, and a cosmic finger is coming to pop it.

The tree is burning now. This never happened, they both know that. This is the iteration of the future they're trying to reach, plucked not from memory but from the far stranger fields of hope. Crane suffers because her physical body is bound inside the tree—to destroy the tree would release her and end her pain. The men with fire for hair stuck her in there because they needed a new god, and great suffering was how they'd been told to make one. What was the most efficient way to make her suffer with the materials on hand? The spears, the nine horrible spears. Yat is crying and doesn't know why. Luis puts a hand on her shoulder and doesn't know why, either, but it seems to bring her comfort, so they sit together and watch the tree burn. When the tree is ash and the spearheads no longer hold their captive, Yat asks the question she's been preparing for what feels like a million years.

"What *happened* to you?"

Luis long ago taught himself to ignore all this, but for the first time, he's forming shapes in the dark water to show history playing out: his soul chipping away piece by piece, how he became everything he'd set out to destroy, how people became nothing but numbers and tools. In their eternity together, he and Yat have shaped each other like the wind shapes a mountain, like a mountain shapes the wind.

"I was a good man once, a good doctor," he says. "A lot has happened since then. The farther you go down a particular road, the harder it is to go home. I don't know if I can ever go home, if there's even a home to go to."

"Who cares?" says Yat. It is the most emotion he's heard from her in an eon together, gravid with the bitterness and hurt he knows she's been holding back.

He stares. "I . . . I guess I deserve that. You can go," he says. "I'm done. I'll stay here. I can't—"

He waits for her to fill the silence, but she says nothing. He knows she's seen the very pit of his suffering, knows his secrets, could walk away and leave them with him. She doesn't. Instead, she just sits and stares out across the lake.

"How are you this fucking *nice*?" he asks.

She shrugs. "I'm really not. Even less now. You rubbed off on me, but I was never all that nice to begin with. And I don't need to forgive you. Nobody should forgive you. That's not the point. I don't give a damn about whether you're redeemed—I care about whether you're still hurting people. You're not forgiven; you're just getting started, and it *doesn't matter*. Justice, forgiveness, they come when you fix what you broke, and you can't fix everything you break, not even close, but you're not staying here, because wallowing is selfish. If you have any fucking integrity, you'll fix what you can, because the end was never the point, redemption was never the point. *Redemption* is fucking selfish. We care too much about the soul who inflicted the damage and don't stop to think about the victims. You're going to help me save the world, and when you're done, we'll still call you a monster, and you'll be happy with that, because despite all the fucking evil, in the end, you did what you could. I'm giving you the chance because you were a good man once, and maybe there's enough of him left in there to start fixing what he broke. You'll never be redeemed, and it doesn't matter, because the only moral thing left is to act as if you could be. Start with me. It's easy, I'm right here. Now help me."

"How?"

"*Wake up.*"

NOW

Ajat sits outside the brig door, staring through the bars. Yat is still asleep, though the paralytic stillness has left her and she lies on her side, curled up around a wodge of blankets. The doc's notes said she must not have slept in weeks, which can't be right, but it's the only thing that makes sense with her condition. Poor kid. Ajat had known what she was getting into when she signed on with the gods, had been briefed by Sibbi about the possibility and the cost, and she still wasn't sure she'd make the same choice again if she had the chance. After the last few months, it's no surprise Yat isn't sleeping, though it's sad she hasn't told anybody how badly she's been hurting. Surely Kiada has noticed? Maybe not—that woman is so wrapped up in her own bullshit, she wouldn't notice a train until it hit her.

The first shout sounds like surprise. Ajat cranes her head upward at the source of the noise and reaches out through the ship. The

Kopek's emotions rush into her, faster and more intense than she's prepared for, and for a moment she's drowning in its alien consciousness: *flesh-not-flesh/ice-bone-leg/beatless breast/head-wreathed-in-sun/spiderlings-seek-my-heart/removal-cleansing/lover-request-aid/removal-cleansing.* She hauls herself back into her own mind. She can't sense more sailors onboard than there were an hour ago, but the ship is screaming, reaching out to embrace her, clinging to her like it was drowning. The shouts from above are getting louder, filled with pain, anger. There's no time for analysis, not even time to take the stairs: she punches her hand into the stoma and hauls on the thick strand of tendon inside. The cabin wall opens up and swallows her, and she's surrounded on all sides by muscle, a system of tensions and contractions that force her upward through the walls. The *Kopek* ejects her on the main deck to total pandemonium.

She's seen dopplers before, but not like this, not even in the Vault. They certainly existed during the war, usually performing menial tasks in the Ladowain camps, but they didn't have combat forms. They were too slow and stupid for it: they needed so much human assistance that it was easier to just use a human. These dopplers are sleek and skinless, with hands terminating in wicked curved steel claws. The crew is trying to fight back, but the grubs from their bio-guns aren't working; it doesn't seem to register to them that they're meant to bite down. Four of the dopplers are on Rikaza, a storm of blades; Riz steps into it, incandescent with golden threads, healing every blow instantly but burning magic too fast to sustain it. They tear a doppler's arm clean from the socket and send the rest of it careening across the deck. Iacci is lying facedown in a pool of blood, trying to crawl away, when a bladed arm comes down on his thigh. He shrieks in agony as a gush of arterial blood sprays upward. Too

many of the crew are dead and dying to process, and Ajat's old reflexes kick in. Each doppler has a spark of magic inside it, a single thread of semiconsciousness, but it's so little to work with. Somebody has to be giving the dopplers orders, and it's the moment after Ajat has the thought that she sees *her*.

She stands to the rear of the mass of metal, dressed in a strange dark coat that seems to gleam in the moonlight. She gives off no magic at all, even less than the dopplers. It's as though she's utterly soulless. Not even a Tiger Weaver could hide that well. Ajat's eyes refuse to focus on her, as though noticing her is an immense physical pain. Their eyes meet, and every doppler stops and stands perfectly still. The only sounds that can be heard are the pained whimpering of the crew and the gentle groan of the ship's boards. The woman takes a step forward. Through the blur, Ajat can make out a writhing moko kauae on her chin, a thing she hasn't seen in years. The islands fared poorly from the war, their people scattered in a thousand directions. Few can remember the language, fewer still what it actually means, and yet the woman speaks it to her, accentless and perfect.

"Ah," she says, "the backup. Tēnā koe, cousin. The ink suits you."

"I'm not your cousin, whaea," spits Ajat.

"Oh, I'm not Auntie," she laughs. "I'm the good one. Call me Wehi." She points a single regal finger. "I hate to burn good data," she says in Radovangi. "Take her alive. Kill the rest."

Three things happen at once: the dopplers charge Ajat, something explodes, and the *Kopek* comes to life. The deck tears itself open, exposing muscle and fat beneath. A doppler raises its bladed arm and swings down at Ajat's chest, but a whip of flagellum-tendon shoots out, grabs the arm, and twists it back with a wrench of metal. All over the deck, the *Kopek* erupts with barbs, whips, and spikes, fighting off

the attackers. A gunshot rings out, and then Wehi's jaw tears away, exposing the metal and wiring beneath. Kiada appears on deck, knife in one hand and shotgun in another, the air around her rippling with Tiger's raw magical power. The scars on her body are open, glowing white bisected by bladelike pupils of pure darkness, a hundred eyes watching every direction at once. A pair of dopplers tries to jump her from behind; she effortlessly sidesteps them and shoots Wehi again. Wehi reels back, but Ajat's shout of triumph is cut short when a doppler sticks Ajat in the side. Its claw rips through skin, through muscle and bone, roughly severing her left arm just below the elbow. Her threads surge into the wound, knitting her veins closed, but she can feel numbness radiating outward from her left side and realizes she is going into shock. Her heart is beating so fast that it rattles her rib cage and makes breathing painful. Cold metal hands grab her and force her to her knees. She looks up.

Yat is walking across the deck, eyes locked on Wehi. She cuts straight through the melee as though she barely even notices it, and the dopplers don't touch her. Then she stops and opens her mouth and says a word that Ajat can't hear over the din. From the shape of her mouth, it looks like *victory*.

Wehi turns just as Kiada manages to lever the muzzle of her gun upward and send a second shell smashing into Wehi's temple, and her head explodes in a shower of sparks. She doesn't collapse, though. Her body rights itself, then opens from the middle. For a moment, Ajat sees thousands of legs, numerous as blades of grass, writhing and roiling, and the beast rises up and disappears over the side of the ship. The dopplers go limp, then collapse like puppets with their strings cut. Yat falls with them, sprawled across the deck and taking shallow gulping breaths like a fish on the dock. Riz is cov-

ered in blood but swearing loudly enough that they're probably okay, though a lot of the crew aren't moving. Counting is difficult, but Iacci is still facedown, pale and still. There's an awful emptiness to him, no golden threads holding him together, just meat. Everything that made him a man is gone. Ajat's vision swims. She becomes aware that she is more tired than she's ever been, and she knows that if she goes to sleep, she might not wake up. Somebody is hauling her to her feet, but she can't process their face, can't understand anything except the awful cold wave rolling over her.

"Hey," somebody is saying, "hey, c'mon, stay with me. No, don't—"

Then Kiada slaps her, and the jolt of pain sends a wave of magic rolling out from her core. She collapses onto Kiada's shoulder, wraps her arm around her and clings to her like she's drowning. Their warmth runs together. Ajat's head hurts like a motherfucker, her extremities filled with pins and needles, but she's alive. After what feels like an age but can't have been longer than a few seconds, she lets go and steps back and her stomach falls.

"Where are the others?" she asks.

Kiada just shakes her head. She pushes Ajat away and starts tending to Yat. "Didn't make it," she mutters.

"What?" says Ajat. She gets no response and hears her own voice rising. "What the fuck happened?"

"Untie her," yells Kiada, only for a cacophony of voices to shout back a dozen different things at once. The tendrils of sinew Ajat managed to coax out of the ship are wrapped so tightly around Yat that she can barely move. One around her throat is tight enough that Kiada can see through her magical threads that the flow of blood and oxygen is

backing up. Yat's face isn't blue yet, but it will be soon. The shotgun is empty, but the others don't need to know that. She raises it and points it at Ajat's chest. Ajat's missing arm has a bladed doppler arm jammed into the stump, visible clusters of nerve and sinew already growing around it and binding it to the arm, a blade sharp enough to take Kiada's head off. She retreated belowdecks briefly to attach it, then came back up, well . . . armed and ready.

"She can't fucking breathe," hisses Kiada. Behind her, she hears the sharp susurration of a dozen people all pivoting in her direction with weapons raised.

Everybody falls silent, and before they can start up again, Ajat raises her remaining hand. The tendril around Yat's throat relaxes, just a bit, and she gasps, which means she *can* gasp, and that's something.

"Put it down," says Ajat. There's a look in her eye that Kiada hasn't seen before, a very real threat. She doesn't lower the shotgun, and they stand there staring at each other for about five seconds.

"I'm going to take a wild guess here," says Ajat, "that the beam is still operational."

"You sent us into a fucking ambush," says Kiada.

"You volunteered," says Ajat. "Now, gun down, and answer my question: What the fuck happened?"

"I just told you, we got ambushed. Sen and Xidaj are dead, and there's a force waiting for us in there that we cannot deal with. This whole thing was a trap, and it's already snapped shut on us. We need to abandon ship, go south on foot down the coast. There've gotta be Dawgae ships doing the run to Hainak and back. I know the coves they use to avoid the navy. We can get another ship there. Steal one if need be."

She lowers the gun a little, and that's when Riz hits her from behind. She sprawls onto the deck and the gun goes flying away, and suddenly the crew is on top of her, pinning her down. A slick wet bone-blade touches the back of her neck just hard enough to let her know the wielder is serious. Ajat kneels down so they're face-to-face.

"*Who* ambushed us? The woman who attacked the ship?"

"Victoria," croaks Yat. It sounds like it hurts to speak, like she's forcing the words through an unfamiliar throat.

Kiada cranes her head to the side as much as she can with somebody's knee on her back.

Ajat laughs. "Auntie Tori? We got ambushed by *God*? Fuck off. Our attacker called herself *Wehi*, the old Taangata word. 'The receptive soul.'"

"Sibyl got ambushed by God," says Yat. "Or at least, a version of God. You're just collateral damage."

"That's not her name," says Ajat, "and what I really want right now is for everybody to have just one name to keep track of, and for prisoners not to speak unless spoken to."

The wind suddenly picks up, roaring around them, then dies away just as quickly. The knee on Kiada's back lifts up as the crew moves to intercept the new threat, but it's too late. The sinew unravels all at once, and some unseen force propells Yat through the air and suspends her a solid foot above the ground so she and Ajat are face-to-face.

"You know who I am," says Luz, "and that I could've killed you by now if I wanted. Or worse. I could cut this girl's throat and reappear in Hainak. If I wanted that, I would've done it, but instead I'm here talking, which means I want you to *listen*." Then he drops to the deck, and Yat's voice says, "Fuck."

After a moment she says, "He won't do the throat thing. But everybody needs to calm down."

"You have no idea what he's capable of," says Ajat.

Yat laughs in two voices at once, in strange harmony with herself. "I've got some idea," she says. "But for now, we need him."

The weapons remain leveled at Yat, and she sighs.

Ajat narrows her eyes, then raises her new blade-arm to Yat's throat. "We most certainly do not need liabilities. What happens if she dies? You both spring back into separate bodies, right? Win-win for me. Yat, you can pull from the city and jump back here. Hells, bring reinforcements."

"You're not cutting my throat!"

"Kid, I didn't intend to give you a say in that."

Behind Ajat, the breech of a shotgun snaps closed. Two barrels push into Ajat's back.

"Don't touch her," says Kiada. "You've killed enough of our crew already today."

Yat feels a monstrous surge of magic tear through her and sees Ajat's eyes widen, the woman's legs and waist turning to strike and—

Kiada drops the gun. Her arms shoot out to her sides, then she does a single jumping jack. She does not at all look happy about it, and she goes limp and dives for the shotgun, but Riz kicks it away and twists her arm behind her back in one fluid motion.

"I could've made her pull the trigger instead," says Luz. "As I said, if I wanted to kill you, I would've done it already. If you insist on killing the girl, then by all means, my spirit is re-formed enough that I'll be back anyway. I lose nothing. I would've killed her myself by now if I intended to leave you here, but despite myself and despite the"—he waves a pontifical hand—"*charming* company, I'm still here because

you're in over your head and you're at profound risk of doing something very stupid that threatens us all. You are colossally out of your depth. If you want to survive, you'll at the very least hear me out."

You wouldn't actually kill me, though, right?

It is just a bluff.

Okay. Don't make me have second thoughts about you.

Dear constable, what does this conversation consist of but second thoughts?

He laughs out loud. Everybody is staring at him.

"All right," says Ajat, "but one wrong move and I take her head off. No hesitation."

"Good," says Luz, "hesitation is the very last thing we need. Can we move on?"

"Fine," she says. "What did you mean by a 'version' of Vic?"

"She called it a fork," says Luz. "The only person Vic trusts is herself, so she made copies. The problem is that consciousness isn't static; you put one out into the world, and it starts getting all *sorts* of ideas. The copy in the Vault was about as close to the original as I've met, but this one we're dealing with? Wehi was . . . a warden, a watcher. Her job was to keep the others in line. The other Vics, the cultists. She alone had the ability to hijack the other shells, to puppeteer them if they got out of line, to have them mete out punishment on themselves. The faith needed an avenging angel, somebody to punish sin, so Vic made one, a patient, lurking spider, a weaver of webs to snare the faithless. Wehi is one of the oldest copies, purged of every emotion that might make her worse at cracking the whip, and it seems like over time, she's purged even more. I don't know where the real Vic is, but even she wouldn't tolerate this. It's not just vicious, it's messy, and she doesn't *do* messy."

"You seem awfully familiar with her," says Riz. They release Kiada, who swears at them but does not go for the shotgun again.

"We were married," says Żu. "Or rather, I was married to a couple of versions of her. She wasn't a Weaver, so she did what she could to ensure continuity. The woman was a genius, you know that? She got ten thousand years of unbroken consciousness from raw copper and a spare roll of duct tape. She was, if you'll permit a pun, the only truly self-made person I've ever met."

"Very funny," says Ajat. She looks ready to slap Yat. "What does she want with my wife?"

"I can't tell you that," says Żu.

"You will," says Ajat.

"You don't understand," says Żu. "It's not that I don't want to tell you, it's that *it* is listening. It's very sensitive to sound, hates it. You can give it a new name for a while, call it the anti-song or what have you, but it's always listening for new names, and it learns fast."

Kiada realizes the sound around them has stopped. There's no wind, no gulls. A chill runs down her spine, and she remembers that moment in the alleyway before she met Tiger. She looks over to the city and sees a distant building on fire, but the flames do not crackle. Her ears pop with sudden depressurization, and it all comes rushing back in. A soft meow comes from her side, and Fea brushes against her leg.

"We're hunting something," she mutters. "A thing we're not allowed to remember." She doesn't mean to say it, but the words fall out.

"No," Żu corrects, "it's hunting *us*. And Vic is trying to do the same thing my brother and I were: deprive it of food. We thought we could keep things low-key, take out any city that grew too big and loud, but she's going a step further, burning every memory of the old

world. That means me, that means Hector, that means Sibyl, and by the transitive property of the self, that means every single one of you. Even a memory of Sibyl is a dinner bell."

"That's cute," says Ajat, "but you're full of shit. *Sibbi* and I were married for ten years, I know her weave better than I know my own. I have gone to sleep beside her and walked through her fucking dreams, and I don't know what the *fuck* you're talking about."

For the first time, Źu seems at a loss for words.

"Impossible," he says, "even if you've vastly overestimated your own abilities. It's not some minor anxiety you can hide; it's countless millennia of lived experience. Even a half-competent Weaver could read it a mile away. She couldn't just put that in a box and lock it awa—"

"Fuck," says Ajat. She's staring at Kiada, eyes wide. She sees a memory stirring unbidden in Kiada's head: gnarled hands clutched over her mouth as she hides from the cops, her bare feet bloody from running, and a phrase that comes to her with the finality of a bullet. *Can you keep a secret?*

"Oh," says Źu, "Tiger Weaving. Hiding herself in plain sight, inside another. Clever."

A lance of pain shoots out from Kiada's sinuses. Something pops inside her nose, and she tastes blood.

"Don't think about it," says Źu. "Whatever you do, do *not* think about it."

"You're not helping," Kiada shouts. Trying not to think about it only brings forth more memory, a million splinters of Sibbi's consciousness nested inside her own, the pain of a second soul that has been suppressed for decades.

"Babe?" says Yat, and it is Yat, her voice, her body language. She

steps forward as Kiada collapses to her knees for what feels like the umpteenth time today. Then Yat kisses her.

It doesn't change the world, doesn't make the ship move again, but it doesn't need to. The iron nail driving itself through the center of her forehead vanishes, and she and Yat are all that matters. When they break apart, the pain is gone.

She does not doubt, even for a moment, that she has just kissed the woman she loves. She needs to ask anyway.

"You're still you, right?"

"Some days," says Yat, "I honestly have no idea. But we're still us."

Ajat steps between them and pushes Yat back. "We don't have time for this. Little Man, that was a neat party trick with the sinews of the ship; you got enough juice to jump us into the city?"

"I'm still unaccustomed to this body," says Źu, "but I can probably make it work. What's your plan?"

"Simple," says Ajat. "God killed my wife, so I'm going to kill God."

"And after that?"

"There's no real test case for this scenario, so I'm just gonna improvise."

"Might I beg you to consider for a moment *why* there's no test case?" says Źu.

"I'm under no illusion about the odds," says Ajat, "but it's what we've got. We've lost too many of the crew to sail, even if we fix the ship. We hit her now, hard and fast, while she's still on the back foot, and we rip her fucking head off."

"Finally," says Kiada, "you're speaking my language."

She reaches out with both her hands. Ajat takes one, and Yat takes the other. Their weave runs together, and they jump.

Radovan is empty and sterile, except for a single glowing point of light that Luis's eye falls on, like a sniper appraising the lit end of an enemy cigarette. There is something wrong with the light: it is ephemeral, but it glows like a Weaver. He reaches into the mind of the Tiger Girl to see what she knows and finds only chaos and pain; digging deeper risks her breaking the connection, and there is no time to ask her about it. They are already hurtling through the void, and it is better to have a target than to spray and pray, so he casts a long golden needle outward, and it sinks into its mark.

He knows instantly that he has made a mistake and tries to whip the needle back out, but the target has sucked it in, greedily devoured it, and now it's pulling on him and the bodies who came with him. He hasn't encountered a trap like this in centuries, and he curses himself for not expecting it: there is only one woman alive who could build such a thing. Vic is hunting a powerful Weaver, and he has blundered right into her snare.

It *is* good, genius in fact, a synthetic soul that she has total

command over. But Luis has not survived an eon by being so easy to catch. He is trained in triage, the art of sacrifice. He regrets that he does not have a belt to bite down on, but there is nothing else for it—he severs the woven braid of their magic as close to the snare as he dares, and five souls in three bodies come tumbling out of the void. Luis hits a cobbled street shoulder-first and Yat takes over, rolling to avoid injury and springing to her feet, but the momentum carries them into a nearby wall. The other two are not so lucky. They hit the ground hard, tumble, and sprawl. He does a quick appraisal and doesn't note any obvious injuries beyond the superficial, so he lets Yat help them up.

The two women are swearing at him. Explaining will only make them angrier, and there is no time for that, so he falls back and lets Yat handle it, all pathetic apologies. The big one is thinking about the mission, and he nudges the threads in her mind back toward it and suppresses a grin as she dusts herself off, turns toward the Kōhiket Maitaz Special Industrial Zone, and marches forward.

"Could've put us inside the fucking wall," mutters Kiada. The skin on her right arm is ripped to shit, but it's not bleeding too badly. She feels so much weaker than she did before, like something important has been taken from her, and she doesn't have the energy to keep healing.

They're in the Ponamet Quarter, about halfway between the corpse-choked alleyway and the Fort. Her skin crawls. She can't handle seeing Sen's body; he would hardly be the first friend she's lost, not even the first she's lost today, but it still hurts to think about. Being aware of it and actually staring it in the face are very different

beasts; once you see it, that's it, you can only lie to yourself so much, and if Sen's dead, then they're all dead. She didn't see any of them die, either, but she is aware, on some level, that it happened.

The Fort is hard to miss, even at a distance. She has no doubt why Ari chose it to squat in; there's something about it that is both homely and strange, making it a cozy, messy place that could never be mistaken for anywhere else. The doppler's light is even brighter than before, and the others clearly notice it, too.

"Is there a way around?" asks Yat. And Kiada nods, grateful she doesn't have to ask not to go in. There's a culvert under the nearby road bridge that'll take them to Hineinui Tepe Station, and she flicks a hand toward it. They start moving on, but her feet are rooted to the ground. If Sen is still alive, then moving on means leaving him behind, but looking will just confirm that he's dead. She can't do it, just can't fucking do it anymore, can't keep leaving people behind. She pinches the bridge of her nose and smells blood, and suddenly she's standing in a café overlooking the sea and she can hear distant yelling, her knees have buckled and the blood is flowing freely from her mouth and nose, she is convulsing, and—somewhere that is not the café, somewhere an eon and a world away—Yat is trying to roll her onto her back, and Sibbi is standing on a balcony looking down at her with a sad smile. She takes a step closer and offers a hand.

"Good girl," she says, "you've been so strong."

She can barely control her own body, but she reaches up a jerky hand, and Sibbi reaches out, and their hands are an inch apart now, and—

Ajat grabs it, and she is pulling Kiada to her feet in a city of smoke and fire, pushing what little magic she has left into Kiada's body,

repairing the elbow she didn't realize she shattered when she fell, banishing whatever strange spell almost overtook her and thrust her into the darkness of memory.

"Bitch," Ajat says, "get up before I have to haul you up myself. And tell me what's happening. I don't like surprises."

She isn't angry, though. Her face is a mask of concern. Kiada finds the strength to speak. It comes from nowhere, anger and pain that she has no idea how to articulate, so she searches for one of Ajat's words, for a metaphor she will understand.

"It's like a . . . partition?" she responds. "Like there's part of me I cut away and put in its own little prison where I never have to look at it, but it's still there weighing on me. And every day, I wake up exhausted because half my soul is working overtime to keep the other half caged."

Her mouth is stronger than her heart, and the words flow free, burning her throat and lips. She hasn't spoken so much in years, and it all comes at once as a wail.

"But I can't stop, I can't just let it out, because if I do, I'll die, I'll fracture, I'll prism, I'll become something I don't even recognize; I've hurt so long I don't know who I am without pain, and I would rather you let me die than take this from me; it'll hurt less. Letting it out will either stop the pain or hurt even worse, and I'm not strong enough and I'll never be strong enough. I don't know how you're meant to live like that; I don't know how you're meant to love like that. I've kept it inside me for almost twenty years, and I'll keep it in for a thousand more."

And like that, the fire is gone, and she feels small and empty. Her chest heaves as though she's been in a fight. She tries to breathe, but the air catches in the cathedral of her mouth, refuses to go down. She slumps against the wall, her head spinning.

"I am a secret," she mumbles. "I don't know how to be anything else."

Yat is hugging her, and Ajat stands back, staring. Then she steps in and pulls the two of them into an embrace.

"If I didn't know better," she whispers, "I'd think you had a very different problem. I lived in fear for such a long time that the new me needed to destroy the old one, and that's not a thing anybody can do. Sometimes you change, but you never stop being you. Not even if you want to. That's what I need you to focus on right now: you are still *you*, you were always you. You've got principles and shit you love and a whole lot of shit you hate, and you've got memories and friends and feelings, and even if you change, that matters, hold on to it. And if you want to change, I'll help, and if you don't want to change, then I'll keep your secret and I'll carry you on my fucking back." She lets Kiada and Yat go and steps back. "You're my sister," she says to Kiada. "I don't always like you, but I love you, and somebody hurt you—a fucking *god* hurt you. So, say the gods are evil and they hate us and they created us just so they could have something to hurl fire at. So fucking what? You catch that fire, and you forge a blade with it, and then you take that blade and quench it in that god's throat. You'll get burned, but you were gonna get burned anyway; may as well do it on your own terms. Now, let's go."

Kiada runs her hand through Yat's hair, then gives her a quick kiss on the cheek, then she nods at Ajat.

"Thank you," she mutters, and sets off walking, leaving the ruin of the Fort behind her.

Hineinui Tepe Station is a twisted ruin of melted steel and glass. It was a modern building, a testament to Radovan ingenuity and

engineering, but it has burned like all the rest. The charred remains of a scaffold run along one side of it, with a dozen bodies hanging from nooses beneath it. Half a dozen armored cars and a single melted tank are spread out around the perimeter, and dead Vuruhi lay everywhere. A ragged wolf banner flies from a flagpole that has melted into a deep kyphoid curve.

They approach carefully, but nobody stops them. Yat mutters something under her breath, and Kiada gives her a puzzled look.

"He recognizes the design," Yat says.

"Does he know how we get in?"

"We need to get into the service tunnels. Best way is to follow the tracks."

The inside of the station is worse than the outside. From the outside, the sun is going down, and the station's lights are all offline, casting long, strange shadows. A small battalion of Vuruhi appear to have taken shelter inside the main platform, and its great skylight rained molten glass and slag down on them, solidifying into a single uneven mass filled with scalded and charred bodies. Trapped in the mass with them is a single ferro-cat, its eyes staring upward. The mass is still warm, and as Kiada climbs over it, it shifts slightly underfoot. In the center of the platform, the mass runs down into a single channel, not as deep as she expected—the liquid glass has flowed down into the tracks and almost filled them up.

She starts down it toward the subway tunnel, but Ajat steps in front of her and shakes her head.

"The tracks are still electrified," she says. "It's not safe."

"Shit," says Yat. "Luz says there'll probably be an admin office with access to the tunnels, but it'll have an electronic lock? Look for

a key . . . card? Little square of plastic. One of the Vuruhi probably has it, an officer."

Kiada looks at the mound of men trapped in the glass like insects in amber. Inside, she catches a glimpse of a pair of epaulettes. She steps to the side to get a better look and sees a piece of melted plastic spread across his breastbone in an awful smear.

"I don't think that's an option," she says, pointing at it.

"Shit," says Ajat. "The lock might be on the main grid, but I doubt it—Auntie doesn't want folks going down there, she'll have covered her bases. If it's anything like the solenoid locks in the Vault, I could probably crack it with a car battery and some copper wire, reverse the current, but I don't think we've got time, and knocking out the power might just seal it shut anyway."

"What about your skin?" says Luis, his voice brimming with something as close to excitement as Kiada has heard from him. "Cuttle-fish graft, right? You're giving off a bioelectric charge. You don't need wiring to blow the lock, you're a magic-to-electricity converter."

Ajat's eyes light up, too, and Kiada realizes she now has two gods-damn geeks to deal with.

"We form a circuit," Ajat breathes. "Two-in-one over here is a battery—one body with two Weavers' worth of wattage—I'm a con-verter, Kiada's a capacitor. Yat sends a charge to Kiada, Kiada accu-mulates it and discharges into me, I turn it into electricity and punch it into the coil. Reverse the polarity, and the dead bolt follows the current along the coil. Won't stay unlocked forever, but it'll give us a couple of seconds, at least. C'mon, Kiada, take my hand."

Ajat places the metal spike that is now her arm against the lock and holds out her free hand to Kiada, who hesitates, then takes it.

Kiada reaches out her remaining hand to Yat, who accepts it, squeezing it gently. "You got this," she says. "I love you."

As Yat says the words, power surges down through her hand and into Kiada, heat building and building until she can't take it anymore, until she feels like she is about to break, until she breathes fire and sweats smoke, and at the point of fracture, where her body is about to break, she releases it all at once. It ejects from her fingers into Ajat's palm, causing Ajat's hair to stand on end; her eyes light with a faint blue. She screws up her face as if undertaking an immense physical effort, then—

Click.

The door opens. The women release each other. Ajat opens the door a crack, and Kiada sticks a boot through, then opens the door fully and holds it open for Yat.

"I love you, too," she says.

Ajat rolls her eyes. "Why do I feel like I need a durry?" she says, and pushs past them.

The Vuruhi in the admin office has been stabbed through the heart. The wound is only a pinprick on the front, but from behind, the gash goes from his shoulder blade almost down to the small of his back. They find another dead man in the security office in front of a bank of monitors showing only static. His throat has been cut, and he died right there in his seat. His blood is tacky to the touch, not entirely dried but far from fresh. He has his pistol half drawn, and Kiada takes it. Ajat gives her a look but doesn't stop her.

"You've earned some trust," she says, "but you'd better not point that thing at me if you don't want it shoved somewhere painful."

"Noted."

The tunnels are deeper and broader than seems possible, and

Kiada doesn't recognize the language on the signs. One room is clearly a dormitory, the ground covered in feathers and blood, the bunks filled with the bodies of dozens of shaven-headed men who were stabbed in their bedclothes. A few of them died on their feet, and their bodies are strewn around the room; it is clear somebody caught them by surprise. The floor is slick with blood, and the trail of footprints leaving the room aren't from big, heavy boots but a mix of bare feet and common soft-soled shoes.

As they follow the trail deeper into the tunnels, it becomes clear from their structure that these weren't built by Radovan hands: it is ancient ferro all the way. Sen told Kiada stories about the tunnels below Syalong Cherta, and they slowly come back to her as they pass more and more rooms with flickering displays and strange devices and many, many dead Vuruhi. Every so often, a doppler or ferro-cat lies smashed and twitching among them. She didn't even know there *were* this many Vuruhi: between the tunnels and the station, she's seen almost a thousand, and not one is alive.

Even the ones with guns up have no shell casings around them, and their weapons are cold. Kiada checks the chamber of one and finds it fully loaded, a misfired round still inside and the barrel entirely blocked: a small metal cylinder built into the chamber has rolled down across it. She passes it to Ajat, who inspects it for a few seconds.

"There's a transmitter and receiver in here," she says. "Remote shutdown for the guns. Gotta admit it's clever. You arm them in a way that they can never turn on you. Let me check your pistol."

Kiada hands it over, and Ajat opens the chamber and peers inside.

"Yep," she says, "it's bricked. Don't suppose you've got a screwdriver?"

"I've got a knife."

"That'll do."

Kiada passes her the karambit with some trepidation. "Careful," she says.

"I'd never clip a tiger's claws," says Ajat. She clicks her tongue and tinkers with the chamber for a few seconds, then pulls out a device about the size of a thumbnail. She drops it on the floor, then stomps on it and hands both the pistol and the knife back. Kiada takes them, and their eyes meet for a second.

"You don't scare me," says Ajat.

"Is that a compliment?"

"Something like that."

They proceed deeper, Kiada at the lead. There are fewer bodies the farther down they go, and they are dressed differently, rough hessian robes printed with the same symbol she saw on the man in the alleyway all those months back, three exclamation marks radiating out in a circle from a single dot. A door ahead has a large glass panel at head height, and a man in hooded robes has died up against it, his skin red-rubbery and liquid, his hair patchy, with chunks of it caught in the folds on his robes. One of his hands was pressed flat against the glass and has slid down, leaving behind a smear of skin, flesh, and muscle. It is still wet. He has burns just like the man in the alley. The same hood and robe, the same patch of hair. A monitor bank shows dozens more of them, hundreds maybe, all dead beyond the blast door. Next to the door, there is a yellow sign. The antechamber has dozens of empty racks in it, the clothes they were meant to hold long since rotted away, except for the lead aprons that lay in piles on the floor.

"She *didn't*," Luis mutters.

They turn to him and see Yat's features filled with fear.

"Didn't what?"

"She built another reactor," he says. "No idea how—she'd talked about it, but I thought she was out of uranium. She cannibalized some from our old NSRO labs, and they didn't exactly have large quantities. That door will be lead lined, but we're probably catching some radiation even on this side."

"This is a little outside my wheelhouse, but I'm gonna take a wild swing here and say," Ajat says grimly, "that if the staff look like that, half the continent is going to be catching some radiation in a couple of hours, depending on the wind."

Xidaj was right all along. She runs her fingers across the scars on her face where her own window shredded her cheek during the Featta explosion. She was two hundred miles away from that bomb when it ruined her life, and now she's standing right on top of another one.

"Not too late to get out," says Luis. "I've got a few beacons around the place for big jumps, places I know well. I can't say I'm in top form, but I can get three bodies to Holbrecht easily enough."

"No," says Kiada. "We're not leaving the crew behind. No more sacrifices. We kill this bitch and shut this thing down. How long till it's safe to go in there?"

Yat purses her lips. "Fifteen, twenty thousand years?" says Luis. "I'm a patient man, but it seems like a stretch."

"I can do it," says Auntie.

They whirl around. Auntie's hands are in the air, and she is looking upward. Half her face has been torn open, exposing the wiring underneath. She is wearing a silk dress with gold embroidery.

"Don't speak," she says softly, "and don't come closer. This thing

237

is loaded with facial and voice recognition tech, and Wehi is looking for you."

It is very hard not to swear at her, but something in her remaining eye makes Kiada stop in her tracks. She recognizes this woman, though she knows she's never met her before—she's spoken to this body, but not this mind. She doesn't lower her gun, but she taps her foot against the steel floor, and Auntie gets the message.

"It's not nuclear," she says, "not really. We ran out of materials, but we got to thinking: whatever power source Weavers use is bottomless and totally untapped. At first, we tried to pierce through into the void between worlds and set up a direct pipeline, but it was like trying to collect oxygen by opening an airplane door at thirty-five thousand feet. Then Wehi realized there was a stable link that existed already, perfect conductors of the weave, made from flesh and blood. There were ten of us then, ten copies of Victoria, and the others tried to stand up to her. I didn't. The reactor burned through more and more weavers, so Wehi had me keep an eye on the streets for folks everybody else forgot, set up situations where they might meet a maker. I couldn't stand it, she had me raising those kids to be batteries. 'Auntie,' she called me, a mother but not quite—her idea of a joke. I tried to build a durable synthetic core, and she used it as fucking *bait*. Sibyl's the biggest game there is, enough power for centuries. She's not who's in there now, though, and that's why I'm going in: I need to shut it down, but first, I need to get Ari out of there."

Kiada nearly curses but stops herself. Instead, she lets out a soft breath. Auntie's head snaps up, and her posture shifts. Her one remaining eye looks right at them, the pupil so dilated that it is almost a single black pit. A curved steel blade slides soundlessly from each fingertip.

"You knew what was coming," she says, no longer the woman who just spoke to them, "and you came anyway. Do you know why? Hope. You let yourselves believe you were in control because you *wanted* to believe it, even if you knew it wasn't true. Hope is a sin, the only virtue is truth, and the only truth is fear."

A half dozen shapes emerge from the darkness behind her: the same face, the same posture, different clothes, different scars. Each is partly faceless, skin torn away in a different place, the mechanisms beneath damaged and twitching.

"You know what keeps us alive? Knowledge and fear. Fear is the thing that teaches you the difference between torchlight and wild-fire. Fear protects, hope destroys. Hope is choosing the tallest build-ing to hurl yourself off, fear is knowing gravity well enough to keep your feet on the ground. Auntie hoped she could trick me, Ari hoped he could save his friends. Ladies, you let yourselves hope, but this is the pavement."

She lunges, and Kiada tries to slip the blow, but her back hits the wall. The claws sink into her, and a gaping wound spreads from her shoulder across her collarbone, all the way through and into the wall behind. She headbutts Wehi and hears her own skull crack as it meets steel. The other dopplers are among them: one tries to grab Ajat by the arm when its body jerks back and falls like a marionette with its strings cut. Yat jumps to the other end of the hallway and turns to strike at Wehi when a dozen more Aunties charge in behind, grab her, and pin her against the wall. She jumps again and ducks a backhand from a doppler, but two more tackle her to the ground. She jumps for a third time, and one of the dopplers unsheathes its claws and swings at a spot of empty air the second before she arrives. The claw takes her in the gut, a second takes her in the ribs. The dopplers

around Ajat are falling but not quickly enough, for each one she shocks into submission, there are two more, and she soon disappears under a pile of them. Kiada's head is spinning, but she isn't done yet. With her free hand, she draws the Vuruhi pistol, points it upward through Wehi's chin, and pulls the trigger.

The bullet detonates inside the chamber. The gun jolts out of her grip and clatters across the floor.

"See?" says Wehi. "That's what hope gets you. Fear builds contingency."

She headbutts Kiada right back, onto the part of her skull that is already stinging. Kiada's vision starts to swim. She is losing too much blood, can't repair her body fast enough; there is no magic to pull from without killing one of her friends, and she'll die before she considers that. The dopplers drag a beaten Ajat over to their leader and pin her against the wall beside Kiada. Ten feet away, which might as well be a mile, Yat is turning pale, lying in a growing pool of blood.

"We don't need the young one," says Wehi. "She's a threat, or has one contained inside her. Plus, we've got you two. One with built-in weave-to-electric conversion, no less. Kill the cop."

The claws of four dopplers rise.

"Vic!" cries Luis, and Wehi's head spins for a second.

"Ajat," spits Kiada through bloodied teeth, "*let's burn.*"

She braces her back against the wall, then leaps forward, driving herself deeper onto the claw. Muscle, flesh, and bone split as the arm open up, but for a split second only, she twists her hand and grabs Wehi's faceplate as her other hand shoots out and grabs Ajat, and their weaves run together in a sudden burst of light and fire.

The world rebuilt itself around Kiada painted in piece by piece, and she found herself standing in a café. The diners didn't seem to notice her. They were dressed strangely, but well—stiff embroidered collars on the men, exquisite jewelry and long flowing dresses on the women. Gulls cried somewhere nearby, and the room smelled of coffee, spices, and sea salt. She moved through them like a ghost and came to a wide-open balcony, where she found herself staring at a woman's back and a girl with red hair and tearstained cheeks. Kiada found her mouth moving soundlessly, repeating words she had pushed down long ago.

"This is the last memory," said the woman. "It's a nice one because I know the rest hurt. This will keep them in, but you have to keep it secret, okay?"

The redheaded girl's throat seemed to seize, but then she nodded. Sibbi leaned in and kissed her on the forehead. Kiada's past self vanished, just walked backward off the balcony and into thin air. Sibbi turned.

"So," she said. She inspected Kiada with pursed lips. "Sealing those memories away gave us, what, twenty more years safe from the Quiet?"

"Seventeen," muttered Kiada.

Sibbi sighed. "Well," she said, "better than nothing. That's what all of this was, you know, just buying time."

"All of what?"

"That's the wrong question."

"Where are we?" said Kiada. That seemed to be the right question, though it hung in the air for a few seconds anyway. The sea outside was so blue it almost hurt to look at; she could see sandstone and cherry blossoms; the sea breeze sent a pleasant chill down her spine. It was a day so perfect it burned.

"This is the last day I was happy," said Sibbi, finally. "August 3, 2083. Café Palatino, in Raoucheh. Tomorrow morning, I'll get a phone call that I never quite come back from. But today? Today I have too much coffee and too many cigarettes, and I read a book, and I wonder whether things are finally looking up."

Sibbi looked out and waved a languorous hand.

"Welcome to Beirut," she said.

They stood and watched the ocean, and Sibbi took out a little cardboard box of cigarettes. She offered one to Kiada, who took it eagerly. She knew it wasn't real, but it felt real, and that was all that mattered. She took a long drag, then turned to speak, but Sibbi shook her head.

"Take your time, dear," she said. "You've got a rough day ahead of you, and tailies are expensive."

"Tailies?" said Kiada. It was the smoothest thing she'd ever smoked. The urgency of the moment tugged at her from somewhere, but no, she knew she could stand here forever and only a second would pass. This had already happened, was happening, would happen.

"Ugh, don't remind me," said Sibbi. She flicked a little ash over the balcony. "Four thousand years of guided development, and still none of your people have found the time to invent a decent filter. Tailies are probably another century away, at least."

It was an incredible cigarette, that much was true; the sort of pleasure that only existed in memory. Kiada wondered how much of this was real, and how many of the cracks were papered over by time and distance. It didn't matter: it tasted exactly like it was supposed to taste.

"Is this home?" said Kiada. Sibbi shook her head.

"Home is farther down the coast," she said. "It was bigger when I grew up there, back when purple dye was the hot commodity. Lovely, ancient, and proud, but they can't make coffee worth a damn. Every good barista moves to the city. I like cities. They have this . . . weight. Beirut isn't *the* city, definite article, but it has its own gravity, its own charm. I hate it when people call it 'Paris of the East'—Paris is all concrete and dog shit; Paris was a hill fort when this place had streets lined in purple and gold; Paris should be honored to be the Beirut of the West. I did my medical residency here, dropped acid for the first time, broke so many hearts I lost track. But of course, none of this means anything to you. It's just words. Everything's just words, you know?"

It was the sort of question that didn't need an answer. They stood there and watched people, cars, and ships in the cool, perfumed air. Behind them, lovers were meeting for the first time, artists were

finding inspiration, people were having a damned good cup of coffee. When both their cigarettes were burned down, Sibbi put a hand on Kiada's shoulder. "I'm truly sorry for everything, but especially what comes next. You are brave, and I'm proud of you, and neither of those things is going to make this hurt any less."

The walls behind them shuddered as the weight of Sibbi's other memories pushed in from all sides. The café stood resolute against the intrusion of the universe, but it didn't seem like it would stand for long.

"What's out there?" said Kiada.

Sibbi looked at the wall, then reached over and placed a hand against it. It warped and rippled outward, and the wall gave way to somewhere else: a storm-dark sea, the boom and rattle of cannons, the creak of rigging, and the screams of dying men. A man in the café was talking excitedly into a little gray box. He held it out at arm's length and pushed a button, then held it low, looked at the screen on the front, and held the box back up to his ear.

"No, baby, *you* look beautiful," he said, and his grin changed the sound of his words, made them rounder and gentler. Through the hole in the wall, a sailor in a small red hat screamed as something quick and heavy slammed into his shoulder, and Kiada saw him fall. The man in the café didn't seem to notice.

"Everything," said Sibbi. "That's the secret, dear: the whole damned world."

She extended her hand, and Kiada took it, and they stepped through the wall and into history.

The memory seemed to recoil as they stepped out onto the deck of the ship, to dissolve and run like somebody had dropped paint thin-

ner on the world, to flee in streaks in all directions until they stood among a grove of olive trees. Sibbi—so young, maybe thirty, smiling and unlined—leaned against one in another woman's arms. They wore white robes with purple accents. They spoke to each other in hushed, low tones, rich with laughter.

The Sibbi standing with Kiada scowled as she stared at the two women beneath the tree, and her voice cracked just a little. "I suppose this is as good a start as any for you to understand. I wasn't a witch yet, hadn't had the epithet thrust on me. Died a few times and came back, but that wasn't special—people used to believe more, and more easily. I was just a woman, and I was in love; Niwahsusar, a mountain girl—she used to talk about the north like it was heaven. After she left, I wandered north to see what it was like. A bit shit, honestly, but it pulled me into the orbit of the City, and I never quite found a way to leave. Lygos, it was called then."

"Where did she go?" said Kiada.

"She chose not to stay. I didn't have much power then, but I used every little piece of it to get her a meeting with one of the big guys, and she just said no and walked away. Said she'd lived enough, that she loved me deeply, but that living forever would just water it all down, spread it thin. She couldn't bear the thought of falling out of love with me. Wanted to leave on a high note. They do that sometimes: with bright eyes and full hearts, they just leave. She wasn't the last, only the first."

Another shift in the world, and they were in a crude house. The woman was much older, perhaps seventy, but she had the same smile. Sibbi was only a child: maybe nine or ten. She screamed and wept as the room took on that specific emptiness of one less set of breathing lungs.

———

The world changed again. The sky was so red, it looked less like the sky than a canvas painted with blood. They stood at the bow of a corvette, flying a red-and-white flag she didn't recognize. All around them, men died. A steamer flying the same flag was going down, close enough to see the sailors jumping overboard, hear their screams as they burned alive. It seemed like the entire horizon was in flames, as if the world itself were burning. The red-and-white flags weren't merely losing, they were being exterminated. Their enemies flew a blue cross on white, and they were now firing across the red fleet to shell the city behind.

"This is it," said Sibbi. "This is where it starts, or where it ends. I've never been sure. Every time a Weaver dies, they come back a little more powerful and a little more broken. November 30, 1853. The day I died a thousand times."

Their own ship was listing hard, almost ready to go over. Other-Sibbi was perhaps forty, dressed in a stiff blue peacoat and a round, flat red hat with a gold tassel. She grabbed ahold of one of the shrouds and hauled herself up so all the crew could see her. Kiada knew what mutiny looked like, and she could see it creeping into the expressions of the crew. They had no morale left to shatter, nothing to do but surrender or die. Sibbi clearly wasn't ready to let that happen.

"SONS OF THE CITY," she roared, "BLOOD OF SULEIMAN, BELOVED OF THE PROPHET."

They turned to her, and Kiada saw light in their eyes. She heard one of them mutter *Blessed be his name.* Embers, perhaps, but better than nothing.

"OSMAN'S DREAM DOES NOT DIE TODAY," said Sibbi, "NOT WHILE I BREATHE. WILL YOU STAND BY WHILE SINOPE BURNS? WILL YOU LEAVE CONSTANTINOPLE UNDEFENDED?"

A sailor stepped closer to her. "It's done, ma'am. One corvette against the entire Russian fleet. What can we do?"

She grinned. "We can capture Admiral Nakhimov," she said.

The men muttered and shook their heads. They began to turn away.

"How?" said one. A nearby explosion rocked their ship, and for a moment they were all bathed in its cruel light—the steamer's engine had finally had enough. The screams stopped abruptly, and for only a moment there was perfect silence before the Russian guns opened up again on the town of Sinope.

"I'll handle that," she said. "You prepare to board."

"Ma'am?"

Out of nowhere, the wind whipped up and the corvette surged forward. Enemy sailors in the water began to scream and writhe, and Kiada could see the life being pulled from them. Sibbi's eyes turned gold. Her crew was fixing bayonets, checking their blades. They had the focus of dead men, but several of them saw their captain, saw the men dying in the water, and started to put two and two together. One raised a blade toward her, but his comrade grabbed his forearm, said something that was imperceptible over the roar of wind and guns.

"I had the weight all wrong," said the second-Sibbi. "I forgot to account for spent powder and iron. Overshot the flagship. I had a long time to sit and think about the math, don't you worry."

The sailor didn't get time to respond before the ship jumped. It emerged from the void with a sickening crash as it collided side-on

with a steamer. The hull buckled and collapsed inward. The sudden onrush of seawater pulled the entire corvette starboard, and Sibbi plunged from the deck into the wintry sea. One of the ship's cannons sank with her, broken free of its mooring, bringing a mass of ropes and chains behind it that wrapped around her and dragged her screaming down into the deep.

She drowned.

Then she drowned.

Then she drowned. She watched herself with a sort of fierce pride, and Kiada did not know what to say. Then she drowned. Then she drowned. Then she drowned. Then she drowned. Then she drowned. Then she drowned. Then she drowned. Then she drowned. Then she drowned. Then she

drowned. Then she drowned. Then she drowned. Then she drowned. Then she drowned. Then she drowned. Then she drowned. Then she drowned. Then she drowned. Then she drowned. Then she drowned. Then she drowned. Then she drowned. Then she drowned. Then she drowned. Then she drowned. Then she drowned. Then she drowned. Then she drowned. They stood together at the bottom of the pit and did not speak as the air bubbled up, as she convulsed, as the chains rusted away. Then she drowned. A loop of perhaps ten seconds—for there was no air in her lungs when she drowned—where she floated up and free, kicked toward the surface, never quite made it. Then she drowned. Then she

drowned. Swimming against inevitability while the years turned to decades. Then she drowned. For years at a time, she stopped and let it happen, let herself fall to the floor of the bay and let the darkness in. Then she drowned. Then she

drowned. Then she drowned. Then she drowned. Then she drowned. Then she drowned. Then she drowned. Then she drowned. Then she drowned. Then she drowned. Then she drowned. Then she drowned. Then she drowned. Then she drowned. Then she drowned. Then she drowned. Then she drowned. Then she drowned. Then she drowned. "Why are you making me watch this?" said Kiada. Sibbi did not look at her, couldn't look at anything but her own thrashing body. Then she drowned. For a few weeks she would kick against the darkness, launch herself upward, drown, and re-emerge from the void and drown again. Then she drowned. Then she drowned. Then she drowned. Then she drowned. Then she drowned. Then she drowned. Then she drowned. Then she drowned. Then she drowned. Then she drowned. Then she drowned. Then she drowned. Then she drowned. Then she drowned. Then she drowned.

Then she drowned. Then she drowned. Then she drowned. Then she drowned. Then she drowned. Then she drowned. Then she drowned. Then she drowned. Then she drowned. Then she drowned. Then she drowned. Then she drowned. Then she drowned. She broke and broke again, put herself back together only to break again, and put herself back together only to break again—then she drowned. Then she drowned. Then she drowned. Then she drowned. Then she drowned. Then she drowned. Then she drowned. Then she drowned. Then she drowned. Then she drowned. Then she drowned. "Thirty years," she said, "give or take." No question had been asked. Then she drowned.

"After a few dozen times, I didn't recognize myself," said Sibbi. "That's the thing about pain; it changes you bit by bit until you're not the same person anymore. Sometimes it's the big things, sometimes it's all the little things adding up until there's more scar tissue than skin." Then she drowned. "Sometimes, if you've spit on the wrong altars, it's both," she said. "The catastrophe drags all the little fishhooks behind it. The moon crashes into the sea and the ripples carry on over land and into the horizon, and it's impossi-

ble to say when they stop." Then she drowned. Then she drowned. Then she drowned. Then she stepped closer to herself, knelt down, reached out to touch the memory, and recoiled. They were both crying, down in the darkness with nobody else to see. Then she drowned. "Pain is transformative," she said, choking through her words, "but what that means depends on you." Then she drowned. Then she drowned. Then she drowned. Then she drowned. Then she drowned. Then she drowned. Then she drowned. Then she drowned. Then she drowned. Then she drowned. Then she drowned. Then she drowned. They stood in darkness for so long that light lost all meaning, that time crushed down into a pinprick and thirty years tore through them until at last there was a net, and a light, and a rising, and then screams.

Sibbi hurt the fishermen on that boat in ways that Kiada could not bring herself to name. She kept them alive long past the point where their bodies should've given out, and when the pain became so much their hearts stopped, she brought them back again so she could destroy them all over again. She conducted a symphony of their screams, flayed their exposed muscle like catgut, made them as monstrous on the outside as she was on the inside. When another ship came to investigate, she fed greedily on its crew, and by the time the authorities realized what was happening, she had jumped away into a forest whose ground was wet with young, half-formed snow.

"Two more years," she said, "before I was able to speak again. Ten before I remembered my name. I remembered nothing but water and death, and so I went north and spread as much death as I could. Took a name from a storybook, Kashchey, though they never called me that, they called me Yaga, they called me witch or rusalka, the

Wraith of the Volga. I already knew how to sail, and I could jump away if anybody came close to catching me, and besides, water was comfortable. It's funny how that happens: some people hurt and then spend their lives getting as far away from the source as possible. For some people, it works the other way: it's magnetic, it's a part of you now that calls out to the rest. I get uncomfortable if I spend too long on dry land. It feels wrong somehow, like something's missing.

"It was another forty years before I could stop hurting people, before I could control the compulsion. It didn't go away. I've relapsed, and I'll relapse again. The sea is part of me, in all its vicious, empty glory. When that happens, I'm down in the pit again, the dark water my entire world. And that's why I chose you, how I knew: you are a knot, you are a burning brand, you are in so much pain, but you can be *saved*. That's all this is about: saving the people who refuse to save themselves."

A town burned around them. A man in an olive uniform ran at past-Sibbi, and she skinned him to ribbons with a flick of her wrist, degloving him entirely. His momentum carried him forward another few wet red steps, and then he came apart. His comrades broke formation and fled. Kiada could see children peering out of windows, and she did not want to witness what was about to happen.

"Enough," she said.

"No," said Sibbi, "I want you to see what happens if you become like me."

"Enough," spat Kiada. "This isn't your memory anymore. When you gave it to me, you brought me into it. I've seen enough, and I say we're done."

The memory shattered, and they stood ankle-deep in black water.

"You still don't understand."

"Understand what? That you're old? That you've sinned? Anybody who's had lunch with you knows that. Fun history lesson, but if you'll excuse me, I need to go save your wife."

"It's not history," said Sibbi. "At least not of this place. It's . . . somewhere else. The next house over. A world that belongs to the dead now, or something like it. Swallowed up by the Quiet."

She said the words, and the darkness in the distance rippled.

"That's the secret," said Sibbi, "the whole damn world. The Quiet sniffed this new one out somehow—it was heading our way. I thought maybe it was coming after me, caught the scent of familiar prey, so I plucked the memories from my head and put them into you, then wrapped them up tight in your threads and used you to hide this whole beautiful rotten place."

"What *is* the Quiet?"

"It's, it's . . . it's hard to explain without showing you. It's like emptiness with teeth. It's the inverse frequency of existence. It's anti-history. A temporal seam ripper. It is the most vicious nothing that never lived. We are everything it's not: life, noise, color. I don't know whether it's capable of emotion any more than a storm is, but Luis once called it the Silence That Hates, and that feels right."

Kiada sighed. "Okay, fine," she said. "Show it to me, but no more pain. I'll come with you if you can promise me that."

"Nobody can promise you that," said Sibbi, "but I'll do my best."

"Good enough," said Kiada. She took the woman's hand and stepped out into the world that was.

They stood in a stately ship's cabin. One wall was lined with screens that, for only a moment, reminded Kiada that her body was

somewhere else, that there was something she needed to be doing. She tried to grasp at it, but it vanished under the onslaught of other memories. The doors to the cabin burst open, and Sibbi stomped in, followed by a small man in round glasses. Luz from another life.

"No, no, unacceptable," she spat. "Hector almost blew our cover, and now there are six dead bodies in the Spree. You think I can just jump to the North Sea every day? I could've died, but it was that or get captured. Do you know what happens if the Stasi picks us up, Luis? They'll kill us before we can say a word. That man Hector drained was KGB—they probably think we're American now, carrying some experimental weapon. If some camera got me, if some Stasi man was quicker than we thought to get to the scene, they'll find out who I am and see Harvard, and then we've turned the Cold War hot. Hector couldn't keep a cool head, and now we might just wake up to the sound of Geiger counters. He's a monster, and if you don't put him down, I will."

Kiada didn't recognize the names, but something from drifting through Sibyl's memory (Sibyl, Sibyl—it fit better but still wasn't quite right) gave them weight, made a chill run down her spine.

"Monster, monster," Żu said, like he was tasting the word. "Do you know what a monster is, Dr. Tiryazan?"

Żu, or Luis, or whatever his name was, let the words hang in the air. He stepped behind the bar and started mixing himself a drink. Kiada was standing close enough to him to see the labels on the bottles: gin, vermouth, Campari. He poured them each first into a little spoon from a ring of little spoons, held it up to his eyeline before dropping it into the glass. He finished and turned the glass around in his hands, looking dissatisfied.

"I was in India in '71," he said, "keeping the peace, moving folks

from safety to safety, and a man told me a story about a demon that came for his grandfather's village. It would attack women and children in broad daylight, kill them and drag their bodies into the jungle before anybody could even raise the alarm. When men from the village went to hunt it down, they found nothing. It looked like a tiger, but the men knew better: they were hunting a wraith, some divine vengeance. It was too quick, too clever, too deadly to be anything else. For almost ten years, it hunted them. In that time, it killed nearly five hundred people, and anyone who attempted to catch it was left grasping at shadows."

He sniffed the drink. "God," he said, "what I'd do for an orange right now. Remind me to stock up on fruit the next time we're at port; I'm not happy with our vitamin intake."

In silence, he put the glass down, held the tiny spoon up to his face, filled it perfectly with something from a fourth bottle, then lowered it and tipped it into the glass. He took a sip, paused, then smiled.

"Eventually," he continued, "the Empire sent a very clever man from London with a very big gun, and he went into the jungle of Champawat and came out with a single dead tiger. It turns out that a month before the attacks began, a big-game hunter shot her in the mouth, shattering her canine teeth. Sheared one of them off right at the gum line. The teeth never grew back: she couldn't hunt properly, had to take whatever food she could, and there was so little food left. The expansion of the Raj had hacked away at her home, piece by piece, until there was barely anything left. I suppose if that tiger were a utilitarian, she might've just let herself starve. Outside of that, I don't think she had a lot of other options."

He let the silence hang again. He seemed comfortable with it, and Sibyl did not.

"So your brother's a wild animal; that doesn't change anything," she said. "The tiger would've kept killing, you know. Do you think it was wrong to shoot her?"

"No," he said, "I think it was wrong that she was placed in the position where she needed to be shot in the first place."

He examined his glass for a moment, then threw his head back, downed the whole thing, and returned it to the table with barely a clink. It was the largest and heaviest single movement Kiada had seen him make, but it didn't lose its watch-like precision.

"Which is to say," he said, and for the first time there was a tremor of something in his voice—perhaps grief, perhaps rage?—"if I had the power to go back, I'd park a nuclear submarine off the coast of Cebu and not stop firing until every last Spaniard was on the bottom of the strait. I'd plant plastique in every East India Company warehouse from Hong Kong to Karachi. I'd give the Māori machine guns, helicopters, and Hellfire missiles. I'd take a súndang and cut the throats of Christopher Columbus and Hernán Cortés myself. I can't do that. Instead, I must simply survive. That's what you've never understood. Despite all your years, despite all the places you've called home, you remain a daughter of empire. You've been Phoenician, Carthaginian, Roman, Byzantine, Ottoman, American, always on to the next big thing like the crown was your birthright. Hector and I never had the privilege."

The world seemed to slow, to break apart. The memory held together, but just barely. The other-Sibyl spoke now, memory-Sibyl. "He wasn't wrong," she said. "Not back then, anyway. God, I was so young, playing with so much power. I look at myself, and it's like watching a child play with a hand grenade."

The last words came through almost-tears.

"Saw that happen once," said Sibyl, "in Belfast, a decade after things calmed down. I was in town meeting old friends, only realized what it was later: some kid had found an old nail bomb stashed in an alleyway, didn't recognize it, gave it a kick. Worst sound I ever heard. You'd think it would boom, but it just sort of popped, like a firework, then a drumroll of nails driving into brick. The blast mostly stayed in the alley, didn't even touch the second-floor windows. Took a good ten seconds for the screams to start. Kid wasn't even born when they declared a cease-fire, and the Troubles came for him anyway. We're caught in this, you know, the cascade of history. You can sign treaties and repaint the fences, but history is still there: not just in books but in living, breathing action. If you're born into enough power, you get to ignore it, but that's no comfort for the kid who kicks a bomb. This whole thing was meant to be a fresh start, a new world, a better place. I should've known better. I should've realized that if there's one fucking truth, it's that history never stays in the past. You can't outrun the world."

Even as the memory broke apart, it continued to move, and Luis spoke.

"I do not wish to wage war with you, Sibyl; it will go poorly for us both. You aren't the first imperial killer sent for me, and you won't be the last, but if there is a choice, I'd rather have you on my side. So, let me put this question to you: Did we fail today?"

"That depends on your parameters for failure," said young-Sibyl.

"That isn't an answer. Did we achieve our strategic objective?"

"We got what we came for, and we weren't identified," said Sibyl, slumping a little.

"Then we have succeeded," said Luis. "The plan changed, and Hector made the hard choice to keep our identities concealed. My

mother always used to say that God gives us imperfect tools and the strength to raise them. If I thought either of us lacked the strength, I wouldn't be here."

"So, what now?" said Sibyl. She crossed her arms and leaned against the cabin's polished wooden walls. The light from the monitors cast itself across her face, playing out a dozen little scenes.

"Now," said Luis, "we do what we've been trained to do: we analyze the data."

The memory broke away entirely, leaving only new-Sibyl and Kiada standing ankle-deep in dark water.

"That was where it started," said Sibyl. "French passenger jet went missing over the Atlantic in '79. Cuban weather station picked up an unknown atmospheric disruption seconds before the plane lost contact. The Americans thought it was the Soviets, the Soviets didn't know what it was. They were moving a hard copy of the readings through Berlin. We'd all been having dreams about it for months, knew exactly where to be to intercept. Turned out we weren't the only ones: KGB had a goddamn Weaver, too, some old oprichnik, real bastard. Hector handled the situation, but we had to lie low until the Berlin Wall fell, and then a few more decades just to play it safe. The data kept us busy for almost that long anyway."

"What was it?" said Kiada. Her voice seemed to echo, warp in the air, and come back to her as mockery.

Sibyl gave a sardonic smile and took Kiada's hand. They were back in the café, and another wall opened up. The memory looked different, colder, inhuman somehow. "Oh, not much," she said, "just the end of the world. Ajat was a gift, you know—I'd never found a way to merge the organic and the synthetic. She let me grab memories from machines, which I'd once thought to be totally off-limits. It . . .

went poorly. Every time I tried to access the synthetic memories, they changed; it was like a body fighting off infection. Whether our organic memory corrupted the synthetic or vice versa, I was never really sure. I had you make Ajat forget because it was killing her, so I stored the memories in here with my own. But they matter to our story. Come."

The archway in the wall glowed a cold neon white. Together, they stepped into someone else's memory.

Vic watches a gull fly over the pylon and get eaten by the empty air. There are no feathers, no blood—one moment there is a gull, the next, she almost forgets there was ever a gull at all. Between the nearest two pylons is half of a vape shop. It makes her head hurt. She went there once to get Luis his awful butterscotch vape juice; she remembers that, but the memory gives her a migraine. The shop simply terminates halfway. Vic is an engineer who has built her life around precision; you can't afford to fudge the numbers on a bridge. The cleanness of the cut unnerves even her, right down the middle of individual bricks so perfectly it cannot be the work of men or nature. On one side of the pylons there is half of a vape shop, on the other, there was never a vape shop at all. It is caught perfectly between existing and not existing; her memory of the place aches like a rotten tooth. A woman is standing at a distance, staring to her right, wearing what looks like an Ottoman cosplay dress. Her face doesn't register; it hurts to look at.

Vic turns back from the awful shop-not-shop and sees a little

Pākehā girl in filthy rags crying in the middle of the street. For a moment, the skyline seems to warp and shimmer, and she glimpses something organic, immense, alien; then soot-stained brick, which soon returns again to chrome and glass. The same girl is older now, perhaps thirty, but she still weeps in a child's voice: awful, hitching, wounded sobs. Vic takes a step forward, then kneels down and puts her hand on the girl's shoulder.

You're not meant to be here, she doesn't say. A glitch in the memory, perhaps, whether from bit rot or actual physical rot in the server room. She files away the thought for later.

She settles on, "Where are your parents?"

The girl stares up at her with eyes as orange as firelight. She opens her mouth to scream, and as she screams, a torrent of black smoke pours from her mouth.

"Stop," says Vic. "Rewind."

The recording does not stop. Smoke fills Vic's vision, and she begins to choke. She cannot remember how long it has been since she lost control of her own domain, but she knows she is safe, that it's all just data for later, so she lets the smoke take her.

Vic is passing through the Boğaziçi checkpoint. Her moko gives her away as a foreigner—and therefore likely a refugee—and the security guard is giving her shit about it. *Timeloose, timeloose,* he's saying, *no good.* She waves her ID in his face and he goes white, shuts the fuck up, and waves her through. The crowd of refugees tries to surge behind her, but security whip out their retractable batons and start shouting. Vic feels something tug on her jacket, and she turns to see a little girl with red hair before the roiling crowd snatches her away

and the guards hustle Vic onward and away from what is quickly turning into a riot.

"Rewind," she says, louder this time.

The recording does not rewind. Vic stares right at the sun and gives it the ol' Kahungunu Wave, her override in case of lockout, but the riot continues unabated. She remembers it well, knows that before it's over, the guards will fire live rounds into the crowd—the bullets will kill eight, and the resulting stampede will kill hundreds. It's not as though she can change history, but she cannot bring herself to watch it again, so she turns and heads deeper into the guts of the City.

Vic arrives at HQ five minutes late. Since the riot, things have gotten worse, the municipal council has added more checkpoints, the journey from Alibeyköy is a massive faff. Hector is at the front doors tapping his foot, but his judgmental look melts when she reaches into her bag and chucks him a siopao from the Flip place across town. "Boss lady's mad," he says as he peels off the plastic wrap.

"E hoa mai, when is she not?" says Vic.

"Okay, but like, *actually* mad," he says, "not just like . . . Sibyl."

Vic sighs. "Thanks for the heads-up, big man," she says.

"Anytime," he mumbles through a mouthful of sweet pork.

"We live in an era of hope," she says sardonically. It's her least favorite word. Hector buzzes her through to decontamination. She taps her foot while the seals do their business and wonders why on earth they bother, but Luis insisted. Yadda yadda, *it's not to keep things out, it's to keep them in.* What things? The paperwork to get the drill powered has been stuck in red-tape hell for months—they

needed the civic grid, but so did the pylons, and the pylons won every time.

She finds Dr. Sibyl Tiryazan at the monitor banks.

"You're late," the doctor spits in that clipped accent Vic was forced to file as Levantine (misc). "And time is the one thing we don't have."

"We're all doomed anyway," says Vic. She waves her hand at the nearest security camera, activating her system. Every monitor flicks over to the exospace she's dubbed 118-6-Pakiunui. Rolling plains divided by a colossal mountain range, hunters in furs crossing vast tundra, a group of pale-skinned people dancing around a fire. She grins.

"But I have a plan."

Out of the corner of her eye, beside the roaring campfire, she swears she can make out a few lonely pixels of red hair.

Luis has sent Vic another biology meme she doesn't quite *get*. The mission is doomed, but damned if she's going to act like it. She throws Luis a heart react, then returns to the monitors. Her phone buzzes again: a notification pops up from a dating app she doesn't really use anymore. She reads it: she mentioned Rumi in her profile, and all the boys quote Rumi at her now; this one is sending her each line as an individual message. She's about to put her phone on silent when she gets a very different notification from a very different screen, but she ignores it—another false-positive, no doubt. She's watching 118-6-Pakiunui again and hasn't seen any hunters for centuries. The cross-dimensional monitoring hardware can't pick up sound, and that leaves the possibility open that any viable plane is Quiet. The plague was cross-dimensional. Her phone is still buzzing every few

seconds as the horniest man alive sends her line after line after line of poetry, but she's too transfixed by the monitors to care.

Emerging from a floodplain on 118-6-Pakiunui is some sort of pillar of dark basalt, at least ten meters tall, slightly pointed. Vic slows down the feed, slow enough to make out the cycle of night and day. A piece of basalt doesn't mean much: could just be a splinter thrown up by a volcano. The planet is young, after all, and a tectonic nightmare. Reminds her of the motu, which barely exists anymore in her memory, but enough to hold on to, and she holds on to it desperately. The satellite is too high in orbit to make out much detail. She stares at the feed, pupils dilated, hands shaking. Her phone buzzes and she ignores it. She is so close to the monitor that her breath fogs it up, and she is rubbing it with her sleeve when a single figure steps out of the jungle, stares up at the monolith, and—as a factor of the time, and the hardware, and a million other little factors that make it impossible to see in the same phase as that figure—vanishes.

"Kore*take*," says Vic, in a single breath. Her supervisor, Ghassan, is never in this early (always precisely on time, the *other* sort of engineer, one who leaves at five p.m. sharp and lacks dark circles under his eyes and talks a lot about his family) and doesn't speak Te Reo, but she scans the room quickly anyway, to make sure nobody heard, then she checks her phone (five new notifications, God, Luis is needy) and realizes it's almost eight a.m. and she's been staring at the screen all night, long past her shift's end. Which means—

The doors swing open, and the boss, Dr. Tiryazan, shoulders her way through the door, whistling something with too many quartertones. She has two paper cups, and bags under her eyes. She smiles and proffers one. "Coffee, Dr. Lim?"

It's the grainy stuff from the brass container, the unsweetened

Turkish shit that tastes like river mud, but proper sweet vending machine coffee vanished along with the rest of Singapore and the Kent Ridge campus where she'd done postgrad, so Vic takes it and sculls it all at once, then points at the monitor and tries to let the caffeine rush cover up the bitterness. Her phone buzzes yet again, and while Sibyl fusses at the controls, Vic checks her messages.

The latest one blinks out at her, not a dating app message but a frantic DM from a friend down south.

Damascus is gone.

The message swoops away, and another message sits down on top of it, more fucking Rumi. She scrambles for the DM to make sure she read it correctly, confirms it. Her veins run ice water. They thought they had another few years before Damascus, at least. The Quiet ate through young cities like worms going through an apple, leaving the harder parts untouched. Damascus was ancient. The Quiet ate new time but had little appetite for history. It wouldn't have touched Damascus a year ago—it must be starving, whatever it is. It has proven impossible to create a taxonomy of the Quiet; how do you describe something that, by definition, isn't? Just a great emptiness, spreading across worlds, unwriting history and leaving behind strange false memories of cities that never existed.

The City is old. Sibyl talks about it a lot, especially when she's drinking. *And you see, my dear, before it was Istanbul it was Constantinople, and before it was Constantinople it was Byzantium, and before it was Byzantium it was Lygos, and for millennia before it was Lygos it was the place between places, the town where worlds met. If only one city could ever exist, it would span the Bosphorus, and that's why we call it the City, definite article. Even its latest name, Istan Bul, just means the City; it doesn't matter who holds the City, it is eternal,*

which is why, according to the mission brief, they moved mission HQ there in the first place—there was only one data point they'd been able to gather about the Quiet, and that's that it choked on old bones. It is impossible to think the City could fall, but Damascus is gone, and that means something is changing. Vic looks up at the screens and sees New Olduvai still bustling, sees a busy train station in Cairo, sees the break room at the base in Luoyang, where the staff—the last eastern island against the rising Quiet, cut off from supply, still hoping against hope to find a viable jumping-off point—are running low on canned goods but are apparently in good spirits. There's a vending machine at the back of the room, almost empty, but she sees a can of coffee inside and her mouth waters.

It is good to know that that four-cups-of-sugar canned coffee still exists. The Quiet unravels history, turns her memories into lies—she has names and places and smells all catalogued in her head, but they are as substantial as dreams, and she worries that a strong wind might blow them away. They have those coffee cans in the vending machines in Singapore, and that means Singapore still exists somehow. It feels like a dream, but she knows it is real. She can't bring herself to turn the monitor over to the Bugis channel, and nobody on staff will make her—even the locals have lost memories to the Quiet. Sibyl did her PhD in Baghdad, and Ghassan's father was out there on some geoengineering project, and when that screen went dead, the office stopped a full hour to grieve. It was so fast. There'd been scattered reports all morning, something chewing around the edges, and then—the jaws of a trap snapping shut too fast to perceive—the Tigris was alone on the plain. Three thousand years of history, gone. No sound from the feed, but of course there was no sound. They still don't know why it did that: whether it was intentional or part of the

digestive process. The sound came back eventually, but there wasn't much left to make it, just river water and wind. It left the cameras behind, almost as if to taunt them. The last rubbish of mankind, broadcasting to an ever-shrinking ring of research bases.

"Vicky," says Sibyl. Vic almost snaps at her for being informal (as if it were ever a formal office, as if it were anything other than a group of overpaid engineers spitballing at the end of the world, trying to do the impossible because they've run fresh out of the possible), but there's something in Dr. Tiryazan's voice that stops her. She turns to the screen and sees the other city in the other place, spread out across the floodplain, reaching to the jungle. She sees the unmistakable shape of train lines unfurling like the legs of a spider across the land. They are at 100x speed. For only a second, the city burns, then builds again, strange and green, and then—

Quiet. An empty floodplain.

It is past nine a.m., and Ghassan is usually in by now, but he's Syrian and he's probably heard the news. Vic doesn't blame him for staying home, but she needs him right now to do that thing where he takes off his glasses and cleans them and explains very calmly that they're going to need another six months of tests and not to get their hopes up. She needs him to tell her that so her heart can come down from her throat.

Sibyl puts the video on every screen and plays it back. The penetration point is one hundred thousand years before the Quiet reaches them; more than enough time to get that civilization up to speed to fight the Quiet. The membrane is thin enough to breach, but it's not thin—they're going to need a major power source, and she doesn't think the base generators are going to cut it. They're going to need to hook up to the city grid, and the mayor has been a pain in the ass

about it on previous attempts: he doesn't like the project, thinks it's pointless hubris that eats up his power and stops him from running his beloved fences. They'd need another six months of testing, at least, not even accounting for the infamous bureaucracy of the City.

The door opens, but it's not Ghassan, it's Luis and Hector. Hector is carrying a box of custard squares, and he has some custard and coconut on his lower lip, and Luis is saying something (Vic catches a string of Tagalog, then the English words "dog cum" and a snort-laugh), and they notice the monitors at the same time and stop dead.

"Fuck," says Luis, repeating Vic's earlier word in English. She doesn't know how they can even still speak it: England is gone, America is long gone, all the great young colonial powers eaten by the Quiet, all flash and expansion and cruelty and then just silence. English remains, as a thing they were all made to share.

Vic's phone buzzes again. She is about to ignore it, but she is familiar with her phone's buzz from a thousand notifications before, and something isn't quite right. It is a fraction of a second too short, and when she takes out her phone with trembling hands, she sees no new messages. There was never a boy sending her Rumi at all.

Hector and Luis are shouting, Sibyl is shouting, they're embracing, Luis is rushing off to get the last bottle of champagne, but Vic stands looking down at her empty phone and she starts to cry. It is ugly and painful, and the more she tries to stop it, the heavier it becomes. She can't stop, she can't say why, and everybody thinks it's because she's happy and they're embracing her and patting her on the back, and it's only when Luis comes back with the bottle that she manages to squeeze out the words between ragged breaths.

"It's here," she says.

Sibyl checks her phone, and Hector does the same. It is amazing

how little it seems to register on their faces. Sibyl looks up and says the words that will change worlds. There is no hesitation in her voice, only a grim resolve.

"Fire up the drill," she says. "We're going through."

There's not enough power, Vic knows that, but Hector is ordering Luis around, telling him what to carry, and Vic wonders for the thousandth time why they let a doctor's dipshit brother get the security contract, but those two are inseparable, and it's not like there's an HR department to get upset about it.

They're moving together toward the drill, Vic at the back, at that sort of brisk walk of people in work clothes who really need to be running. This jump needs four months' testing before they'd even send a mouse, but they've all decided as one that it's happening now. Vic is still crying, and she has given up trying to control it, but she can walk and cry, despite the pain in her throat and her chest. They come through the doors so close together that Vic almost knocks Hector down. The drill doesn't look like a drill: it looks like a ring of gigantic diodes and wiring, twenty feet tall, the fluorescent lights throwing its shadow long across the back wall. The interior walls are lined with EM shielding. They're not even meant to be in here without protective gear, but there's no time.

The room is powered now, but there's no telltale ripple in the heart of the drill. Vic can hear the generators straining from somewhere within the walls, but it's not happening. The drill is designed to open a permanent hole, to transport a minimum of forty thousand persons for recolonization. They don't need to keep it open forever; they have four.

Vic pulls herself together and manages to say through an aching throat, "Cut the power to the rest of the base," but Sibyl shakes her head.

"Not enough," she says. She gets a look in her eye that Vic has seen a few times before, before something strange happens, the same something she's observed before somebody who steals her special coffee gets bitten by a cat, before a journalist won't stop asking questions about the base and later finds his home filled with termites. It's a gleam, something golden, a little bit of makutu. Vic doesn't believe in witchcraft, but she knows it when she sees it. She takes Hector by the hand—a strangely familiar gesture for work colleagues—and he takes Luis by the hand, and they kneel together. Sibyl places a single hand against the stainless steel floor.

Vic does not have any special sense, but the hairs on the back of her neck stand up, and she asks herself in that moment just how well she really knows her colleagues. Then the rush hits, and she screams.

A million voices, shrieking, torn from their mouths and pulled into the machine, a roiling mass of life as the City flows through them, dying anyway, being eaten by the Quiet, torn between two damnations, and Sibyl is stealing them from the Quiet, taking them into herself and pushing them into the machine as electrical current, tens of thousands of megawatts, in the multi-gigawatt range of a fusion reactor, making mockery of the EM plating, and Vic can feel it rushing past her and knows if she tries to touch Sibyl, she'll blow like a bad fuse, but the horror almost turns her inside out and she is empty from crying, and all she can do is moan *Stop please stop* and it's not even in English anymore: she's switching to Te Reo, to Malay, to Mandarin, Cantonese, the Hokkien she only ever heard her father speak, trying anything at all to make the great horrible tide stop, and then the roar drops off and there is a ripple at the heart of the drill, and the three are already moving toward it, but Vic is paralyzed, muttering (or shouting? Hard to tell, her own sense of

sound is blown out, but whatever she's doing hurts her throat like she's shouting), and Sibyl turns back to her with those golden eyes and extends a hand.

Sibyl's face is a mask of grief, and Vic realizes that they've both been crying, and somehow that breaks down the last wall inside her. She rises to her feet (when did she fall? She does not remember falling) and steps forward and takes Sibyl's hand.

There is something maternal to Sybil in that moment, and Vic needs a mother more than anything right now.

"C'mon, kid," says Sibyl, "let's save the world."

The four of them walk together through the portal, and it closes behind them soundlessly.

Less than an hour later, the Quiet catches up, and the Bosphorus is just a river.

The City has never existed.

You can't just take millions of souls and smash them together into a single bullet and fire it at the universe itself and not leave anything behind. In the new place, as they find their feet, Vic's first impression is of meat. Monstrous, spread out for miles across the floodplain, pulsing and bleeding and screaming, and Vic is screaming with them while the other three do something she doesn't understand, but in time the meat coheres into a single form, an immense human heart. Vic touches her chest to make sure her own heart is still beating. She has seen many strange things in her time, but this is by far the strangest. When the work is done, she walks over to Luis and slaps him; she doesn't need to understand what he just did to know it's wrong. She is overwhelmed; she walks away from them and does not

come back for weeks. Traveling north, she finds an island with a system of deep caves through a mountain of iron, copper, and bauxite. The people there do not understand what they're sitting on, and she doesn't trust the others, so she keeps it a secret, gently feeding this new society information to help it advance, helping to keep it tika. Luis finds out eventually but agrees to leave her secret world alone— he tells her he owes her that much, at least. In time, her pain will cool, and she will process it as she processes everything: breaking it down into smaller and smaller pieces until she doesn't recognize it anymore. The scar never heals, but she gets very good at ignoring it.

Vic is jumping for the first time since the drill breached through between worlds. She's held off letting Luis do it for years, but she needs access to an NSRO base that's been buried in ice for decades, and the motherfucker can teleport; he's seen her naked a hundred times and somehow never told her he could fucking *teleport* until after the apocalypse. (You can't love somebody who keeps a secret that big, no matter how bad your heart wants to.) He tells her he has to hold her hand while they do it, and she suspects it's koretake but lets him do it anyway. She gasps as their hands meet and she feels the organic current flowing between them; she knows a circuit when she sees one. The space they pass through is incomprehensible, a million shades of writhing black, and then they're standing in a filthy server room. Most of the hardware is ruined, but she's still able to salvage more in an afternoon than her little cult could build in a decade. She can hear moaning from outside the doors, but they're depowered and locked, and there's no way the Ferguses are getting in.

One of the servers is still functional, running on reserve power.

More important than the doors. Ripping it out of the wall isn't going to be great for it, but she's confident she can fix it. She is, after all—she laughs bitterly to herself—the best engineer in the universe. She turns to Luis. "Baby, can we jump with that? Take it with us?" she asks, putting a little flirty twang into her voice. For a moment he stiffens, mumbles something about how it could be difficult, though he immediately relents when she shoots him the ol' doe eyes.

"I can't promise it won't break," he says.

It's a risk she'll need to take; it's amazing it lasted this long in the ruins of the base at all.

"Do it," she says. He places a hand against the server rack, then grabs her rakishly around the waist and pulls her in.

"Just like old times," he says, and she can't help but smile as they hurtle through the endless dark.

Vic is bent over double with age, the steel of her prosthetics gleaming orange in the light of the forge. She cannot believe what she has been told, that the path to immortality is to suffer and die over and over. Sounds too much like Pākehā religion for her taste, and besides, who needs God when you have a hammer? Robed attendants scrape and bow as they approach the fire to feed it, and she tries her best not to scowl; they are only doing as she taught them, after all. Easier to tell them God wanted some metals to burn than explain why she needed a shitload of aluminum. She needs to replace her spine to stay mobile; she's struggling to make it with the local metals but feels a wheelchair is beneath her somehow, so she shuffles bent-backed around the tunnels and lets the legs she's built do the work. It's a stopgap, and it's failing. She considers, for a moment only, tak-

ing Luis up on his offer. *Low chance of success, guaranteed chance of suffering, but surely better than death?* Fuck off, nothing wrong with dying. She could become an ancestor. Maybe she'll float back to Hawaiki like her dad told her she would—float on a strange dark starless current, farther than any tupuna in history. She's learned in her time that death can be kind.

Still, there is work to be done and little time to do it. She grabs a nearby monitor and tunnels into the server where she stored her backups. It's all code, but she knows it so well that she can watch it breathe. There are dozens of Vics now, most of them here clusters of gibbering junk data locked inside their own partitions. Failed experiments. Wehi is still the only functional shell, and Wehi scares her. There is one she doesn't recognize, with the hair cells #A52A2A, red. Vic has not seen her in an eon. "Help," says the girl. Vic makes a copy of her, moves it into its own partition for observation, then deletes the original.

This isn't how it happened, but it's close enough, and it's what's in front of her now.

The line of code that has one of the Vics walking in a circle breaks, the word HELP cutting a function in half. Within seconds, it dominates the screen, wiping and mutating the backups: HELPHELP-HELPHELPHELPHELPHELPHELPHELP. Dozens of nascent minds dying in an instant, all of them versions of Vic. It is as though slivers of her soul are being cut away. She panics and tries to roll the changes back, but the codebase is so thoroughly corrupted that even its core functionality is starting to break down. She's screaming now, hammering the keyboard, trying to do something, *anything*. Dozens of cultists have rushed to her side, and as they lower their cowls, she sees red, red, red, and then she sees, standing among them, *Sibyl*.

Her eyes narrow.

Of *course.*

A thousand years pass for Vic in an eyeblink, it seems. Her body fell away long ago, but her memory remains in the machine, mad and wandering, one woman living as a thousand broken sisters. It is statistically improbable, but eventually it happens: one of them returns to sense. Cities have risen and fallen in her absence; her enemies are nowhere to be found. She recognizes nothing, but this is not a problem; her technology has promulgated itself across the planet, though advancing incredibly little—it is scripture, after all, and you don't refactor scripture. Since she wrote the code, she can inhabit it, move through it, watch, learn, rebuild. It takes years, but in time, she repairs her sisters and teaches them to watch for their great enemy. She takes on the name Wehi, *the soul that receives another's intent.* She likes how precise it is, how English lacks the word entirely. It just makes sense to her; she called one of her copies that once. She considers for a moment that it's strange that her memories seem to stop the moment Wehi is created, and become identical to the memories of Wehi, but she erases the thought; it is junk data that will slow her down. The name is good. There is no other word for Wehi, for there is no other sister like her. She sees through all their eyes, receives their minds and is changed by them. They will obey; how can you disobey yourself? Her sisters know what she knows, and know what she will not admit: that more often than not, Wehi actually means *the soul that receives fear.*

In the bright white possibilities between semiconductors, the Spider begins to weave. She reaches out toward Sibyl with no natural

read on the weave but something better, a machine-mind that *understands* it through millennia of study. It is analogous to electricity, and she knows her hardware. She reaches out across space and finds her prey, finds some old Hainak wiring in a part of town Sibyl walks regularly, and settles in to wait. When Sibyl finally comes to her, she is holding hands with a woman Vic recognizes from her memory banks: a Vault archivist, but it doesn't matter. Their behavior is strange, they too seem patient, they are arrayed like a circuit, but they could not possibly be moving to strike back at her, they do not have the tools. The other woman is a nonfactor, nothing more than a lover, a lever to be pulled at a later date. Vic strikes, and in a moment of victory forgets one very basic fact: the current runs both ways.

Kiada's eyes snap open in a hallway that reeks of blood.

Wehi stands before her, looking down at her almost pityingly. "I possess no organic parts," she says. "I knew you'd be back, so I culled that weakness centuries ago; all that time and all that power locked within you, and you can't even roll over a stone."

"No," says Ajat, "*she* can't."

It starts in the room itself: the dopplers holding Kiada sag and drop her, the monitors behind them flicker and warp in rainbow whorls, a loose screw on the floor begins to chatter and rise. Ajat is pulling power from Kiada, from the unsealed memory vault in its entirety, tearing the splinters from her and embedding them in her own flesh. The surge starts somewhere behind Ajat's navel, arcing up through her chest and shoulders, rolling gold that unravels and turns white-hot. It flows down the bridge running between them, crashes into Vic in a shower of sparks, erupts out of her spine and shoulders in great plasma arcs that sear the floor and walls, fills the air with a reek of ozone and burning copper and then—through Wehi's feet,

into the steel floor and the wiring, surging along the path of least resistance, as unstoppable as the dawn—it hits the monitors. The wave of electric weave rolls up them row by row, blowing out each one in turn, filling the air with a thousand shards of molten glass. Kiada lunges, wrapping her arms around Yat to shield her from the burning shrapnel that instead enfilades her own back. They hit the ground together and lie there, smoking and warm. The only lights left are the emergency LEDs on the floor and the dim glow of cooling metal.

Yat stares at her, eyes wide with shock. "You all right?" she says.

Kiada nods. It is a lie: her back is screaming at her, and she doesn't have the magic to push the glass out. She can feel it cooling, can feel the heat moving from the shards into her flesh. Distantly, she can smell cooking meat. She sees a look in Yat's eye and turns over just in time to catch the entire right side of Ajat's body as a mess of cuts and burns, half her face entirely gone, a leering mask of charred flesh. But just then, the last of the titanic wave of magic rolls through and reknits her, building her body back anew. If Kiada had looked up a half second later, the only damage she would've seen would be the burns on the woman's clothes. Ajat's limp and boneless hand, a blade still protruding awkwardly from it, is already being covered in new flesh, the tattooed organic components regrowing, spreading down her arm like ivy across an old house. Wehi's blackened shell twitches once, twice, then hits the floor amid the mess of metal and glass and lies in a smoking ruin.

Ajat strides over to them, still smoking, and extends her flesh hand. Kiada tries to lift her arm to take it, but the muscles in her shoulders refuse to comply, and she groans. Yat is still wrapped around her, their fragile magic running together, and she reaches

out on their behalf, grasps Ajat around the wrist and lets the embers move between all three, warming and healing. Some of the glass is too deep to simply eject and makes new wounds tearing its way out, and Kiada does what she has not done in many, many years: she weeps openly and feels safe. The shards make music against the steel floor as her body pushes them out, one by one. She just lies there, a mess of tears and blood and broken glass, until two pairs of strong hands haul her to her feet. She didn't even register Yat standing up, too consumed by pain to notice. She notices now and throws herself into Yat's arms and feels the pain purging itself, tearing out of her in great ragged gouts. She knows they don't have time to cry, so she sucks it all back up, pushes it down. "I hate that you had to see that," she says. To her surprise, Yat rolls her eyes.

"Quit that whole bulletproof thing," she says. "I've been trying to tell you for months: you're strong, and you're brave, and being a human on occasion doesn't change that. A wall might be strong, but you can't love it. I'm not in love with your strength, I'm in love with *you*, the whole woman. It's exhausting to always be the Strong One; sometimes it's okay to pass me the slack. Trust me, I've got you."

"You're in love with me?"

"I appreciate that this is a moment, sisters," interrupts Ajat, "and I'm proud of you both, but we gotta fucking move. If she doesn't have backups, I'll eat my arm off, and I don't think I can turn my wife's trapped memory into a bullet twice."

Emergency lighting on the floor has come on, three different-colored lights: green leading back the way they came, red into the reactor, and yellow going deeper into the tunnels.

"Same as the Vault," says Ajat. "Yellow leads to the server rooms, administration, the nerve center. We want to take her out for good,

we follow the yellow. If we do that, though, I don't think we're getting out of here before the reactor goes."

"Ari's in there," says Kiada. "We jump in, pull him out, problem solved."

"He is dead, and the radiation will kill you in seconds," says Luis, "and we've spent too long here already."

He pushes past them, following the yellow lights off into the darkness. Ajat follows him without a word. Kiada lingers for only a moment. The dead man at the door has started to fall to pieces, clotting and running like cream left in the sun. He's slid perhaps an inch down the door since she last looked at him, leaving a dark smear on the port. She reaches her weave into the reactor but finds nothing except thousands upon thousands of tumors that haven't quite gotten the message about their hosts. The others have already vanished into the darkness of the tunnels, the clack of their boots on the steel floor getting quieter. It is done. Ari is dead. Kiada steels herself, takes a breath, and follows the yellow lights away from their failure.

Auntie wakes in a pile of broken dopplers, her own ruined face reflected at her again and again and again. Her limbs aren't functioning properly, but for the first time in years, she cannot feel an awful cluster of eyes peering over her shoulder. She knows she doesn't have long before Wehi reboots, but it's more of a chance than she's ever had before. A pistol lies on the floor, and she takes it and removes the misfired round, then quietly deactivates the redundant jamming mechanisms. She cannot hear any other human footsteps for miles, so she jerks herself over to the blast door and enters the code.

It slides open, and the technician inside falls out. What remains of his face is a mask of horror, and she wonders for a second whether he realized, in his dying moments, that his life was a lie. His cult was taught that radiation sickness was a gift, that they attended a holy fire and to burn in it was to be touched by heaven. Not one of them even knew a city existed above them. She steps as carefully over his corpse as her failing form will allow, then makes sure to seal the

door behind her. It slides home with a reassuring pneumatic hiss, though it takes a few seconds longer than it should, and she worries the mechanisms are starting to fail. She walks quicker through the plant, around and over bodies, hundreds and hundreds of men, women, and children whose only sun was an electric bulb. Millennia of work training them to know only the reactor, all wasted in a single meltdown.

She realizes she is being followed, which is impossible. For a moment she worries that Wehi has rebooted faster than expected, but this is something else, a shimmering patch of air that seems to be trailing her. She pretends not to see it and marches onward to the reactor core. When she reaches it, she stops.

She doesn't want to look at what has been done to Ari, the places where the wires have pierced his skin, where connectors and ports have been drilled into his flesh with the knowledge that he can take more punishment than most. The radiation has done awful things to him, but the generator keeps cycling his own weave back into him, healing him again and again. She looks up, and his eyes swivel down.

"*Kopek*'s in the harbor," she says to him. "Nor-nor-east, got it?"

He cannot respond; he does not look grateful, only tired and scared. She raises the pistol and fires a single shot right into his head. It falls, and his body slumps in its harness. The shimmer behind her coheres slightly, and she smiles.

"Sergeant," she says, "a friend once told me something about old dogs and new tricks: You're not about to make him a liar, are you?"

"Whoever said the universe had rules never met me," says Sen. "'Oh, you gotta come back in a body, it's not *stable*, you'll only have a few hours and the exertion could wipe you out, just gone entirely in the ether,' and all that. Live forever in a perfect body, become a god's

perfect vessel. Everybody's chasing immortality, mate, it's a fuckin' rort. Whatever game they're playing, I'm not."

"You just . . . opted out? I didn't think that was possible."

"Happens all the time, you've just never met anybody who did it."

Auntie's eyes shine; there is something about her of a teacher who is good at finding common ground with naughty boys.

"What's your plan?" she asks. "If you're going to melt down the reactor, it seems like that party's started without you."

"Well," he says, "there isn't exactly a big red button for that, so I'm just sort of improvising. For what it's worth, I was thinking less 'melt down' than 'break forever.'"

"It would make life a lot easier," she says, "if there were more big red buttons. Not necessarily better, just more . . . dynamic. But I'm afraid we didn't design the power grid's control software with that in mind. And at this stage, it's meltdown or nothing, and I do suspect we've run out of nothing. If you'd like, I can check in the back?"

"If you're here to stop me, love, you'd best fuckin' do it already."

"I'm not here to stop you," she says. "Hell, mate, I'd gladly do it for you. But first I want to know you understand what you're getting into; you're about to start coming back from the dead in the middle of a fallout zone. Again and again. Even if you get out, the radiation gets you and you pop right back. I've met exactly one human who got caught in a loop like that, and it took her a thousand years to recover. You reckon you can handle that, Sen? Because Sibyl's a tough lady, and she spent the entire 1950s slaughtering her way across the Western Steppe. You're about to hurt far, far worse than you've ever thought you could hurt. Maybe you'll go mad, maybe you'll become a god, maybe b—"

"You do it, then," snaps Sen.

———

Auntie looks momentarily taken aback. Sen has the impression she is unaccustomed to being interrupted.

"Just like that?" she says.

"Just like that. My girls will pop back up in Hainak, and your sisters have done a bloody good job of making sure there are no civilians left to worry about. This place is gonna blow eventually, best do it while it's swarming with fascists. They want fuckin' purity? Give them exactly what they want: silence."

She tilts her head, then takes a step forward.

"All right," she says. "I'll do it. This experiment has failed." She pauses, seeming to tamp down some emotion. "*I've* failed," she says. "But we can fix this."

Sen doesn't know what to say. It's just all so . . . big. He's used to grappling with morality, but always at street level, always one-to-one. He can't get his head around the scale of the damned thing, but he's seen enough to know that nothing good will come from letting this wound fester. The dead man's body is slumped in its rigging. Sen steps aside from the console and lets the woman approach. As she types, the warnings on the screen become more urgent. She opens several more windows onscreen, dances between them. He isn't sure whether it's his imagination, but the whole structure seems to shudder like it's trying to shake off a fever. After a minute or so, she looks up at him.

"This is it," she says. "I fire off this script, and this whole place is a crater. If you've got anything you want to ask me, ask it now."

"Just one thing," he says. "How do you rate my odds?"

She squints and purses her lips. Her face is so *human*, especially

after everything he's seen from the others. Maybe they were all like this, once.

"A lot of this world descended from us," she says. "We walked the earth as gods and rewrote half the place. But you people? You were here before us, and you were always like this. I don't know whether it was a miracle or some god having a laugh at my expense, but I traveled farther from Australia than just about any human in existence, and when I arrived at my destination, I found they'd independently developed fuckin' *Australians*. I tried to teach you people cricket, and you were awful at it; it's uncanny, and they say history never repeats. But look at you, bringing home the ashes."

"That's not an answer," says Sen.

She laughs. "Mate, that's the point exactly. How do I rate your odds? A billion to one. But shit, you've beaten worse."

"Now, then?" says Sen. Auntie shakes her head.

"Give it a couple minutes. Your friends might find an escape route."

"Don't know if we've got a couple minutes," says Sen.

Auntie laughs. "What else is new?" she says. The lights above them flicker. Sen floats forward. Auntie's set up the console for one-click confirmation, blazing red. Sen is struggling to hold his form; he can feel the dark place calling to him. He has the unpleasant feeling that he's missing a meeting he didn't remember putting on the calendar, one that he's already attended and already missed. He raises a single finger, and despite all he's been through, it's hard to finish the job, even as his spectral body begins to break apart.

He thinks about how badly it will hurt, even if the girls pop back up. Yat told him about her nightmares of being shot, and he knows what Kiada went through as a kid. What if they don't die right away?

What if they get trapped down here while the air runs out and the radiation ravages their bodies? There are worse ways to die, but not many. He bites his tongue—or at least bites down with spectral teeth on a spectral tongue—and hits the button.

Kiada thinks she's imagining it at first, but as they follow the yellow lights, the static gets louder and louder. It is coming from everywhere at once now, a dull, constant hiss. A thought comes to her unbidden in a voice that isn't quite her own: *It's to keep the Quiet out*. Deterrent and early warning signal rolled into one. Constant rolling background noise to make it harder for silence to slip in.

The tunnels give way to bare stone, the emergency lighting to a series of electric lamps marking a single path through the darkness. They follow it until at last they come to a room with a single plain wooden door set right into a cave wall. The hiss is so loud it is almost unbearable. The door isn't locked. The room inside has a single bed, a desk, and photographs and paper over every single wall. On the desk, there is a single glowing monitor.

Luis is inside before any of them can react. He takes a photo off the wall, and for a moment, a spasm of powerful emotion crosses his face, and it is impossible to tell whether he or Yat is in control of her body.

"You can't look at any of this," he says, his voice thick with rage and sadness. "We need to just burn it and go."

Kiada sighs. "Bit late for that," she says. "The Quiet's onto us."

"Oh. Well, then, the end of the universe it is," says Luis. He holds up the photograph, the picture facing away from him. "Can I keep this?"

"Anything we should know about it?" says Ajat.

Yat shakes her head. "Important to him," she says, "not to us."

Ajat has taken a piece of paper from the wall. It's hard to make out the detail at a distance, but it looks like a diagram of some sort of large fish tank. "NSRO," she says. "You used that name before—who are they?"

"North Sea Research Organization," says Luis. "Ostensibly a climate change think tank based out of Oslo. We thought they'd been taken out early in the crisis with the rest of northern Europe, but they managed to get a small team through about a year before us, which amounted to thousands of years on this side, and not a Weaver among them. They had . . . other methods for keeping themselves alive, but it got ugly by the end. The old lab's still up there at the pole—Victoria took a lot of it as scrap, but the tanks were too hard to shut off. That's . . ." His voice falters. "That's where Crane is."

"What do you mean? Crane doesn't have a body, she's a god," says Ajat.

"Crane does," says Luis. "Constable Yat has seen it through my eyes. Like Sibyl, Crane was once human. Her name was Sigrid. She isn't like the others . . . Crane happened on purpose. They killed her at the roof of the world, beyond the Iron-That-Walks: she sits within a tree inside a chapel, run through by nine iron spears for eternity. That's why she screams. She's asked me to end her suffering so many times, but I can't. If she dies, then I die, Hector dies, and every Crane Weaver loses their gift. You've dreamed about it, right? The tree that screams. It got into Sibyl's head a thousand years ago on Dawgar, and they're still dealing with the aftermath; it got into my head in Suta. It got into Hector's, too, eventually, though I think I'm to blame for that. If you haven't yet heard her screams, Miss Ajat, you will."

As they speak, Kiada goes over to the computer. She isn't very familiar with the technology and can't read the language onscreen, a single line in large print.

"Will this shut her down?" she asks.

Ajat leans over her shoulder. "I am scared," she read aloud. Kiada vacates the single rickety chair, and Ajat swiftly sits and begins to work at the computer, bringing up more and more text, new panels and colors.

"It looks like," she says, after a minute or so, "the Vault was the primary server, the Radovan lab was the backup, and this is yet another backup. Auntie took a copy home with her. Unbelievable, deeply irresponsible—not tika at all. If we can knock out both this server and the lab servers, then she'll be down to whichever body she's currently in."

"All right," says Kiada, "but how do we knock them out?"

Yat has been rummaging under the bed. She holds up an ancient-looking wooden cricket bat, preserved by some unknown chemical process that has left it shinier than day-old chitin.

"Will this do?" she says. Ajat nods, and Yat hands her the bat.

"She's *your* auntie," she says. "You wanna do the honors?"

Ajat takes the bat, but then shakes her head and passes it to Kiada. "Sounds like I already need to kill one god, don't know if I've got it in me to kill two. All yours, Kiada."

Kiada takes it, holds it high over her head, and brings it down on the monitor.

Ari lands on his feet. The dopplers are waiting for him again, but they do not reach for him. They are as still as the statues, and for

a moment, he wonders whether they'll stay that way forever, when Radovan rebuilds: awful things that one day become curiosities for lovers to kiss beside. But he doesn't have a lot of time to sit with this thought; one of the dopplers jerks its head toward him, and a set of awful claws slides out with a rasp.

"Mine," says Wehi. "MINE."

The dopplers on the ground say it, too, but Ari is already running through the park he knows so well. It is one of the few places he's seen that hasn't been reduced to a burned ruin—perhaps there was nobody in it to kill. As he runs, he passes hundreds more dopplers, maybe thousands, that were converging on the same point before something knocked out all their systems at once. As they reboot, they sprint at him, shrieking *MINE, MINE, MINE* in awful chorus. He reaches the crest of the hill, and in the distance he can see the harbor and one ship that stands out from the rest; even this far away the biowork is unmistakable. He pauses for only a second to determine whether it's the *Kopek*, and in that moment a doppler tackles him to the ground, clawing and shrieking at him, and suddenly he is surrounded. They're still moving wrong, still in the middle of rebooting.

"You can't escape me," they say in unison. "I built the greatest surveillance network in history. A thousand eyes, a thousand hands, invisible and obedient. I am on every house in this city, and once I have rebuilt, I will be in every house in the continent, in the world. I will take from them, and they will love me for it. Do you know what that is, Ari? That's *power*."

He reaches into his pocket for a blade, something, anything, and his hand clasps around a toy car.

"I know everything," says Wehi. "I see everything: what makes

people tick, which buttons to push to make them scared and make them love me—and if they don't love me, I'll destroy them. They think you win wars with bullets, with boots and steel; no, you win wars by knowing everything and never firing a shot. I *am* this city, and you will never escape. *That's* power."

"No, *bitch*," he spits, "that's attack surface."

His thumb pushes the button Mārū installed so long ago. Across Radovan, in a thousand houses, a thousand random knickknacks and trinkets and bits of random crap come online. A thousand tiny EMPs, a thousand tiny impact points, a thousand memories of a thousand friends; in Mr. Kanikai's little flat, a lightbulb blows; in Jules's attic garret, an old radio momentarily forgets to scan the airwaves; in Auntie's tea shop, a rainbow sheen spreads across a surveillance monitor, and as half the city shuts down at once, the electricity surges back through the wires, down into the plant, burning through capacitors of a network already stretched to breaking point, Mārū's last reckoning; a thousand little knickknacks forged together; a million memories of days lost and songs sung; a single nail right through the eye of a god.

The lights go out, and Sen swears. The reactor is silent. He turns to Auntie. Her expression flickers for a moment; she looks punch-drunk, then rights herself.

"Did you know that was going to happen?" he says.

She shrugs. "I suspected, but it's always good to cover your bases. Wehi didn't, of course. She knew everything about everything, but that's the problem with big datasets: it's just more crap to sift through to figure out what matters. Trinkets, gifts, ephemera,

they didn't matter to her. She saw them and chose to forget about them."

"No idea what you're talking about," says Sen.

"Sorry," she says, "sometimes I forget not everybody is networked up. Anyway, you want to push the button?"

"How about," says Sen, "we don't blow it all up, but if anybody asks, we say we did?"

"Didn't we?" says Auntie with a faraway smile.

"You reckon," says Sen, "we could at least break this thing so they can't put anybody else in it?"

Auntie purses her lips. "Any solution I can think of, Wehi can think of, too. There's no factor she didn't account for, there's—" She stops and stares at him, eyes wide, then laughs.

"Well, blow me down," she says. "What are the odds? Trillions to one. You're pure void energy, highly unstable, liable at any minute to get torn back through the other side. Can't guarantee it would even try to pull power from you, because there's absolutely no precedent, which is sort of the point. She can't prepare for something that's never happened."

"Worth a shot," says Sen.

His feet are on the ground, but they don't need to be; he knows he isn't standing in the room any more than the night sky stands on the earth. He drifts off the ground, and for a moment he's superimposed on Ari's body in the harness. It tickles a little, and he feels himself being pulled, weakly but insistently, into the machine.

"You sure about this?" he says.

Auntie shakes her head. "Not even a little. You can come down if you want."

"Yeah nah," says Sen, "but thanks."

And then he is gone.

Dearest daughter,

At last, it is time to roar. There is blood on your teeth, can you taste it? Isn't it glorious? The world must know. You are a star, and in your burning heart is the forge of new worlds. Appreciate this moment, because soon they will come for you with blades and bullets. Let them come; many seek fire, only the least lucky catch it. When the time comes, dear daughter, shout. Show them exactly who you are.

Kiada brings the bat down again and again, and for a moment the screen flickers to life with a dozen new programs, something impossibly complex roaring to life, and then wood strikes metal and it all goes dead.

The reactor roars to life, then splutters, then starts to whine. As Auntie watches, the reality around it begins to warp. The point where Sen sits is the new center of a hungry void. Metal twists and screams; a thousand shadowy figures fill the room, then vanish as a single shadow eclipses them all, and Auntie hears the distant chattering of monkeys. The pull of the hole is immense, and she is struggling to keep her feet on the ground.

Suddenly, she feels an eye looking over her shoulder, feels her synthetic muscles stiffen, hears the roaring voice of Wehi in her ears taking back control of her shell just as the vortex rips her off her feet.

In the second she has before her body meets the emptiness, with her final fiber of strength, Auntie grins.

All around Ari the dopplers fall, and this time they don't look like they'll be getting up again. Silence reigns, and Ari realizes it is the first time in months that he hasn't heard the awful hum from the tower at Kōhiket Maitaz. He kneels next to a doppler and removes its faceplate. The circuitry is a blackened, fused mess. He replaces the faceplate, gently closes its eyes, and sets off for the docks.

There is a distant roar, and a sudden blossom of weave energy, the formation of a new magical sun in the heart of the reactor. It is getting larger, closer, tearing through the facility. Kiada turns to the others, who are already linking hands, preparing to jump.

She joins the circle, sees them homing in on the light of the *Kopek*, but the heart is giving off the same worrying light as the trap in Fort Tomorrow. There is something hungry about it, so she pulls her vision back and finds four living souls, likely Vuruhi, all converging on the same point, some faster than others. She vaguely recognizes all four, but she cannot determine why. She knows the docks like the back of her hand, knows exactly which alleyways and roads they're moving down. Two of them have come together at the water and stopped moving. They're on the street outside an abandoned warehouse she knows Ari liked to use. She passes the information to the other Weavers. There is a momentary resistance, but then they jump together.

As their feet crash down on the pavement in the Moazi Ward,

Kiada collides with the Vuruhi with the baby face from so long ago, the one whose threads she pushed back down to get him to leave Ari's place. For a moment, as they find him in the weave, she gets flashes of the last few months of his life. Mocked and rejected by the other Vuruhi for his many failures, growing more hateful and not less, stealing a rig from the quartermaster before selling Malatenki's secrets to a strange woman in a tea shop, surviving in ruined houses by eating rats. He has lost his mind, but he has finally, finally, found his man. He is going to kill Ari, and they'll let him into the bunker; they'll take him back and hold him up on their shoulders. He can even hear reinforcements on their way, a roaring motorbike coming closer and closer.

She hits him squarely in the chest, and he staggers back, slashing wildly with a blackened shiv, and when he sees his other quarry delivered to him by heavenly providence, he roars in victory. A motorbike is tearing down Victory Boulevard, a driver with a passenger clinging to them with one arm, and in their other arm—

"I've found you," says Babyface, and he smiles as Mr. Kanikai's lance strikes his back with such force that it lifts him off the ground and hurls him headfirst into the redbrick wall of the warehouse. His head hits the wall at a bad angle, and his feet fly up, his spine shattering as the vertebrae twist and collide. He is dead before he hits the ground. Ms. Kalpona swerves the bike to a halt with a drawn-out screech of tires. She takes the cigarette out of her mouth and ashes it.

"Friends of yours, Ari?" she says. Ari turns to Kiada.

"Friends of *yours*?" he asks.

"Uh," she says, "sure."

Ari grins.

She wraps him in an embrace, and he squeaks in protest. She lets

him down but keeps her hands on his shoulders, not quite ready to let him off on his own again.

"Motherfucker," she says, "I thought you died."

"Me too," he says. "It's a long story, and we don't got time. That's your ship out there?"

"That's *my* ship," says Ajat, and Ari sticks out a hand. She doesn't seem to know what to do with that, so Ari grabs her hand from her side and shakes it vigorously. There's a tension to him that he's pushing down, a pain. Kiada considers helping him for a moment, but she's had enough of changing minds with her magic—she'll talk to him when they have time.

"Miss Ajat, Kiada has told me so much about you," he says, "but you exceed even those high expectations. Fwoof, just appearing outta nowhere, all regal. Love it. That's your ship, then?"

"It is," she says, and Ari extends his free hand to point to a small dinghy roped to the docks.

"This one's mine. It's not as big, just closer. Shall we?"

Nobody needs to be told twice, and they descend the ladder one by one. Kiada tries to keep her balance in the overloaded little boat while helping Ms. Kalpona and Mr. Kanikai down the ladder, the man grumbling something fierce.

"Did anybody else make it?" she asks Ari. He shakes his head. That's it, then. Nyree is dead. The Nightingale of Radovan died in a fire, curled around a woman she couldn't hope to protect but tried to anyway. Kiada isn't going to cry over something that never happened, but it twists inside her all the same.

"I left you behind," she says. Mr. Kanikai has been successfully lowered into the boat, and Yat and Ajat take the oars. The rowboat cuts quietly through the water toward the *Kopek*.

"Really?" says Ari. There isn't enough room in the boat to gesture, but she can see his hands firmly pinned at his sides, desperate to gesticulate. "Doesn't look like it."

"I didn't do everything I could've," she says.

Ari chuckles. "Nah, but you did what you did, and if you want to stay sane in a crazy world, you need to find peace in it. The past is never really behind us, you know; Auntie once told me that we looked at time wrong, that we're walking backward into the future and the past is the one we can see. It's impossible to know exactly when the future might throw a branch underfoot, but if you don't look at the past, you won't even know branches exist."

"Ari, when did you get so wise?"

"I ain't saying nothin'," says Ari. He looks at Yat, then back to Kiada. "That one looks like a cop," he whispers loudly.

"I can hear you," says Yat.

"I know," says Ari, and he sticks his tongue out at her.

They bicker as the little boat—rowers looking backward, as they always do—pulls its way through the past and into the future.

The *Kopek* limps to safety, its engines hitching and stuttering. They pull into a cove on the Oxhead, an old Tangata port fallen to ruin, the tunnels below heading Vaultward having long since caved in. Ajat knows the place, says she learned to sail there. It's a scrap heap now, nothing left even for scavengers. The great wooden arch over the entrance is one of the few things left, carved with the face of an ancestor who utterly failed to protect the place. Ajat says a few words of acknowledgment anyway as they pass beneath him. This place was a hive of activity before the war with Radovan, and the silence burns.

Ajat doesn't comment on it. What little she's heard about the expedition into the city lets her know it isn't the time, that her quiet sorrow spoken aloud would trigger a louder pain.

There's no rahui on this place, but nonetheless it belongs to the dead, and she knows it is unwise to linger. It is a good place, perhaps, to leave their own dead behind. She lowers the anchor and calls the crew.

They stand together on the ruined remains of the *Kopek*'s deck. Riz has wrangled up all the rum from the bar. Kiada has gone to Iacci's bunk, found his violin, and brought it up.

"Does anybody know how to play?" she asks.

The new woman, Ari's friend, raises her hand. "Not well, but enough to carry a tune."

She takes it, tests the strings with the bow, then smiles and starts to play. She isn't as good as Iacci, not by a long shot, more of a fiddler than a violinist, but the first notes almost break Kiada nonetheless. It's a song she heard played on street corners in Radovan at dusk, a song for homecomings. Nobody dances or taps their feet; they just stand there in silence. Riz takes a bottle of rum, pops the cork, and upends it over the side of the ship. Once the bottle is drained, Riz drops it over the side. The rest of the crew follows suit. Fifteen bottles in all over the side, one for each of the dead. Ari has managed to get his hands on a flask of palm wine, the kind Sen always drank, and is clutching it tightly. He has found a knife somewhere and carved the word *wlne* into the glass. Kiada approaches him and puts a hand on his shoulder. He nods.

"I know," he says. "Just give me a minute?"

"Sure," says Kiada. All the bottles but one are overboard, the music

has finished, and Ari still holds tightly on to the rattan-wrapped bottle. Everybody is looking at him. Kiada puts her hand on top of his, and together they wrap their hands around the neck.

"Ripeki," says Ari, "can you play something Mārū would've liked?"

The woman starts up something quick yet somber, in a minor key but with little sharp edges and nimble, clever fingers.

"C'mon," Kiada says, and she and Ari walk over to the side of the ship and turn the bottle upside down, its contents sloshing out.

"I had a friend who would've liked this song," she says, and she feels Ari choke back tears. She puts an arm around him, then lets go of the bottle. He holds on to it for another second, then drops it. It lands neck-down, the ocean quickly fills it, and then it is gone. The song finishes, and the spell holding them in place breaks, the crew returning to watch and repairs and sleep.

"The past is in front of us," says Ajat from behind them, "which means nobody ever really dies. If you can see them, they're still there. The houses we build, the lives we touched, they tend to outlast our bodies. This isn't real death, it's life's last act. I hope Auntie didn't leave that part out."

"Same field, different game, right?" says Kiada.

"Something like that," says Ajat. Her eyes are red. "Now if you'll excuse me," she says, "I need to be alone."

She turns to leave, but Kiada stops her.

"You could've overwritten me, you know," she says. "Made me into her."

"No," says Ajat, "I couldn't. Good night."

She disappears down the stairs.

––––––––

Yat is alone in her room, but of course she isn't. Luis stands across from her, less solid than he was before, more shadow than anything else. She finds it hard to tell where he ends and she begins anymore, but that doesn't scare her.

I want to show you where this started, he says. *I need you to understand.*

To the observer, she is sitting alone, staring at the floor, and she nods ever so slightly.

The chair, right? she asks.

The chair, he confirms.

The dark place inside him, the endless reservoir of fury. She has seen pieces of it, knows that he thinks it's the same thing that turned Auntie into Wehi. When she reaches for the thought, though, she sees teeth and smells burning. Luis holds out an ethereal hand, and she stands and takes it. A slit in reality opens, and they step into it together.

Luis had fine hands. His tutor in Madrid had praised them, said they were almost too good to waste on an Ilustrado. God had graced him with quick fingers and an inquiring mind: if he'd been born into wealth, he might've become a pianist, but instead he'd fought his way up to become a surgeon. The American cavalryman held one of his fine hands down on the table, fingers splayed, while a second gently placed the ball of a hammer against Luis's fifth metacarpal. They had strapped him into the dentist's chair so tightly he could barely move.

Their sergeant stood facing the window, looking down on the streets of San Fernando below. The American vanguard had arrived in Pampanga only that morning, but they were already setting to their grim work. The sergeant turned. He had removed his hat and put on a pair of small round glasses. He looked more like a priest than a soldier, possessing a preacher's energy: that strange mix of calm and fire.

"I take no pleasure in this, Dr. Ortega," he said. "In fact, I am

impressed that a man of your breeding has done so well for himself. I'm told your mother was a washerwoman and you taught yourself to read in her master's house. What intellect, Doctor! What fierce dedication. God, what an example the Filipino might become! Except, of course, for the issue of your brother. It is imperative that we capture him, for his own good; any man who has taken up with Aguinaldo is half-savage already. And I must ask what that says of you, Doctor. You are a man of medicine, so I'm sure you understand that blood does not lie. A true man of civilization would've given the savage up, but there is something in even you that resists civilizing. It's the devil half. Tell me where Hector is, dear Doctor, or I will be forced to punish you. For your own good, I will not withhold the rod."

He didn't know, he honestly didn't. The Spanish colonial governor had assigned him to Pampanga. He had last spoken to Hector almost ten years ago, in Cebu, before their paths diverged so wildly. God, they had been so close. Where had he gone wrong? He'd heard rumors that Hector was in Manila, then in Bulacan, and then nowhere—disappeared into the jungle like a phantom. He'd long thought about leaving his practice and going to find him, but he had patients who would suffer without him. His practice served a dozen towns, and finding a replacement in the middle of a war would be next to impossible.

"I don't know," he said.

The sergeant shook his head. "I hate that you're making me do this," he said. He nodded, and his man brought the hammer down. Luis pulled his breath into his stomach and tried not to focus on the pain. Messy fracture on the fifth metacarpal, like you'd see after a street fight. Painful, but not career-ending. He breathed through the pain. Somewhere, on the edge of sense, he could hear the American

begin to recite something. He looked out the window once more, a blue shadow lined in the Luzon sunlight.

"'Go bind your sons to exile,'" he said, "'to serve your captives' need.'"

He turned away from the city, stepped smartly to Luis's side, then leaned in. His breath stank of salted fish and rum.

"Let me help you, Doctor," he said. "Your people could've remained savages, but instead, God created the United States of America. I come from there with good news, with civilization! If only you would let me uplift you. Now tell me: Where is Hector?"

Speech was hard. Speech meant breathing through his nose, and breathing through his nose meant letting the pain from his finger pierce through the calm he was desperately clinging to. He had to give them something, and it didn't matter if he was wrong: all he needed to do was stop them from moving on to his other fingers. He could maybe, maybe lose the fourth metacarpal and keep his practice, but if they moved on to the third, he'd never hold a scalpel again.

"Malolos," he said.

"Doctor," said the sergeant, "why are you lying? Malolos fell weeks ago. Our scouts saw Hector and his comrades on horseback heading for Pampanga, and here you are, his beloved brother. If anybody knows where he is, then it's you," he said, then stepped back and nodded to his man. Luis didn't have time to suck in breath this time, didn't have time to brace. The ball of the hammer struck him right on the knuckle, and he felt bone shatter and muscle tear. All the pain he'd been holding back came crashing down at once. Whatever he'd been holding together broke with his finger.

"I don't know," he shrieked, "I don't know, please, I don't know, no se, no se, wala ko kabalo, please, God, I don't know."

"Why cling to this?" said the sergeant. Through the haze of pain, his features seemed to melt and twist. "War has come, and your people need a doctor. You could be their shepherd, but instead, you hold fealty to the wolves. Corporal, the middle finger, if you would."

The cold ball of the hammer brushed against his third proximal phalanx.

"My man is going to destroy that finger," said the sergeant. "When I tell him to, he is going to beat it until it turns black and I can pluck it off like a Georgia peach. You may find this extreme, but you were given a choice once, twice, and for the third time I am granting that to you. I am asking you only to banish barbarism, to answer freedom's call. Is that so very hard?"

Luis tried to spit at him, but it just dribbled down his chin. "Pisting yawa," he said. As close to *fuck you* as he could approximate without dignifying the man with his own tongue.

"'By all ye cry or whisper,'" said the sergeant, "'by all ye leave or do, the silent, sullen peoples shall weigh your gods and you.' Very well. Gentlemen, punish this savage. Teach him our manners."

The cold iron of the hammer lifted off his finger, and Luis set his mouth to a rictus. If it was going to end, he was not going to let them enjoy it. He was going to seize whatever control he could, even strapped to a chair.

"Do it," he said.

Nobody spoke. One of the men looked to the sergeant. His face was unreadable.

"Corporal Landry," he said, after a time, "did you bring a rope? I think we need to set an example."

"Yes sir," came the reply.

He tried to fight them off as they unstrapped him from the chair,

but they were fit from months of training and he was weak with pain. They dragged him across the tiled floor and down the staircase, laughing as he hit his head on the top stair and the world spun around him. He tasted copper. They loosed their grip for a moment at the bottom of the stairs, and he fell. He tried to put a hand out to stop the fall, but his ruined finger touched first, took too much weight, and the arm collapsed beneath him. Somebody hooked a hand under his elbow and hauled him out through the doors and onto the dusty street. They dropped him again, and he did not make the same mistake twice. He lay on his face in the dirt and felt a thin trail of drool escape his lips.

He saw several pairs of shoes, not all of them American. Locals. Not many, and certainly not enough to fight off a group of soldiers. Nobody stepped in to save him; nobody even said a word. He was an outsider in Pampanga, another colonial import. They liked him because he kept their children healthy, but they never let him forget that he wasn't from around here.

"By the power vested in me by the executive of the United States of America," said the sergeant, "for the crimes of providing comfort and lodgings to rebel forces, I, William Joseph Jones, hereby condemn the guerrilla Luis Ortega to death by hanging. Let it be known that any persons who assist the Katipuneros in any fashion are liable to the same. Dr. Ortega, do you have anything to say in your defense?"

They hauled him to his feet. The crowd had grown now, and he saw fear in their faces. He had treated many of them, and he knew they did not hate him, they simply didn't love him enough to take an American bullet. The sergeant stared at him. In the light of day, his features were clearer. He looked like a very ordinary man, with a

pinched face and watery blue eyes. Less of a priest, more of a clerk. Even the name on his uniform was forgettably ordinary. Bill Jones. There were a million more Bill Joneses in a dozen countries. It was common, and that was what made it terrifying—if you killed Bill Jones, another would be right along to fill his shoes. If you didn't kill him, he'd go on doing his evil work, and a hundred more Bill Joneses would sign the paperwork and say it was the right thing to do. In that moment, Luis Ortega saw a great machine of steel and teeth looming over the world, but he did not allow himself to weep: to do so would give too much to the beast. Instead, he raised his head and stared Bill Jones right in the eye. He'd never been a man of theatrics, but it seemed like a fairly unique occasion. The words came out through bloodied teeth that he did not remember bloodying.

"Bury me deep," he spat, "wrap me in ten shrouds and twelve chains and throw me in the ocean; put my carcass in your largest cannon and fire it at the sun; put as much distance between me and your God as possible, because if you don't, I will come back as a curse. I swear on my blood and the blood of my people, I will be there when your children are buried; I will be there when their children are buried; I will be there a thousand times over, until the stars lose their fires. I bestow my soul to whichever god or spirit is clever enough to find it; I bestow my curse upon Empire and all her vicious children. Now, hurry up and kill me—I've got places to be."

It was nothing other than bravado, but he thought he'd earned it. He did not know it at the time, in the dirt, but his words would set the course for eleven thousand years of human history. He knew it now, in memory, of course, though memory is always younger than the thing it remembers, and never quite the same.

When he called out for a spirit, the spirits heard him, and when

the noose hauled him up onto a shop awning—they could find no tree branch stout enough—they swarmed around him, pushing at the fabric of the world like children driving their fingers into wet clay. He could not have known that high above the universes, vast skeins of membrane and bone unfurled to catch the cosmic winds, a creature very much and yet totally unlike a crane would hear him call out and would descend and reach out a single monstrous claw into the shadow world beneath Luzon to catch him. There was no drop, not in the real world, anyway: Luis Ortega died of strangulation almost precisely one minute before the first Philippine bullet smashed into one of the American cavalrymen, bisecting his face from chin to widow's peak. One minute late for the first scouts, with Hector at their lead, roaring, charging down the street, firing as he came. He was shot three times almost immediately: once in the belly, once in the leg, and once in the throat. He died instantly and fell through the world, and in that moment his fate was entangled with that of his brother, who was also falling through the night. Crane had snatched at one and come away with two.

In the world, it was barely a flicker. Hector Ortega fell back, then reappeared and kept coming. Luis appeared in the air, beside his own hanging body, fell and hit the ground at a bad angle and felt bones shatter. The Americans were all firing at Hector, or trying to stop their horses from bolting, or panicking at the approaching demons, and each time he died, a body would slump, and then he would reappear in the same spot where he'd first been hit and continue his advance. Each time, he would have a few seconds to whip off another shot before he died and returned with a full rifle.

At a distance, it was hard to tell exactly what was happening. It was only when the Americans ran out of ammunition that they

realized that the dozens of bodies on the ground were all those of the same man, and that man was still advancing, still wailing in grief at his brother's body on the gibbet, blind to the wounded man on the ground.

The Americans broke. It wasn't an orderly retreat, but a panicked rout. One of the faster soldiers reached the horses and tried to mount, but the beasts were panicking, pulling against their reins, all tied together around the same stout botong branch. As the first rider reached his horse, it jerked its head back and snapped the reins. The knot fell away and the horses bolted. The rider tried to grab a rein, but the horse was moving too quickly and hauled him off his feet. He fell awkwardly into the crush of equine bodies and disappeared beneath their hooves. In less than a second they were gone, and something that once looked like a man in blue lay shattered on the street. Seeing the horses flee, the remaining riders turned to face their assailant, but then Hector was among them with bayonet and bolo, an eagle with red talons descending. Those who tried to run were cut down by bullets from the remaining scouts.

As the Katipuneros secured the street, Hector Ortega approached his brother's body on the gibbet, fell to his knees, and saw his brother's other body on the ground. He blinked once, twice, then extended a hand.

"You too, huh?" he said.

"Me too," said Luis.

"You saw her? God?"

Luis took his brother's hand and hauled himself to his feet.

"Dear brother," he said, "I am proud to say I am a man of inquiring mind who considers every possibility equal. I have read many

descriptions of God and the cosmos and all creation, and in none of them did God look like that."

He hadn't had the courage to look it fully in the eye, if that was even possible. He had seen it in all his peripheries, in pieces, fractured like a reflection in a broken mirror. Parts of it were almost right: immense wings, something pale and almost robe-like, but denser, with thousands of tiny veins that seemed to writhe like worms after rain. It was not like God, but like a bird, yet entirely unlike a bird, nothing but gargantuan hollow bone and the distant sound of wingbeats.

"An angel, then," said Hector.

Fire from heaven, brass and thunder, Galgalim with a thousand eyes. Like the angels that came to Ezekiel. Terrible things, the first-wrought, the things God made when he was still learning to work clay. Where was he now, in heaven? Could a place so dark be heaven? But ah, he had seen it, hovering above: crystals, pink and gold, the titanic stained glass window that put all man's cathedrals to shame. He had seen exposed sinew and bone, smelled fertilizer, acid, and snowmelt. He looked up and saw that his corpse had broken itself, and he was not sure it was from the hanging. He turned away from it, toward the sun. The men were raising the Philippine flag the Americans had torn down. It had a little mud on it, but it flew true. God's works were not always beautiful, but they were always good.

"Yes, Hector," he said at last. "It could have been an angel."

He turned and looked his brother in the eye. Hector was going slightly bald, and his eyes were lined with crow's feet. He didn't know what to say, how to bridge the years.

"It's good to have you back," he mumbled.

Hector lunged forward and embraced him with both arms, lifting his feet off the ground. For the first time, their memories ran

together into one, and they both knew they would never let each other go again.

They've drawn up a plan to kill God. It mostly involved a lot of bickering. Kiada has never seen a good map of the North before; she only knows it as the place raiders came from, but Luis has drawn it in extraordinary detail, rail lines and stations, towns ("ghost towns not even the ghosts have time for"), what looks like a thriving continent; then one by one he went over major locations and crossed them out with red pen. At the center of it all, at the pole, he drew a tree and circled it twice.

"So we jump there," says Kiada. "Burn the tree down. Her spirit goes free to the other side, we're done, right? Break our connection with . . . the other place."

It hurts to even think about.

"Break that connection, and whatever's following us loses the scent," she says.

"Jump right to her? Impossible," says Luis. "It is one thing to navigate by the stars, it is another entirely to sail into one. The human mind has limits: very few who've spent even a moment in her presence have survived unscathed. She gets inside your head, her pain becomes your pain, and you'll do anything to make it stop."

"Mad as shithouse rats," mutters Ajat.

Luis ignores her.

"The only safe approach," he continues, "is through the NSRO tunnels under Crow Hearth—they're deep, they're shielded, and they run from the labs, right into the heart of the township. Used to be a train running directly from Holbrecht, but scavvers have torn the

track to pieces. There's functional track from the station at Wirriwon that Hector likes to use, but it's four hundred miles across the taiga on foot, and you'll have the Iron to deal with."

"That's a *myth*," Ari scoffs.

"The Iron-That-Walks? I assure you, it is not. The proper name is Biomass Agent: Wandering, Secure. BAWS, for short. But I refuse to dignify Fergus by playing into his little jokes, so Iron it is. There used to be hundreds of them, but the cloning vats needed a lot of raw material. The North used to be inhabited, you know? There weren't any nice beaches, but it was hardly a wasteland. Good forests, good lakes, good hunting and fishing, all the wood and fur you could ever need. They ran out of biomass at some point in the last millennium, and they've spent centuries since cannibalizing each other, cutting the machine up for spare parts and feeding its crew into the tanks. There's a reason there's only one Iron left: it's the most efficient machine with the most ruthless crew. New crew grown from the onboard vats and trained by the old ones. It's been running low on fuel and crew for a long time; it's a shadow of its former self, but I would still recommend avoiding it at all costs. You're food, and they're starving."

"So," says Ajat, "avoid the Iron, get to this inland station, ride the train north, send a non-Weaver up with a can of gasoline and a box of matches. Difficult, but we've got Weavers, and once we're on the train, we're safe, right?"

"*Then* we have to deal with Fergus," says Luis.

"Just . . . a guy?" says Ari. "*One* guy? Can't we just bribe him? Shout, 'Look, over there,' then sneak past him?"

"No," says Luis, "the *same* guy, but there's a lot more than one of him. Like Wehi."

"Just how many more?" asks Ajat.

Luis holds out a hand. "Let me show you."

They walk down a chrome-lined hallway under the dim glow of electric lamps. Amazing how well equipped a team can be with proper preparation for their jump. How the NSRO managed to avoid the Quiet is a question for another day; Luis has a more pressing inquiry. Dr. Fergus McCullough walks beside him. The man is six-three, maybe six-four, with a thick blond beard and deep laugh lines. His lab coat is too short, and his glasses have clearly been repaired many times.

"Anyway," he says, "good to know somebody else made it. I've been stuck here for twenty thousand years with the fuckin' Scandis. You wanna know what purgatory looks like? An epoch with only a Norwegian for company. I reckon she was lookin' at the screens goin', 'Which place looks the most shit? That one's got a nice beach, it's right out. That one's a barren desert but it's still got sunlight, keep moving, lads. Polar fungal caves? Perfect, reminds me of Oslo.' Fifteen clones of one woman, all united in their shared lack of any fuckin' patter. Tell any of those lasses a joke and they'll stare at you for ten seconds, then ask if the chicken made it across the bloody road in one piece. Utterly joyless. Didn't even think to pack snakes and ladders."

Luis nods, makes a small sound of affirmation from inside his throat. More input seems unnecessary; McCullough seems very experienced at holding one-sided conversations. He's probably forgotten what the surface even looks like. They come to a stop in front of a key card door, and McCullough swipes them through. The blast of cool air from inside makes Luis shudder. For a moment, the hulking tanks inside the room look almost organic, like boils roiling with

pus. The lights flicker on as they step inside, revealing row after row of water tanks, each one containing a single human body bound up in wires and pipes. Luis can not see the end of them; the room is truly immense, the nexus of a system of caves and tunnels that stretches under the entire polar region.

A second Fergus McCullough floats in one nearby, eyes closed, bobbing gently up and down.

"Not really immortality," the conscious McCullough says from behind Luis, "but it does the job in a pinch."

"Are they alive?" says Luis. "Are they conscious?"

Fergus comes to stand beside him, and they share a glance. Their breath crystallizes in the air in front of them, and Fergus shivers.

"Yes, and uh . . . sort of," he says. "We tried to grow them without consciousness, but they were all inviable. They're not human, if that helps, not anymore. They're about as smart as the average Yorkie after we hit 'em with the mind wipe, and we keep them sedated anyway. It's upsetting, you know? They're just sort of not there, sort of . . . blank. It's nae pretty, but when you're saving the world, you've got to take what you can get."

Luis has seen maybe thirty staff in the entire facility. Well, two staff really, copied over and over again, as many times as needed to keep the lights on.

"I get it, uh, pal," he says, "I really do."

"You'll get there, too, pal," says the Scotsman with a sardonic grin. Luis does his best to shoot one back.

"What do you need from me?" he says.

"Well," says McCullough, "we build the backup from aggregate data. We'll find you a room in the complex, you just wear a tracking badge and be yourself and it'll figure you out from there. Sigrid

has been refining the tech over time; it'll take somewhere between a week and a month. The first version took years, couldn't stand it, having to look down at my lapel and shout every time I had an emotion. 'Your heart rate is elevated, Fergus? What are you doing, Fergus?' I'm having a wank, fuck off. 'Tell me, Fergus, what is a wank?' Anyway, we'll take some stem cells during your surgery tonight, grow you another shell, keep it in storage. From there, we'll put in a heart monitor implant: if your heart stops for more than twenty-four hours, the system'll reinstall your consciousness into your shell from the backup. Installation can take up to a month, depending on how developed the blank is. You're overriding the existing consciousness, even with our special fungal brew, and that's going to take time. We get an alert when the upload starts, so I'll be along to monitor the situation and make sure you come out in one piece. There'll be an adjustment period: we do our best to keep the shells in good condition, but there's unavoidably some atrophy."

Luis rubs his thumb against his forefinger.

"Hmm," he says, "all right. I'll need to return to my team before spring, but I can spare a month or two. You'll provide Vic with the same treatment? Her body is . . . not in great condition."

Fergus laughs.

"You'd be surprised at how little we can work with," he says.

Thousands of tanks stretch off into the darkness, each one holding a growing clone, each one capable of running forever so long as the BAWS are able to find biomass and the systems stay well maintained. If they can't? Likely a catabolysis of sorts, system degradation, auto-cannibalism. It doesn't bear thinking about; he needs to change the subject.

"Excellent," he says, "we have a deal. Now tell me about this lichen."

————————

Ajat is alone with the heart. There is no knot at its center anymore, and she knows Sibbi is fully gone, but she is first and foremost an engineer, first and foremost about solutions. She reaches into the heart's threads and forces it to grow a cellulose polyp, and she takes the polyp in her hands and wrenches it away from the rest of the body in a single twist. Then she reaches into the recesses of her own mind, into the memories she shared with Kiada, and pushes them all into its threads. For a moment nothing happens, then a slit forms on the surface of the polyp, and a single familiar eye opens. Ajat smiles. She does not know whether this will be the same woman, whether this will even work at all, but she cannot bring herself to let go. She takes the polyp to her room, places it near the porthole, where it can see sunlight, and waits for the growth to begin.

Sen is Sen is Sen is Sen is Sen. Sen looks at Sen, who is looking at Sen while a Sen on the ceiling stares down sadly, smoking a cigarette whose smoke drifts down among the hundreds of identical men. They are in the docks ward station in Hainak, they are at his mum's house, they are in an alleyway choked with melting flesh, shifting from place to place with no structure. The Sens aren't all uniform; some are dressed differently, some have more or less biowork, and many of them are simply corpses held up like puppets.

"Brother," says a voice from behind them, behind all of them at once somehow, "this is the part where you say yes."

"Yeah nah," says Sen, "I'm good. And I don't have a brother." The mirror versions of him disagree, a dense thicket of false echoes saying *yes, yes, yes, yes.*

The man who steps in beside him does look a little like Sen, inasmuch as any underfed soldier looks like another. There are as many of him as there are of Sen, each one of his counterparts next to one of Sen's.

"Not yet, that's the thing you say yes to," he says, and waves a hand at the other Sens. "You've done so in every loop so far."

"You make a convincing argument," says Sen, deadpan.

The man screws up his face. "Really? It's normally harder than that."

"Of course not really, ya fuckwit," says Sen, rolling his eyes. "What is this creepy shit, anyway? I thought I was gone. I was somewhere nice and peaceful. Unburdened. I felt like light."

The man sighs. "You can call me Monkey," he says. "All this 'creepy shit,' as you call it, is what happens when you're outside the loop. This is the point in the loop when we're two different men. Every time you come here you say no, and we have a lengthy, tiresome argument, and then I just say, 'If you don't, Yat will die,' and you fold instantly. The last Sen helps me save the next Yat. If you break the chain, she dies in the harbor and nobody ever finds out why, and then, presumably, we find ourselves back here again, and the next Sen saves the Yat after that. If Yat dies, we are—as I believe you're going to call it—fucked; she's the key. Futures are harder than pasts, I don't know how, but the weave all points to it—we get Yat in a room with Crane, and we can *finally* escape samsara. Simple enough?"

"Yeah, mate," says Sen, "clear as houses."

"This is where I ask whether you're being sincere and you say no again."

"Yes. Anyway, the fuck do you need me for? Can't you just"—he waves his hands in the air—"wooo, *magic* it?"

"Believe me, I've tried. Do you think I'd come to you if I didn't need you? You're a deeply irritating man—"

"Thank you."

"—and if you're not there, she says no. It's too alien, she's too scared, there needs to be someone who loves her in there, or she'll pass on, and we'll have to wait for this whole awful process to end

again, as it always does. You need to love each other; there are loops where you have a daughter and she has a father, and they're all dead ends. So we kill them. Reduce the possibility space. Which seems unforgivable, unless you know the stakes."

They're standing atop a dam. On one side is a barren valley, on the other a roiling lake, the waters glowing soft white.

"The only thing I've ever said that makes sense to you," says Monkey, "is 'It's like time's thrown a clot, history is hemorrhaging, and sooner or later, probably sooner, we're looking at brain death.' You can survive one stroke; you can't survive a million. Time's tougher than the human body, but it's reaching breaking point. Part of me fears we cannot endure another loop. We cannot afford experimentation; we do what we know works. Yat says yes, you say yes, we proceed on the path that gets us closest to escape."

"Clots happen, but dams get *built*," says Sen. "What is this place?"

Monkey sighs. "The clot is an imperfect metaphor—it's just the one your fool mind can grasp. The condition is autoimmune. Somebody broke the rules, ripped open something that wasn't meant to be ripped open, and now the white blood cells are swarming. There is a moment in time beyond which this world ends. Actually ends. Undone, eaten by itself. Never existed at all. Time knows what's coming, it's scrambling to protect itself. We're doing everything we can to help it, for the sake of everybody in there. For Yat. For Kiada. For Ajat, who you've admitted to me a few times you actually like quite a lot. For your old mum, and for everybody's old mum. Gone for good. Unwritten from time, never existed at all. No songs, no games, no jokes. Just silence, and silence is the one thing I know you can't stand, that you feel obligated to fill whether you've got anything to say or not. You once called it 'an eternity with no fucking

bants.' Like I said: this is the part where you say yes. Every single time, for an eon. I'm offering you godhood and the chance to save everybody you love. You're a deeply annoying man, but not a stupid one. Take the deal."

Monkey sticks out his hand. All around them, Sens and Monkeys are shaking hands, most of the Sens somewhat reluctantly, and vanishing. Only one other pair remains. The Sen turns to him. "I spoke to your Yat," he says. "You did good." Then he takes his Monkey's hand, and they disappear together.

"You didn't," spits Sen at the empty air. The last pair of them are alone. Monkey's smile is fixed and empty. Sen sees the animal in him for a moment and does not like it.

"Yat says yes, I say yes," Sen says. "You've tried it a thousand times, and you've failed. You've killed my daughter how many times for this?"

He can feel himself coming apart, whatever magic brought him to this place finally losing its grip on him. Monkey takes a step forward.

"We don't have *time*," he pleads.

"Brother," says Sen, "you've had nothing but. I'm not playing your game. You want my help? I give you instead the strongest curse of my people: *yeah nah, I'm good.*"

Sen raises a middle finger, and Monkey is alone atop the dam.

He looks up at the sky and sees a million pairs of conjoined heads staring down, gibbering madly.

Yeah nah, cunt, everything's sixes and elevens and shit mate mate maaaaaaaaaaaate, the psychic damage of merging a man with a god and letting them both see the myriad of awful possibility spread out in every direction.

He lowers his proffered hand, then sighs in relief.

Finally.

ACKNOWLEDGMENTS

Oh God, acknowledgments are always the most nerve-racking part of a book. Everybody I thanked in book one, you're still in there. Special shout-outs to Sara, Amara, and Dave, the musketeers protecting me while I walk around in an iron mask bumping into things.

To Hannah, my dearest, who kept me together and helped me break some of the more intractable blocks while writing this book, and to Hannah and Lou for helping me navigate The Subtext, and to Rivqa Rafael for letting me ask my terrible goy questions about golems.

To Ilya and Andrei for getting drunk with me and getting emotional about Russia, about Ukraine, about love and art and the deeply sketchy vodka I found at that truck stop dairy in the Wairarapa.

To Paolo for making sure I didn't fuck up the Filipino stuff, and also for making absolutely incredible adobo.

To Metl and all the hackers who let me pick their brains about exactly how they'd shell a robot. I have never met a group of individuals who—when given such an absurd hypothetical—seriously just put their heads together and, well, cracked it.

I guess I should thank Andrew Hussie or something; I still have not

read The Great Work—I'm sorry, my TBR is huge—it's just that I'm continually surrounded by excitable Homesticks who keep telling me OH SIBBI IS PLAYING SPURB? and AUNTIE DID NOTHING WRONG, and I feel at this point I must've just absorbed the entirety of *Homestuck* via memes and osmosis, or somehow via psychic emanations from the dream battles neither of us remember having. [EDIT: I AM INFORMED THESE ARE BOTH IN *HOMESTUCK*. GO TO HELL.] I don't understand what quadrant we're in and I refuse to learn, but I must assume we're somewhere in the mix.

To Emmy, who I kiiiiiind of based Ajat on, then became friends with after *The Dawnhounds* came out, and it was one of the most low-key mortifying moments of my life that we ended up laughing about—I really don't know any other whakawahine Māori, much less ones with my exact sense of humor, and also you're literally Dr. Rockets now? Like, your surname means "rockets" and you have a PhD? You're Doctor Rockets now. I'm putting it in a book, so it's a matter of public record and you can't escape it.

To Seth, for being an incredibly incisive beta reader, and also for at times being the only thing keeping my ego from collapse; every time my demons started rearing up I could just yell at them SETH DICKINSON LIKED IT and for a hot minute it was the only thing keeping me from a breakdown. Also *Exordia* was tika; you and the Māori people are cool.

To Olive and the Ironfolk, for honestly being one of the few things keeping my fragile psyche together, and for tolerating both my rambling about Thibault and the fact that a five-foot-six girl with short limbs keeps insisting she's going to make sabre her *thing*.

To everybody who stuck with me this far. It has been a lonely, scary, isolating tranche of years. There are a lot of people who don't talk to me anymore. God knows, I haven't always been the easiest to talk to. If you're here, you're here, and it means the world to me.

MĀORI GLOSSARY

e hoa mai: Friend(s).

Kahungunu: A Māori tribe.

kahurangi mai: Dearest, beloved. *Literally*: my blue.

kokiki: Trash brought down by a flood.

koretake: Useless.

moko: Traditional Māori tattoo.

moko kauae: A moko on the chin of a woman.

Pākehā: Foreigner, often referring to Europeans living in New Zealand.

pīwak: Short for pīwakawaka, a species of fantail local to New Zealand. Known in some Māori myths to bring news of death from the gods.

pono: Correct, honorable.

rāhui: Temporary ritual prohibition placed on an area, often linked to death or tragedy that has taken place there.

Taangata: People (usually meaning Māori people).

Te Reo: Māori language.

tēnā koe: Hello.

tika: Righteous, just.

tungāne: Brother or male cousin of a female.

wehi: To be in awe, to be enthralled. *Or*: to fear.

whaea: Auntie.

All other terms in this book are of non-Māori origin or were invented by the author.